The
Black Heart

THE COLLECTED SCIENCE FICTION & FANTASY
OF STANLEY G. WEINBAUM: VOLUME 4

The
Black Heart

Classic Strange Tales Including:
the Complete Novel *The Dark Other*,
Plus *Proteus Island* and Others

Stanley G. Weinbaum

LEONAUR

The Black Heart: Classic Strange Tales Including:
the Complete Novel The Dark Other,
Plus Proteus Island and Others
by Stanley G. Weinbaum

FIRST EDITION

Published by Leonaur Ltd

Material original to this edition and this editorial selection
copyright © 2006 Leonaur Ltd

ISBN (10 digit): 1-84677-054-8 (hardcover)
ISBN (13 digit): 978-1-84677-054-8 (hardcover)

ISBN (10 digit): 1-84677-049-1 (softcover)
ISBN (13 digit): 978-1-84677-049-4 (softcover)

http://www.leonaur.com

Publisher's Notes

In the interests of authenticity, the spellings, grammar and place names
used by the author have been retained.

The views expressed in this book are not necessarily
those of the publisher.

Contents

The Dark Other

1. Pure Horror

"That isn't what I mean," said Nicholas Devine, turning his eyes on his companion. "I mean pure horror in the sense of horror detached from experience, apart from reality. Not just a formless fear, which implies either fear of something that might happen, or fear of unknown dangers. Do you see what I mean?"

"Of course," said Pat, letting her eyes wander over the black expanse of night-dark Lake Michigan. "Certainly I see what you mean but I don't quite understand how you'd do it. It sounds—well, difficult."

She gazed at his lean profile, clear-cut against the distant light. He had turned, staring thoughtfully over the lake, idly fingering the levers on the steering wheel before him. The girl wondered a little at her feeling of contentment; she, Patricia Lane, satisfied to spend an evening in nothing more exciting than conversation! And they must have parked here a full two hours now. There was something about Nick—she didn't understand exactly what; sensitivity, charm, personality. Those were meaningless clichés, handles to hold the unexplainable nuances of character.

"It is difficult," resumed Nick. "Baudelaire tried it, Poe tried it. And in painting, Hogarth, Goya, Dore. Poe came closest, I think; he caught the essence of horror in an occasional poem or story. Don't you think so?"

"I don't know," said Pat. "I've forgotten most of my Poe."

"Remember that story of his—'The Black Cat'?"

"Dimly. The man murdered his wife."

"Yes. That isn't the part I mean. I mean the cat itself—the second cat. You know a cat, used rightly, can be a symbol of horror."

"Indeed yes!" The girl shuddered. "I don't like the treacherous beasts!"

"And this cat of Poe's," continued Nick, warming to his subject. "Just think of it—in the first place, it's black; element of horror. Then, it's gigantic, unnaturally, abnormally large. And then it's not all black—that would be inartistically perfect—but has a formless white mark on its breast, a mark that little by little assumes a fantastic form—do you remember what?"

"No."

"The form of a gallows!"

"Oh!" said the girl. "Ugh!"

"And then—climax of genius—the eyes! Blind in one eye, the other a baleful yellow orb! Do you feel it? A black cat, an enormous black cat marked with a gallows, and lacking one eye, to make the other even more terrible! Literary tricks, of course, but they work, and that's genius! Isn't it?"

"Genius! Yes, if you call it that. The perverse genius of the Devil!"

"That's what I want to write—what I will write some day." He watched the play of lights on the restless surface of the waters "Pure horror, the epitome of the horrible. It could be written, but it hasn't been yet; not even by Poe."

"That little analysis of yours was bad enough, Nick! Why should you want to improve on his treatment of the theme?"

"Because I like to write and because I'm interested in the horrible. Two good reasons."

"Two excuses, you mean. Of course, even if you'd succeed, you couldn't force anyone to read it."

"If I succeed, there'd be no need to force people. Success would mean that the thing would be great literature, and even today, in these times, there are still people to read that. And besides—" He paused.

"Besides what?"

"Everybody's interested in the horrible. Even you are, whether or not you deny it."

"I certainly do deny it!"

"But you are, Pat. It's natural to be."

"It isn't!"

"Then what is?"

"Interest in people, and life, and gay times, and pretty things, and—and one's self and one's own feelings. And the feelings of the people one loves."

"Yes. It comes to exactly the point I've been stressing. People are sordid, life is hopeless, gay times are stupid, beauty is sensual, one's own feelings are selfish. And love is carnal. That's the array of horrors that holds your interest!"

The girl laughed in exasperation. "Nick, you could out-argue your namesake, the Devil himself! Do you really believe that indictment of the normal viewpoint?"

"I do—often!"

"Now?"

"Now," he said, turning his gaze on Pat, "I have no feeling of it at all. Now, right now, I don't believe it."

"Why not?" she queried, smiling ingenuously at him.

"You, obviously."

"Gracious! I had no idea my logic was as convincing as that."

"Your logic isn't. The rest of you is."

"That sounds like a compliment," observed Pat. "If it is," she continued in a bantering tone, "it's the only one I can recall obtaining from you."

"That's because I seldom call attention to the obvious."

"And that's another," laughed the girl. "I'll have to mark this date in red on my calendar. It's entirely unique in our—let's see—nearly a month's acquaintance."

"Is it really so short a time? I know you so well that it must have taken years. Every detail!" He closed his eyes. "Hair like black silk, and oddly dark blue eyes—if I were writing a poem at the moment, I'd call them violet. Tiny lips, the sort the Elizabethan called bee-stung. Straight nose, and a figure that is a sort of vest-pocket copy of Diana. Right?" He opened his eyes.

"Nice, but exaggerated. And even if you were correct, that isn't Pat Lane, the real Pat Lane. A camera could do better on a tenth of a second's acquaintance!"

"Check!" He closed his eyes again. "Personality, piquant. Character, loyal, naturally happy, intelligent, but not serious. An intellectual butterfly; a dilettante. Poised, cool, self-possessed, yet inherently affectionate. A being untouched by reality, as yet, living in Chicago and in a make-believe world at the same time." He paused, "How old are you, Pat?"

"Twenty-two. Why?"

"I wondered how long one could manage to stay in the world of make-believe. I'm twenty-six, and I'm long exiled."

"I don't think you know what you mean by a make-believe world. I'm sure I don't."

"Of course you don't. You can't know and still remain there. It's like being happy; once you realize it, it's no longer perfect."

"Then don't explain!"

"Wouldn't make any difference if I did, Pat. It's a queer world, like the Sardoodledom of Sardou and the afternoon-tea school of playwrights. All stage-settings and pretense, but it looks real while you're watching, especially if you're one of the characters."

The girl laughed. "You're a deliciously solemn sort, Nick. How would you like to hear my analysis of you?"

"I wouldn't!"

"You inflicted yours on me, and I'm entitled to revenge. And so—you're intelligent, lazy, dreamy, and with a fine perception of artistic values. You're very alert to impressions of the senses—I mean you're sensuous without being sensual. You're delightfully serious without being somber, except sometimes. Sometimes I feel a hint, just a thrilling hint, in your character, of something dangerously darker—"

"Don't!" Said Nick sharply.

Pat shot him a quick glance. "And you're frightened to death of falling in love," she concluded imperturbably.

"Oh! Do you think so?"

"I do."

"Then you're wrong! I can't be afraid of it, since I've known for the better part of a month that I've been in love."

"With me," said the girl.

"Yes, with you!"

"Well!" said Pat. "It never before took me a month to extract that admission from a man. Is twenty-two getting old?"

"You're a tantalizing imp!"

"And so?" She pursed her lips, assuming an air of disappointment. "What am I to do about it—scream for help? You haven't given me anything to scream about."

The kiss, Pat admitted to herself, was quite satisfactory. She yielded herself to the pleasure of it; it was decidedly the best kiss she had, in her somewhat limited experience, encountered. She pushed herself away finally, with a little gasp, gazing bright-eyed at her

12

companion. He was staring down at her with serious eyes; there was a tense twist to his mouth, and a curiously unexpected attitude of unhappiness.

"Nick!" she murmured. "Was it as bad as all that?"

"Bad! Pat, does it mean you—care for me? A little, anyway?"

"A little," she admitted. "Maybe more. Is that what makes you look so forlorn?"

He drew her closer to him. "How could I look forlorn, honey, when something like this has happened to me? That was just my way of looking happy."

She nestled as closely as the steering wheel permitted, drawing his arm about her shoulders. "I hope you mean that, Nick."

"Then you mean it? You really do?"

"I really do."

"I'm glad," he said huskily. The girl thought she detected a strange dubious note in his voice. She glanced at his face; his eyes were gazing into the dim remoteness of the night horizon.

"Nick," she said, "why were you so—well, so reluctant about admitting this? You must have known I—like you. I showed you that deliberately in so many ways."

"I—I wasn't quite sure."

"You were! That isn't it, Nick. I had to practically browbeat you into confessing you cared for me. Why?"

He stepped on the starter; the motor ground into sudden life. The car backed into the road, turning toward Chicago that glared like a false dawn in the southern sky.

"I hope you never find out," he said.

2. Science of Mind

"She's out," said Pat as the massive form of Dr. Carl Horker loomed in the doorway.

"Your treatments must be successful; mother's out playing bridge."

The Doctor gave his deep, rumbling chuckle. "So much the better, Pat. I don't feel professional anyway." He moved into the living room, depositing his bulk on a groaning davenport. "And how's yourself?"

"Too well to be a patient of yours," retorted the girl. "Psychiatry! The new religion! Just between friends, it's all apple sauce, isn't it?"

"If I weren't trying to act in place of your father, I'd resent that, young lady," said the Doctor placidly. "Psychiatry is a definite science, and a pretty important one. Applied psychology, the science of the human mind."

"If said mind exists," added the girl, swinging her slim legs over the arm of a chair.

"Correct," agreed the Doctor. "In my practice I find occasional evidence that it does. Or did; your generation seems to have found substitutes."

"Which appears to work just as well!" laughed Pat. "All our troubles are more or less inherited from your generation."

"Touché!" admitted Dr. Horker. "But my generation also bequeathed you some solid values which you don't know how to use."

"They've been weighed and found wanting," said Pat airily. "We're busy replacing them with our own values."

"Which are certainly no better."

"Maybe not, Doc, but at least they're ours."

"Yours and Tom Paine's. I can't see that you young moderns have brought any new ideas to the social scheme."

"New or not, we're the first ones to give 'em a try-out. Your crowd took it out in talk."

"That's an insult," observed the Doctor cheerfully. "If I weren't acting *in loco parentis*—"

"I know! You'd give me a few licks in the spot popularly supposed to do the most good! Well, that's part of a parent's privilege, isn't it?"

"You've grown beyond the spanking age, my dear. Physically, if not mentally—though I don't say the process would hurt me as much as you. I'd doubtless enjoy it."

"Then you might try sending me to bed without my dinner," the girl laughed.

"That's a doctor's prerogative, Pat. I've even done that to your Mother."

"In other words, you're a complete flop as a parent. All the responsibilities, and none of the privileges."

"That expresses it."

"Well, you elected yourself, Doc. It's not my fault you happened to live next door."

"No. It's my misfortune."

"And I notice," remarked Pat wickedly, "that you're not too thoroughly in *loco* to neglect sending mother a bill for services rendered!"

"My dear girl, that's part of the treatment!"

"So? And how?"

"I furnish a bill just steep enough to keep your mother from indulging too frequently in medical services. Without that little practical check on her inclinations, she'd be a confirmed neurotic. One of those sweet, resigned, professional invalids, you know."

"Then why not send her a bill tall enough to cure her altogether?"

"She might change to psychoanalysis or New Thought," chuckled the Doctor. "Besides, your father wanted me to look after her, and besides that, I like having the run of the house."

"Well, I'm sure I don't mind." observed Pat. "We've a dog and a canary bird, too."

"You're in fine fettle this afternoon!" laughed her companion. "Must've been a successful date last night."

"It was." Her eyes turned suddenly dreamy.

"You're in love again, Pat!" he accused.

"Again? Why the 'again'?"

"Well, there was Billy, and that Paul——"

"Oh, those!" Her tone was contemptuous. "Merely passing fancies, Doc. Just whims, dreams of the moment—in other words, puppy love."

"And this? I suppose this is different—a grand passion?"

"I don't know," she said, frowning abruptly. "He's nice, but—odd. Attractive as—well, as the devil."

"Odd? How?"

"Oh, he's one of those minds you think we moderns lack."

"Intellectual, eh? New variety for you; out of the usual run of your dancing collegiates. I've often suspected that you picked your swains by the length and lowness of their cars."

"Maybe I did. That was one of the chief differences between them."

"How'd you meet this mental paragon?"

"Billy Fields dragged him around to one of those literary evenings he affects—where they read Oscar Wilde and Eugene O'Neil aloud. Bill met him at the library."

"And he outshone all the local lights, I perceive."

"He surely did!" retorted Pat. "And he hardly said a word the whole evening."

"He wouldn't have to, if they're all like Billy! What's this prodigy's specialty?"

"He writes. I think—laugh if you want to!—I think perhaps he's a genius."

"Well," said Doctor Horker, "even that's possible. It's been know to occur, but rarely, to my knowledge, in your generation."

"Oh, we're just dimmed by the glare of brilliance from yours." She swung her legs to the floor, facing the Doctor. "Do you psychiatrists actually know anything about love?" she queried.

"We're supposed to."

"What is it, then?"

"Just a device of Nature's for perpetuating the species. Some organisms manage without it, and do pretty well."

"Yes. I've heard references to the poor fish!"

"Then they're inaccurate; fish have primitive symptoms of eroticism. But below the vertebrates, notably in the amoeba, I don't recall any amorous habits."

16

"Then your definition doesn't explain a thing, does it?"

"Not to one of the victims, perhaps."

"Anyway," said Pat decisively, "I've heard of the old biological urge before your kind analysis. It doesn't begin to explain why one should be attracted to this person and repelled by that one. Does it?"

"No, but Freud does. The famous Oedipus Complex."

"That's the love of son for mother, or daughter for father, isn't it? And I don't see how that clears up anything; for example, I can just barely remember my father."

"That's plenty. It could be some little trait in these swains of yours, some unimportant mannerism that recalls that memory. Or there's that portrait of him in the hall—the one under the mellow red light. It might happen that you'd see one of these chaps under a similar light in some attitude that brings the picture to mind—or a hundred other possibilities."

"Doesn't sound entirely convincing," objected Pat with a thoughtful frown.

"Well, submit to the proper treatments, and I'll tell you exactly what caused each and every one of your little passing fancies. You can't expect me to hit it first guess."

"Thanks, no! That's one of these courses where you tell the doctor all your secrets, and I prefer to keep what few I have."

"Good judgment, Pat. By the way, you said this chap was odd. Does that mean merely that he writes? I've known perfectly normal people who wrote."

"No," she said, "it isn't that. It's—he's so sweet and gentle and manageable most of the time, but sometimes he has such a thrilling spark of mastery that it almost scares me. It's puzzling but fascinating, if you grasp my import."

"Huh! He's probably a naturally selfish fellow who's putting on a good show of gentleness for your benefit. Those flashes of tyranny are probably his real character in moments of forgetfulness."

"You doctors can explain anything, can't you?"

"That's our business. It's what we're paid for."

"Well, you're wrong this time. I know Nick well enough to know if he's acting. His personality is just what I said—gentle, sensitive, and yet—It's perplexing, and that's a good part of his charm."

"Then it's not such a serious case you've got," mocked the doctor.

"When you're cool enough to analyze your own feelings, and dissect the elements of the chap's attraction, you're not in any danger."

"Danger! I can look out for myself, thanks. That's one thing we mindless moderns learn young, and don't let me catch you puttering around in my romances! *In loco parentis* or just plain loco, you'll get the licking instead of me!"

"Believe me, Pat, if I wanted to experiment with affairs of the heart, I'd not pick a spitfire like you as the subject."

"Well, Doctor Carl, you're warned!"

"This Nick," observed the Doctor, "must be quite a fellow to get the princess of the North Side so het up. What's the rest of his cognomen?"

"Nicholas Devine. Romantic, isn't it?"

"Devine," muttered Horker. "I don't know any Devines. Who are his people?"

"Hasn't any."

"How does he live? By his writing?"

"Don't know. I gathered that he lives on some income left by his parents. What's the difference, anyway?"

"None. None at all." The other wrinkled his brows thoughtfully. "There was a colleague of mine, a Dr. Devine; died a good many years ago. Reputation wasn't anything to brag about; was a little off balance mentally."

"Well, Nick isn't!" snapped Pat with some asperity.

"I'd like to meet him."

"He's coming over tonight."

"So'm I. I want to see your mother." He rose ponderously. "If she's not playing bridge again!"

"Well, look him over," retorted Pat. "And I think your knowledge of love is a decided flop. I think you're woefully ignorant on the subject."

"Why's that?"

"If you'd known anything about it, you could have married mother some time during the last seventeen years. Lord knows you've tried, and all you've attained is the state of *in loco parentis* instead of *parens*."

3. Psychiatrics of Genius

"How do you charge—by the hour?" Asked Pat, as Doctor Horker returned from the hall. The sound of her mother's departing footsteps pattered on the porch.

"Of course, Young One; like a plumber."

"Then your rates per minute must be colossal! The only time you ever see mother is a moment or so between bridge games."

"I add on the time I waste with you, my dear. Such as now, waiting to look over that odd swain of yours. Didn't you say he'd be over this evening?"

"Yes, but it's not worth your rates to have him psychoanalyzed. I can do as well myself."

"All right, Pat. I'll give you a sample analysis free," chuckled the Doctor, distributing his bulk comfortably on the davenport.

"I don't like free trials," she retorted. "I sent for a beauty-culture book once, on free trial. I was twelve years old, and returned it in seven days, but I'm still getting sales letters in the mails. I must be on every sucker list in the country."

"So that's the secret of your charm."

"What is?"

"You must have read the book, I mean. If you remember the title, I might try it myself. Think it'd help?"

"Dr. Carl," laughed the girl, "you don't need a book on beauty culture—you need one on bridge! It's that atrocious game you play that's bothering Mother."

"Indeed? I shouldn't be surprised if you were right."

"Save your surprise for when I'm wrong, Doc. You'll suffer much less from shock."

"Confident little brat! You're apt to get that knocked out of you some day, though I hope you never do."

"I can take it," grinned Pat.

"No doubt you can, but you're an adept at handing it out. Where's this chap of yours?"

"He'll be along. No one's ever stood me up on a date yet."

"I can understand that, you imp! Is that the famous Nick?" he queried as a car purred to a stop beyond the windows.

"No one else!" said the girl, glancing out. "The Big Thrill in person."

She darted to the door. Horker turned casually to watch her as she opened it, surveying Nicholas Devine with professional nonchalance. He entered, tall, slender, with his thin sensitive features sharply outlined in the light of the hall. He cast a quick glance toward the Doctor; the latter noted the curious amber-green eyes of the lad, set wide in the lean face, deep, speculative, the eyes of a dreamer.

"'Evening, Nick," Pat was bubbling. The newcomer gave her a hasty smile, with another glance at the Doctor. "Don't mind Dr. Carl," she continued. "Aren't you going to kiss me? It irks the medico, and I never miss a chance."

Nicholas flushed in embarrassment; he gestured hesitantly, then placed a hasty peck of a kiss on the girl's forehead. He reddened again at the Doctor's rumble of "Young imp of Satan!"

"Not very good," said Pat reflectively, obviously enjoying the situation. "I've known you to do better." She pulled him toward the arch of the living room. "Come meet Dr. Horker. Dr. Carl, this is the aforesaid Nicholas Devine."

"Dr. Horker," repeated the lad, smiling diffidently. "You're the psychiatrist and brain specialist, aren't you, Sir?"

"So my patients believe," rumbled the massive Doctor, rising at the introduction, and grasping the youth's hand. "And you're the genius Patricia has been raving about. I'm glad to have the chance of looking you over."

Nick gave the girl a harassed glance, shifting uncomfortably, and patently at a loss for a reply. She grinned mischievously.

"Sit down, both of you," she suggested helpfully. She seized his hat from the reluctant hands of Nick, sailing it carelessly to a chair.

"So!" boomed the Doctor, lowering his great bulk again to the davenport. He eyed the youth sitting nervously before him. "Devine, did you say?"

"Yes, sir."

"I knew a Devine once. Colleague of mine."

20

"A doctor? My father was a doctor."

"Dr. Stuart Devine?"

"Yes, sir." He paused. "Did you say you knew him, Dr. Horker?"

"Slightly," rumbled the other. "Only slightly."

"I don't remember him at all, of course, I was very young when he—and my mother too—died."

"You must have been. Patricia claims you write."

"I try."

"What sort of material?"

"Why—any sort. Prose or poetry; what I feel like writing."

"Whatever inspires you, I suppose?"

"Yes, sir." The lad flushed again.

"Ever have anything published?"

"Yes, sir. In Nation's Poetry."

"Never heard of it."

"It has a large circulation," said Nick apologetically.

"Humph! Well, that's something. Whom do you like?"

"Whom do I like?" The youth's tone was puzzled.

"What authors—writers?"

"Oh." He cast another uncomfortable glance at Pat. "Why—I like Baudelaire, and Poe, and Swinburne, and Villon, and—"

"Decadents, all of them!" sniffed the Doctor. "What prose writers?"

"Well—" He hesitated—"Poe again, and Stern, and Rabelais—"

"Rabelais!" Horker's voice boomed. "Well! Your taste can't be as bad as I thought, then. There's one we agree on, anyway. And I notice you name no moderns, which is another good point."

"I haven't read many moderns, sir."

"That's in your favor."

"Cut it!" put in Pat with assumed sharpness. "You've taken enough whacks at my generation for one day."

"I'm glad to find one of your generation who agrees with me," chuckled the Doctor. "At least to the extent of not reading its works."

"I'll teach him," grinned Pat. "I'll have him writing *vess libre*, and maybe even Dadaism, in a week."

"Maybe it won't be much loss," grunted Horker. "I haven't seen any of his work yet."

21

"We'll bring some around sooner or later. We will, won't we, Nick?"

"Of course, if you want to. But—"

"He's going to say something modest," interrupted the girl. "He's in the retiring mood now, but he's apt to change any moment, and snap your surly head off."

"Humph! I'd like to see it."

"So'd I," retorted Pat. "You've had it coming all day; maybe I'll do it myself."

"You have, my dear, innumerable times. But I'm like the Hydra, except that I grow only one head to replace the one you snap off." He turned again to Nicholas. "Do you work?"

"Yes, sir. At my writing."

"I mean how do you live?"

"Why," said the youth, reddening again in embarrassment, "my parents—"

"Listen!" said Pat. "That's enough of Dr. Carl's cross examination. You'd think he was a Victorian father who had just been approached for his daughter's hand. We haven't whispered any news of an engagement to you, have we, Doc?"

"No, but I'm acting—"

"Sure. *In loco parentis.* We know that."

"You're incorrigible, Pat! I wash my hands of you. Run along, if you're going out."

"You'll be telling me never to darken my own door again in the next breath!" She stretched forth a diminutive foot at the extremity of a superlatively attractive ankle, caught Nick's hat on her toe, and kicked it expertly to his lap. "Come on, Nick. There's a moon."

"There is not!" objected the Doctor huffily. "It rises at four, as you ought to know. You didn't see it last night, did you?"

"I didn't notice," said the girl. "Come on, Nick, and we'll watch it rise tonight. We'll check up on the Doctor's astronomy, or is it chronology?"

"You do and I'll know it! I can hear you come home, you imp!"

"Nice neighbor," observed Pat airily, as she stepped to the door. "I'll bet you peek out of the window, too."

She ignored the Doctor's irritated rumble as she passed into the hall, where Nick, after a diffident murmur of farewell to Horker, followed. She caught up a light cape, which he draped about her shoulders.

"Nick," she said, "suppose you run out to the car and wait. I think I've stepped too hard on Dr. Carl's corns, and I want to give him a little cheering up. Will you?"

"Of course, Pat."

She darted back into the living room, perching on the arm of the davenport beside the Doctor.

"Well?" she said, running her hand through his grizzled hair. "What's the verdict?"

"Seems like a nice kid," grumbled Horker reluctantly. "Nice enough, but introverted, repressed, and I shouldn't be surprised to find him antisocial. Doesn't adjust easily to his environment; takes refuge in a dream world of his own."

"That's what he accuses me of doing," grinned Pat. "That all you've got against him?"

"That's all, but where's that streak of mastery you mentioned? You lead him around on a leash!"

"It didn't show up tonight. That's the thrill—the unexpectedness of it."

"Bah! You must've dreamed it. There's no more aggressiveness in that lad than in KoKo, your canary."

"Don't you believe it, Dr. Carl! The trouble is that he's a genius, and that's where your psychology falls flat."

"Genius," said the Doctor oracularly, "is a sublimation of qualities—"

"I'll tell you tomorrow how sublime the qualities are," called Pat as she skipped out of the door.

4. The Transfiguration

The car slid smoothly along a straight white road that stretched ahead into the darkness like an earth-bound Milky Way. In the dim distance before them, red as Antares, glowed the tail-light of some automobile; except for this lone evidence of humanity, reflected Pat, they might have been flashing through the cosmic depths of interstellar space, instead of following a highway in the very shadow of Chicago. The colossal city of the lake-shore was invisible behind them, and the clustering suburbs with it.

"Queer, isn't it?" said Pat, after a silence, "how contented we can be with none of the purchased amusement people crave—shows, movies, dancing, and all that."

"It doesn't seem queer to me," answered Nick. "Not when I look at you here beside me."

"Nice of you!" retorted Pat. "But it's never happened to me before." She paused, then continued, "How do you like the Doctor?"

"How does he like me? That's considerably more to the point, isn't it?"

"He thinks you're nice, but—let's see—introverted, repressed, and ill-adjusted to your environment. I think those were the points."

"Well, I liked *him*, in spite of your manoeuvers, and in spite of his being a doctor."

"What's wrong with being a doctor?"

"Did you ever read *Tristram Shandy*?" was Nick's irrelevant response.

"No, but I read the newspapers!"

"What's the connection, Pat?"

"Just as much connection as there is between the evils of being a doctor and reading *Tristram Shandy*. I know that much about the book, at least."

"You're nearly right," laughed Nick. "I was just referring to one of Tristram's remarks on doctors and lawyers. It fits my attitude."

"What's the remark?"

"Well, he had the choice of professions, and it occurred to him that medicine and law were the vulture professions, since lawyers live by men's quarrels and doctors by men's misfortunes. So—he became a writer."

"And what do writers live by?" queried Pat mischievously. "By men's stupidity!"

"You're precious, Pat!" Nick chuckled delightedly. "If I'd created you to order, I couldn't have planned you more to taste—pepper, tabasco sauce, vinegar, spice, and honey!"

"And to be taken with a grain of salt," retorted the girl, puckering her piquant, impish features. She edged closer to him, locking her arm through his where it rested on the steering wheel.

"Nick," she said, her tones suddenly gentle, "I think I'm pretty crazy about you. Heaven knows why I should be, but it's a fact."

"Pat, dear!"

"I'm crazy about you in this meek, sensitive pose of yours, and I'm fascinated by those masterful moments you flash occasionally. Really, Nick, I almost wish you flamed out oftener."

"Don't!" he said sharply.

"Why not?"

"Let's not talk about me, Pat. It—embarrasses me."

"All right, Mr. Modesty! Let's talk about me, then. I'll promise we won't succeed in embarrassing me."

"And it's quite the most interesting subject in the world, Pat."

"Well, then?"

"What?"

"Why don't you start talking? The topic is all attention."

He chuckled. "How many men have told you you were beautiful, Pat?"

"I never kept account."

"And in many different ways?"

"Why? Have you, perchance, discovered a new way, Nick?"

"Not at all. The oldest way of any, the way of Shappho and Pindar."

"O-ooh!" She clapped her hands in mock delight. "Poetry!"

"The only medium that could possibly express how lovely you are" said Nick.

"Nicholas, have you gone and composed a poem to me?"

"Composed? No. It isn't necessary, with you here beside me."

"What's that? Some very subtle compliment?"

"Not subtle, Pat. You're the poem yourself; all I need do is look at you, listen to you, and translate."

"Neat!" applauded the girl. "Do I hear the translation?"

"You certainly do." He turned his odd amber-green eyes on her, then bent forward to the road. He began to speak in a low voice.

"In no far country's silent ways
Shall I forget one little thing—
The soft intentness of your gaze,
The sweetness of your murmuring
Your generously tender praise,
The words just hinted by a breath—
In no far country's silent way,
Unless that country's name be Death—"

He paused abruptly, and drove silently onward.

"Oh," breathed Pat. "Why don't you go on, Nick? Please."

"No. It isn't the mood for this night, Dear. Not this night, alone with you."

"What is, then?"

"Nothing sentimental. Something lighter, something—oh, Elizabethan. That's it."

"And what's stopping you?"

"Lack of an available idea. Or—wait. Listen a moment." He began, this time in a tone of banter.

"When mornings, you attire yourself
For riding in the city,
You're such a lovely little elf,
Extravagantly pretty!
And when at noon you deign to wear
The habit of the town,
I cannot call to mind as fair
A symphony in brown.
Then evenings, you blithely don
A daintiness of white,
To flash a very paragon
Of lightsomeness—and light!
But when the rounds of pleasure cease,

And you retire at night,
The Godling on your mantelpiece
Must know a fairer sight!"

"Sweet!" laughed Pat. "But personal. And anyway, how do you know I've a godling on my mantel? Don't you credit me with any modesty?"

"If you haven't, you should have! The vision I mentioned ought to enliven even a statue."

"Well," said the girl, "I have one—a jade Buddha, and with all the charms I flash before him nightly, he's never batted an eyelash. Explain that!"

"Easily. He's green with envy, and frozen with admiration, and struck dumb by wonder."

"Heavens! I suppose I ought to be thankful you didn't say he was petrified with fright!" Pat laughed. "Oh Nick," she continued, in a voice gone suddenly dreamy, "this is marvelous, isn't it? I mean our enjoying ourselves so completely, and our being satisfied to be so alone. Why, we've never even danced together."

"So we haven't. That's a subterfuge we haven't needed, isn't it?"

"It is," replied the girl, dropping her glossy gleaming black head against his shoulder. "And besides, it's much more satisfactory to be held in your arms in private, instead of in the midst of a crowd, and sitting down, instead of standing up. But I should like to dance with you, Nick," she concluded.

"We'll go dancing, then, whenever you like."

"You're delightfully complaisant, Nick. But—you're puzzling." She glanced up at him. "You're so—so reluctant. Here we've been driving an hour, and you haven't tried to kiss me a single time, and yet I'm quite positive you care for me."

"Lord, Pat!" he muttered. "You never need doubt that."

"Then what is it? Are you so spiritual and ethereal, or is my attraction for you just sort of intellectual? Or—are you afraid?" As he made no reply, she continued, "Or are those poems you spout about my physical charms just—poetic license?"

"They're not, and you know it!" he snapped. "You've a mirror, haven't you? And other fellows than I have taken you around, haven't they?"

"Oh, I've been taken around! That's what perplexes me about

you, Nick. I'd think you were actually afraid of kissing me if it weren't—" Her voice trailed into silence, and she stared speculatively ahead at the ribbon of road that rolled steadily into the headlights' glare.

She broke the interval of wordlessness. "What is it, Nick?" she resumed almost pleadingly. "You've hinted at something now and then. Please—you don't have to hesitate to tell me; I'm modern enough to forgive things past, entanglements, affairs, disgraces, or anything like that. Don't you think I should know?"

"You'd know," he said huskily, "if I could tell you."

"Then there is something, Nick!" She pressed his arm against her. "Tell me, isn't there?"

"I don't know." There was the suggestion of a groan in his voice.

"You don't know! I can't understand."

"I can't either. Please, Pat, let's not spoil tonight; if I could tell you, I would. Why, Pat, I love you—I'm terribly, deeply, solemnly in love with you."

"And I with you, Nick." She gazed ahead, where the road rose over the arch of a narrow bridge. The speeding car lifted to the rise like a zooming plane.

And suddenly, squarely in the center of the road, another car, until now concealed by the arch of the bridge, appeared almost upon them. There was a heart-stopping moment when a collision seemed inevitable, and Pat felt the arm against her tighten convulsively into a bar of steel. She heard her own sobbing gasp, and then, somehow, they had slipped unscathed between the other car and the rail of the bridge.

"Oh!" she gasped faintly, then with a return of breath, "That was nice, Nick!"

Beyond the bridge, the road widened once more; she felt the car slowing, edging toward the broad shoulder of the road.

"There was danger," said her companion in tones as emotionless as the rasping of metal. "I came to save it."

"Save what?" queried Pat as the car slid to a halt on the turf.

"Your body." The tones were still cold, like grinding wheels. "The beauty of your body!"

He reached a thin hand toward her, suddenly seized her skirt and snatched it above the silken roundness of her knees. "There," he rasped. "That is what I mean."

"Nick!" Pat half-screamed in appalled astonishment. "How—" She paused, shocked into abrupt silence, for the face turned toward her was but a remote, evil caricature of Nicholas Devine's. It leered at her out of bloodshot eyes, as if behind the mask of Nick's face peered a red-eyed demon.

5. A Fantasy of Fear

The satyr beside Pat was leaning toward her; the arm about her was tightening with a brutal ruthlessness, and while still staring in fascination at the incredible eyes, she realized that another arm and a white hand was moving relentlessly, exploratively, toward her body. It was the cold touch of this hand as it slipped over her silk-sheathed legs that broke the chilling spell of her fascination.

"Nick!" she screamed. "Nick!" She had a curious sensation of calling him back from far distances, the while she strove with both hands and all her strength to press him back from her. But the ruthless force of his arms was overcoming her resistance; she saw the red eyes a hand's breadth from her own.

"Nick!" she sobbed in terror.

There was a change. Abruptly, she was looking into Nick's eyes, bloodshot, frightened, puzzled, but indubitably Nick's eyes. The flaming orbs of the demon were no more; it was as if they had receded into Nick's head. The arm about her body relaxed, and they were staring at each other in a medley of consternation, amazement and unbelief. The youth drew back, huddled in his corner of the car, and Pat, breathing in sobs, smoothed out her rumpled apparel with a convulsive movement.

"Pat!" he gasped. "Oh, my God! He couldn't have—" He paused abruptly. The girl gazed at him without reply.

"Pat, Dear," he spoke in a low, tense murmur, "I'm—sorry. I don't know—I don't understand how—"

"Never mind," she said, regaining a vestige of her customary composure. "It's—all right, Nick."

"But—oh, Pat—!"

"It was that near accident," she said. "That upset you—both of us, I mean."

"Yes!" he said eagerly. "That's what it was, Pat. It must have been that, but Dear, can you forgive? Do you want to forgive me?"

"It's all right," she repeated. "After all, you just complimented my legs, and I guess I can stand that. It's happened before, only not quite so—convincingly!"

"You're sweet, Pat!"

"No; I just love you Nick." She felt a sudden pity for the misery in his face. "Kiss me, Nick—only gently."

He pressed his lips to hers, very lightly, almost timidly. She lay back against the seat for a moment, her eyes closed.

"That's you again," she murmured. "This other—wasn't."

"Please, Pat! Don't refer to it,—not ever."

"But it wasn't you, Nick. It was just the strain of that narrow escape. I don't hold it against you."

"You're—Lord, Pat, I don't deserve you. But you know that I—I myself—could never touch you except in tenderness, even in reverence. You're too dainty, too lovely, too spirited, to be hurt, or to be held roughly, against your will. You know I feel that way about you, don't you?"

"Of course. It was nothing, Nick. Forget it."

"If I can," he said somberly. He switched on the engine, backed out upon the pavement, and turned the car toward the glow that marked Chicago. Neither of them spoke as the machine hummed over the arching bridge and down the slope, where, so few minutes before, the threat of accident had thrust itself at them.

"We won't see a moon tonight," said Pat in a small voice, after an interval. "We'll never check up on Dr. Carl's astronomy."

"You don't want to tonight, Pat, do you?"

"I guess perhaps we'd better not," she replied. "We're both upset, and there'll be other nights."

Again they were silent. Pat felt strained, shaken; there was something uncanny about the occurrence that puzzled her. The red eyes that had glared out of Nick's face perplexed her, and the curious rasping voice he had used still sounded inhumanly in her memory. Out of recollection rose still another mystery.

"Nick," she said, "what did you mean—then—when you said there was danger and you came to save me?"

"Nothing," he said sharply.

"And then, afterwards, you started to say something about 'He couldn't have—'. Who's 'he'?"

31

"It meant nothing, I tell you. I was frantic to think you might have been hurt. That's all."

"I believe you, honey," she said, wondering whether she really did. The thing was beginning to grow hazy; already it was assuming merely the proportions of an upheaval of youthful fervor. Such occurrences were not unheard of, though never before had it happened to Patricia Lane! Still, even that was conceivable, far more conceivable than the dark, unformed, inchoate suspicions she had been harboring. They hadn't even been definite enough to be called suspicions; indefinite apprehensions came closer.

And yet—that strange, wild face that had formed itself of Nick's fine features, and the terrible red eyes! Were they elements in a picture conjured out of her own imagination? They must be, of course. She had been frightened by that hair-breadth escape, and had seen things that didn't exist. And the rest of it—well, that might be natural enough. Still, there was something—she knew that; Nick had admitted it.

Horker's words concerning Nick's father rose in her mind. Suspected of being crazy! Was that it? Was that the cause of Nick's curious reluctance where she was concerned? Was the face that had glared at her the visage of a maniac? It couldn't be. It couldn't be, she told herself fiercely. Not her fine, tender, sensitive Nick! And besides, that face, if she hadn't imagined it, had been the face, not of a lunatic, but of a devil. She shook her head, as if to deny her thoughts, and placed her hand impulsively on Nick's.

"I don't care," she said. "I love you, Nick."

"And I you," he murmured. "Pat, I'm sorry about spoiling this evening. I'm sorry and ashamed."

"Never mind, honey. There'll be others."

"Tomorrow?"

"No," she said. "Mother and I are going out to dinner. And Friday we're having company."

"Really, Pat? You're not just trying to turn me off gently."

"Really, Nick. Try asking me for Saturday evening and see!"

"You're asked, then."

"And it's a date." Then, with a return of her usual insouciance, she added. "If you're on good behavior."

"I will be. I promise."

"I hope so," said Pat. An inexplicable sense of foreboding had come over her; despite her self-given assurances, something unnamable troubled her. She gave a mental shrug, and deliberately relegated the unpleasant cogitations to oblivion.

The car turned into Dempster Road; the lights of the teeming roadhouses, dance halls, road-side hamburger and barbecue stands flashed by. There were many cars here; there was no longer any impression of solitude now, in the overflow from the vast city in whose shadow they moved. The incessant flow of traffic gave the girl a feeling of security; these were tangible things about her, and once more the memory of that disturbing occurrence became dim and dreamlike. This was Nick beside her, gentle, intelligent, kind; had he ever been otherwise? It seemed highly unreasonable, a fantasy of fear and the hysteria of the moment.

"Hungry?" asked Nick unexpectedly.

"I could use a barbecue, I guess. Beef."

The car veered to the graveled area before a brightly lit stand. Nick gave the order to an attendant. He chuckled as Pat, with the digestive disregard of youth attacked the greasy combination.

"That's like a humming bird eating hay!" he said.

"Or better, like a leprechaun eating that horse-meat they can for dogs."

"You might as well discover that I don't live on honey and rose-petals," said Pat. "Not even on caviar and terrapin—at least, not exclusively. I leave the dainty palate for Mother to indulge."

"Which is just as well. Hamburger and barbecue are more easily budgeted."

"Nicholas," said the girl, tossing the paper napkin out of the car window, "is that an indirect and very evasive proposal of marriage?"

"You know it could be, if you wished it!"

"And do I?" she said, assuming a pensive air. "I wonder. Suppose we say I'll let you know later."

"And meanwhile?"

"Oh, meanwhile we can be sort of engaged. Just the way we've been."

"You're sweet, Pat," he murmured, as the car edged into the line of traffic. "I don't know just how to convey my appreciation, but it's there!"

The buildings drew more closely together; the road was suddenly a lighted street, and then, almost without realizing it, they
were before Pat's home. Nick walked beside her to the door; he
stood facing her hesitantly.

"Good night, Pat," he said huskily. He leaned down, kissing her
very gently, turned, and departed.

The girl watched him from the open doorway, following the
lights of his car until they vanished down the street. Dear, sweet
Nick! Then the disturbing memory of that occurrence of the
evening returned; she frowned in perplexity as the thought rose.
That was all of a piece with the puzzling character of him, and
the curious veiled references he'd made. References to what? She
didn't know, couldn't imagine. Nick had said he didn't know either, which added still another quirk to the maze.

She thought of Dr. Horker's words. With the thought, she
glanced at his house, adjacent to her own home. A light gleamed
in the library; he was still awake. She closed the door behind her,
and darted across the narrow strip of lawn to his porch. She rang
the bell.

"Good evening, Dr. Carl," she said as the massive form of Horker appeared. She puckered her lips impudently at him as she slipped
by him into the house.

6. A Question of Science

"Not that I'm displeased at this visit, Pat," rumbled the Doctor, seating himself in one of the great chairs by the fireplace, "but I'm curious. I thought you were dating your ideal tonight, yet here you are, back alone a little after eleven. How come?"

"Oh," said the girl nonchantly, dropping crosswise in the other chair, "we decided we needed our beauty sleep."

"Then why are you here, you young imp?"

"Thought you might be lonesome."

"I'll bet you did! But seriously, Pat, what is it? Any trouble?"

"No-o," she said dubiously. "No trouble. I just wanted to ask you a few hypothetical questions. About science."

"Go to it, then, and quickly. I was ready to turn in."

"Well," said Pat, "about Nick's father. He was a doctor, you said, and supposed to be cracked. Was he really?"

"Humph! That's curious. I just looked up a brochure of his tonight in the American Medical Journal, after our conversation of this afternoon. Why do you ask that?"

"Because I'm interested, of course."

"Well, here's what I remember about him, Pat. He was an M.D., all right, but I see by his paper there—the one I was reading—that he was on the staff of Northern U. He did some work at the Cook County Asylum, some research work, and there was a bit of talk about his maltreating the patients. Then, on top of that, he published a paper that medical men considered crazy, and that started talk of his sanity. That's all I know."

"Then Nick—."

"I thought so! So it's come to the point where you're investigating his antecedents, eh? With an eye to marriage, or what?"

"Or what!" snapped Pat. "I was curious to know, naturally."

"Naturally." The Doctor gave her a keen glance from his shrewd eyes. "Did you think you detected incipient dementia in your ideal?"

35

"No," said the girl thoughtfully. "Dr. Carl, is there any sort of craziness that could take an ordinarily shy person and make a passionate devil of him? I don't mean passionate, either," she added. "Rather cold, ruthless, domineering."

"None that I know of," said Horker, watching her closely. "Did this Nick of yours have one of his masterful moments?"

"Worse than that," admitted Pat reluctantly. "We had a near accident, and it startled both of us, and then suddenly, he was looking at me like a devil, and then—" She paused. "It frightened me a little."

"What's he do?" demanded Horker sharply.

"Nothing." She lied with no hesitation.

"Were there any signs of Satyromania?"

"I don't know. I never heard of that."

"I mean, in plain Americanese, did he make a pass at you?"

"He—no, he didn't."

"Well, what did he do?"

"He just looked at me." Somehow a feeling of disloyalty was rising in her; she felt a reluctance to betray Nick further.

"What did he say, then? And don't lie this time."

"He just said—He just looked at my legs and said something about their being beautiful, and that was all. After that, the look on his face faded into the old Nick."

"Old Nick is right—the impudent scoundrel!" Horker's voice rumbled angrily.

"Well, they're nice legs," said Pat defiantly, swinging them as evidence. "You've said it yourself. Why shouldn't he say it? What's to keep him from it?"

"The code of a gentleman, for one thing!"

"Oh, who cares for your Victorian codes! Anyway, I came here for information, not to be cross-examined. I want to ask the questions myself."

"Pat, you're a reckless little spit-fire, and you're going to get burned some day, and deserve it," the Doctor rumbled ominously. "Ask your fool questions, and then I'll ask mine."

"All right," said the girl, still defiant. "I don't guarantee to answer yours, however."

"Well, ask yours, you imp!"

36

"First, then—is that Satyro-stuff you mentioned intermittent or continuous?"

"It's necessarily intermittent, you numb-skull! The male organism can't function continuously!"

"I mean, does the mania lie dormant for weeks or months, and then flare up?"

"Not at all. It's a permanent mania, like any other psychopathic sex condition."

"Oh," said Pat thoughtfully, with a sense of relief.

"Well, go on. What next?"

"What are these dual personalities you read about in the papers?"

"They're aphasias. An individual forgets his name, and he picks, or is given, another, if he happens to wander among strangers. He forgets much of his past experience; the second personality is merely what's left of the first—sort of a vestige of his normal character. There isn't any such thing as a dual personality in the sense of two distinct characters living in one body."

"Isn't there?" queried the girl musingly. "Could the second personality have qualities that the first one lacked?"

"Not any more than it could have an extra finger! The second is merely a split off the first, a forgetfulness, a loss of memory. It couldn't have more qualities than the whole, or normal, character; it must have fewer."

"Isn't that just too interesting!" said Pat in a bantering tone. "All right, Dr. Carl. It's your turn."

"Then what's the reason for all this curiosity about perversions and aphasias? What's happened to your genius now?"

"Oh, I'm thinking of taking up the study of psychiatry," replied the girl cheerfully.

"Aren't you going to answer me seriously?"

"No."

"Then what's the use of my asking questions?"

"I know the right answer to that one. None!"

"Pat," said Horker in a low voice, "you're an impudent little hoyden, and too clever for your own good, but you and your mother are very precious to me. You know that."

"Of course I do, Dr. Carl," said the girl, relenting. "You're a dear, and I'm crazy about you, and you know that, too."

"What I'm trying to say," proceeded the other, "is simply that I'm trying to help you. I want to help you, if you need help. Do you?"

"I guess I don't, Dr. Carl, but you're sweet."

"Are you in love with this Nicholas Devine?"

"I think perhaps I am," she admitted softly.

"And is he in love with you?"

"Frankly, could he help being?"

"Then there's something about him that worries you. That's it, isn't it?"

"I thought there was, Dr. Carl. I was a little startled by the change in him right after we had that narrow escape, but I'm sure it was nothing—just imagination. Honestly, that's all that troubled me."

"I believe you, Pat," said the Doctor, his eyes fixed on hers. "But guard yourself, my dear. Be sure he's what you think he is; be sure you know him rightly."

"He's clean and fine," murmured the girl. "I am sure."

"But this puzzling yourself about his character, Pat—I don't like it. Make doubly sure before you permit your feelings to become too deeply involved. That's only common sense, child, not psychiatry or magic."

"I'm sure," repeated Pat. "I'm not puzzled or troubled any more. And thanks, Dr. Carl. You run along to bed and I'll do likewise."

He rose, accompanying her to the door, his face unusually grave.

"Patricia," he said, "I want you to think over what I've said. Be sure, be doubly sure, before you expose yourself to the possibility of suffering. Remember that, won't you?"

"I'll try to. Don't fret yourself about it, Dr. Carl; I'm a hard-boiled young modern, and it takes a diamond to even scratch me."

"I hope so," he said soberly. "Run along; I'll watch until you're inside."

Pat darted across the strip of grass, turned at her door to blow a goodnight kiss to the Doctor, and slipped in. She tiptoed quietly to her room, slipped off her dress, and surveyed her long, slim legs in the mirror.

"Why shouldn't he say they were beautiful?" she queried of the image. "I can't see any reason to get excited over a simple compliment like that."

38

She made a face over her shoulder at the green Buddha above the fireplace.

"And as for you, fat boy," she murmured, "I expect to see you wink at me tonight. And every night hereafter!"

She prepared herself for slumber, slipped into the great bed. She had hardly closed her lids before the image of a leering face with terrible bloody eyes flamed out of memory and set her trembling and shuddering.

7. The Red Eyes Return

"I suppose I really ought to meet you friends, Patricia," said Mrs. Lane, peering out of the window, "but they all seem to call when I'm not at home."

"I'll have some of them call in February." said Pat. "You're not out as often in February."

"Why do you say I'm not out as often in February?" demanded her mother. "I don't see what earthly difference the month makes."

"There are fewer days in February," retorted Pat airily.

"Facetious brat!"

"So I've been told. You needn't worry, though, mother; I'm sober, steady, and reliable, and if I weren't, Dr. Carl would see to it that my associates were."

"Yes; Carl is a gem," observed her mother. "By the way, who's this Nicholas you're so enthusiastic about?"

"He's a boy I met."

"What's he like?"

"Well, he speaks English and wears a hat."

"Imp! Is he nice?"

"That means is his family acceptable, doesn't it? He hasn't any family."

Mrs. Lane shrugged her attractive shoulders. "You're a self-reliant sort, Patricia, and cool as iced lettuce, like your father. I don't doubt that you can manage your own affairs, and here comes Claude with the car." She gave the girl a hasty kiss. "Goodbye, and have a good time, as I'm sure I shan't with Bret Cutter in the game."

Pat watched her mother's trim, amazingly youthful figure as she entered the car. More like a companion than a parent, she mused; she liked the independence her mother's attitude permitted her.

"Better than being watched like a prize-winning puppy," she thought. "Maybe Dr. Carl as a father would have a detriment or two along with the advantages. He's a dear, and I'm mad about

40

him, but he does lean to the nineteenth century as far as parental duties are concerned."

She saw Nick's car draw to the curb; as he emerged she waved from the window and skipped into the hall. She caught up her wrap and bounded out to meet him just ascending the steps.

"Let's go!" she greeted him. She cast an apprehensive glance at his features, but there was nothing disturbing about him. He gave her a diffident smile, the shy, gentle smile that had taken her in that first moment of meeting. This was certainly no one but her own Nick, with no trace of the unsettling personality of their last encounter.

He helped her into the car, seating himself at her side. He leaned over her, kissing her very tenderly; suddenly she was clinging to him, her face against the thrilling warmth of his cheek.

"Nick!" she murmured. "Nick! You're just safely you, aren't you? I've been imagining things that I knew couldn't be so!"

He slipped his arm caressingly about her, and the pressure of it was like the security of encircling battlements. The world was outside the circle of his arms; she was within, safe, inviolable. It was some moments before she stirred, lifting her pert face with tear-bright eyes from the obscurity of his shoulder.

"So!" she exclaimed, patting the black glow of her hair into composure. "I feel better, Nick, and I hope you didn't mind."

"Mind!" he ejaculated. "If you mean that as a joke, honey, it's far too subtle for me."

"Well, I didn't think you'd mind," said Pat demurely, settling herself beside him. "Let's be moving, then; Dr. Carl is nearly popping his eyes out in the window there."

The car hummed into motion; she waved a derisive arm at the Doctor's window by way of indicating her knowledge of his surveillance. *Ought to teach him a lesson some time,* she thought. *One of these fine evenings I'll give him a real shock.*

"Where'll we go?" queried Nick, veering skilfully into the swift traffic of Sheridan Road.

"Anywhere!" she said blithely. "Who cares as long as we go together?"

"Dancing?"

"Why not? Know a good place?"

"No." He frowned in thought. "I haven't indulged much."

"The Picador?" she suggested. "The music's good, and it's not too expensive. But it's 'most across town, and besides, Saturday nights we'd be sure to run into some of the crowd."

"What of it?"

"I want to dance with you, Nick—all evening. I want to be without distractions."

"Pat, dear! I could kiss you for that."

"You will," she murmured softly.

They moved aimlessly south with the traffic, pausing momentarily at the light-controlled intersections, then whirring again to rapid motion. The girl leaned against his arm silently, contentedly; block after block dropped behind.

"Why so pensive, honey?" he asked after an interval. "I've never known you so quiet before."

"I'm enjoying my happiness, Nick."

"Aren't you usually happy?"

"Of course, only these last two or three days, ever since our last date, I've been making myself miserable. I've been telling myself foolish things, impossible things, and it's only now that I've thrown off the blues. I'm happy, Dear!"

"I'm glad you are," he said. His voice was strangely husky, and he stared fixedly at the street rushing toward them. "I'm glad you are," he repeated, a curious tensity in his tones.

"So'm I."

"I'll never do anything to make you unhappy, Pat—never. Not—if I can help it."

"You can help it, Nick. You're the one making me happy; please keep doing it."

"I—hope to." There was a queer catch in his voice. It was almost as if he feared something.

"Selah!" said Pat conclusively. She was thinking, "Wrong of me to refer to that accident. After all it was harmless; just a natural burst of passion. Might happen to anyone."

"Where'll we go?" asked Nick as they swung into the tree-shadowed road of Lincoln Park. "We haven't decided that."

"Anywhere," said the girl dreamily. "Just drive; we'll find a place."

"You must know lots of them."

"We'll find a new place; we'll discover it for ourselves. It'll mean more, doing that, than if we just go to one of the old places where I've been with every boy that ever dated me. You don't want me dancing with a crowd of memories, do you?"

"I shouldn't mind as long as they stayed merely memories."

"Well, I should! This evening's to be ours—exclusively ours."

"As if it could ever be otherwise!"

"Indeed?" said Pat. "And how do you know what memories I might choose to carry along? Are you capable of inspecting my mental baggage?"

"We'll check it at the door. You're traveling light tonight, aren't you?"

"Pest!" she said, giving his cheek an impudent vicious pinch. "Nice, pleasurable pest!"

He made no answer. The car was idling rather slowly along Michigan Boulevard; half a block ahead glowed the green of a traffic light. Faster traffic flowed around them, passing them like water eddying about a slow floating branch.

Suddenly the car lurched forward. The amber flame of the warning light had flared out; they flashed across the intersection a split second before the metallic click of the red light, and a scant few feet before the converging lines of traffic from the side street swept in with protesting horns.

"Nick!" the girl gasped. "You'll rate yourself a traffic ticket! Why'd you cut the light like that?"

"To lose your guardian angel," he muttered in tones so low she barely understood his words.

Pat glanced back; the lights of a dozen cars showed beyond the barrier of the red signal.

"Do you mean one of those cars was following us? What on earth makes you think that, and why should it, anyway?"

The other made no answer; he swerved the car abruptly off the avenue, into one of the nondescript side street. He drove swiftly to the corner, turned south again, and turned again on some street Pat failed to identify—South Superior or Grand, she thought. They were scarcely a block from the magnificence of Michigan Avenue and its skyscrapers, its brilliant lights, and its teeming night traffic, yet here they moved down a deserted dark thoroughfare, a street lined with ramshackle wooden houses intermingled with mean little shops.

"Nick!" Pat exclaimed. "Where are we going?"

The low voice sounded. "Dancing," he said.

He brought the car to the curb; in the silence as the motor died, the faint strains of a mechanical piano sounded. He opened the car door, stepped around to the sidewalk.

"We're here," he said.

Something metallic in his tone drew Pat's eyes to his face. The eyes that returned her stare were the bloody orbs of the demon of last Wednesday night!

8. Gateway to Evil

Pat stared curiously at the apparition but made no move to alight from the vehicle. She was conscious of no fear, only a sense of wonder and perplexity. After all, this was merely Nick, her own harmless, adoring Nick, in some sort of mysterious masquerade, and she felt full confidence in her ability to handle him under any circumstances.

"Where's here?" she said, remaining motionless in her place.

"A place to dance," came the toneless reply. Pat eyed him; a street car rumbled past, and the brief glow from its lighted windows swept over his face. Suddenly the visage was that of Nick; the crimson glare of the eyes was imperceptible, and the features were the well-known appurtenances of Nicholas Devine, but queerly tensed and strained.

A trick of the light, she thought, as the street car lumbered away, and again a faint gleam of crimson appeared. She gazed curiously at the youth, who stood impassively returning her survey as he held the door of the car. But the face was the face of Nick, she perceived, probably in one of his grim moods.

She transferred her glance to the building opposite which they had stopped. The strains of the mechanical piano had ceased; blank, shaded windows faced them, around whose edges glowed a subdued light from within. A drab, battered, paintless shack, she thought, dismal and unpleasant; while she gazed, the sound of the discordant music recommenced, adding, it seemed, the last unprepossessing item.

"It doesn't look very attractive, Nick," she observed dubiously.

"I find it so, however."

"Then you've been here?"

"Yes."

"But I thought you said you didn't know any place to go."

"This one hadn't occurred to me—then."

"Well," she said crisply, "I could have done as well as this with my eyes closed. It doesn't appeal to me at all, Nick."

"Nevertheless, here's where we'll go. You're apt to find it—interesting."

"Look here, Nicholas Devine!" Pat snapped, "What makes you think you can bully me? No one has ever succeeded yet!"

"I said you'd find it interesting." His voice was unchanged; she stared at him in complete bafflement.

"Oh, Nick!" she exclaimed in suddenly softer tones. "What difference does it make? Didn't I say anywhere would do, so long as we went together?" She smiled at him. "This will do if you wish, though really, honey, I'd prefer not."

"I do wish it," the other said.

"All right, honey," said Pat the faintest trace of reluctance in her voice as she slipped from the car. "I stick to my bargains."

She winced at the intensity of his grip as he took her arm to assist her. His fingers were like taunt wires biting into her flesh.

"Nick!" she cried. "You're hurting me! You're bruising my arm!"

He released her; she rubbed the spot ruefully, then followed him to the door of the mysterious establishment. The unharmonious jangle of the piano dinned abruptly louder as he swung the door open. Pat entered and glanced around her at the room revealed.

Dull, smoky, dismal—not the least exciting or interesting as yet, she thought. A short bar paralleled one wall, behind which lounged a little, thin, nondescript individual with a small mustache. Half a dozen tables filled the remainder of the room; four or five occupied by the clientele of the place, as unsavory a group as the girl could recall having encountered on the hither side of the motion picture screen. Two women tittered as Nick entered; then with one accord, the eyes of the entire group fixed on Pat, where she stood drawing her wrap more closely about her, standing uncomfortably behind her escort. And the piano tinkled its discords in the far corner.

"Same place," said Nick shortly to the bartender, ignoring the glances of the others. Pat followed him across the room to a door, into a hall, thence into a smaller room furnished merely with a table and four chairs. The nondescript man stood waiting in the doorway as Nick took her wrap and seated her in one of the chairs.

"Quart," he said laconically, and the bartender disappeared.

Pat stared intently, studiously, into the face of her companion. Nick's face, certainly; here in full light there was no trace of the red-eyed horror she had fancied out there in the semi-darkness of the street. Or was there? Now—when he turned, when the light struck his eyes at an angle, was that a glint of crimson? Still, the features were Nick's, only a certain grim intensity foreign to him lurked about the set of his mouth, the narrowed eye-lids.

"Well!" she said. "So this is Paris! What are you trying to do—teach me capital L—life? And where do we dance?"

"In here."

"And what kind of quart was that you ordered? You know how little I drink, and I'm darned particular about even that little."

"You'll like this."

"I doubt it."

"I said you'll like it," he reiterated in flat tones.

"I heard you say it." She regarded him with a puzzled frown. "Nick," she said suddenly, "I've decided I like you better in your gentle pose; this masterful attitude isn't becoming, and you can forget what I said about wishing you'd display it oftener."

"You'll like that, too."

"Again I doubt it. Nick, dear, don't spoil another evening like that last one!"

"This one won't be like the last one!"

"But honey—" she paused at the entrance of the bartender bearing a tray, an opened bottle of ginger ale, two glasses of ice, and a flask of oily amber liquid. He deposited the assortment on the red-checked table cloth.

"Two dollars," he said, pocketed the money and silently retired.

"Nicholas," said the girl tartly, "there's enough of that poison for a regiment."

"I don't think so."

"Well, I won't drink it, and I won't let you drink it! So now what?"

"I think you'll do both."

"I don't!" she snapped. "And I don't like this, Nick—the place, or the liquor, or your attitude, or anything. We're going to leave!"

Instead of answering, he pulled the cork from the bottle, pouring a quantity of the amber fluid into each of the tumblers. To one he added an equal quantity of ginger ale, and set it deliberately squarely in front of Pat. She frowned at it distastefully, and shook her head.

"No," she said. "Not I. I'm leaving."

She made no move, however; her eyes met those of her companion, gazing at her with a cold intentness in their curious amber depths. And again—was that a flash of red? Impulsively she reached out her hand, touched his.

"Oh, Nick!" she said in soft, almost pleading tones. "Please, honey—I don't understand you. Don't you know I love you, Nick? You can hear me say it: I love you. Don't you believe that?"

He continued his cold, intense stare; the grim set of his mouth was as unrelaxing as marble. Pat felt a shiver of apprehension run through her, and an almost hypnotic desire to yield herself to the demands of the inexplicable eyes. She tore her glance away, looking down at the red checks of the table cloth.

"Nick, dear," she said. "I can't understand this. Will you tell me what you—will you tell me why we're here?"

"It is out of your grasp."

"But—I know it has something to do with Wednesday night, something to do with that reluctance of yours, the thing you said you didn't understand. Hasn't it?"

"Do you think so?"

"Yes," she said. "I do! And Nick, honey—didn't I tell you I could forgive you anything? I don't care what's happened in the past; all I care for is now, now and the future. Don't you understand me? I've told you I loved you, honey! Don't you love me?"

"Yes," said the other, staring at her with no change in the fixity of his gaze.

"Then how can you—act like this to me?"

"This is my conception of love."

"I don't understand!" the girl said helplessly. "I'm completely puzzled—it's all topsy-turvy."

"Yes," he said in impassive agreement.

"But what is this, Nick? Please, please—what is this? Are you mad?" She had almost added, "Like your father."

"No," he said, still in those cold tones. "This is an experiment."

"An experiment!"

"Yes. An experiment in evil."

"I don't understand," she repeated.

"I said you wouldn't."

"Do you mean," she asked, struck by a sudden thought, "that discussion of ours about pure horror? What you said that night last week?"

"That!" His voice was icy and contemptuous. "That was the drivel of a weakling. No; I mean evil, not horror—the living evil that can be so beautiful that one walks deliberately, with open eyes, into Hell only to prevent its loss. That is the experiment."

"Oh," said Pat, her own voice suddenly cool. "Is that what you wish to do—experiment on me?"

"Yes."

"And what am I supposed to do?"

"First you are to drink with me."

"I see," she said slowly. "I see—dimly. I am a subject, a reagent, a guinea pig, to provide you material for your writing. You propose to use me in this experiment of yours—this experiment in evil. All right!" She picked up the tumbler; impulsively she drained it. The liquor, diluted as it was, was raw and strong enough to bring tears smarting to her eyes. Or was it the liquor?

"All right!" she cried. "I'll drink it all—the whole bottle!" She seized the flask, filling her tumbler to the brim, while her companion watched her with impassive gaze. "You'll have your experiment! And then, Nicholas Devine, we're through! Do you hear me? Through!"

She caught up the tumbler, raised it to her lips, and drained the searing liquid until she could see her companion's cold eyes regarding her through the glass of its bottom.

9. Descent into Avernus

Pat slammed the empty tumbler down on the checked table cloth and buried her face in her hands, choking and gasping from the effects of the fiery liquor. Her throat burned, her mouth was parched by the acrid taste, and a conflagration seemed to be raging somewhere within her. Then she steadied, raised her eyes, and stared straight into the strange eyes of Nicholas Devine.

"Well?" she said fiercely. "Is that enough?"

He was watching her coldly as an image or a painting; the intensity of his gaze was more cat-like than human. She moved her head aside; his eyes, without apparent shift, were still on hers, like the eyes of a pictured face. A resurgence of anger shook her at his immobility; his aloofness seemed to imply that nothing she could do would disturb him.

"Wasn't it enough?" she screamed. "Wasn't it? Then look!"

She seized the bottle, poured another stream of the oily liquid into her glass, and raised it to her lips. Again the burning fluid excoriated her tongue and throat, and then suddenly, the tumbler was struck from her hand, spilling the rest of its contents on the table.

"That is enough," said the icy voice of her companion.

"Oh, it is? We'll see!" She snatched at the bottle, still more than half full. The thin hand of Nicholas Devine wrenched it violently away.

"Give me that!" she cried. "You wanted what you're getting!" The warmth within her had reached the surface now; she felt flushed, excited, reckless, and desperately angry.

The other set the bottle deliberately on the floor; he rose, circled the table, and stood glaring down at her with that same inexplicable expression. Suddenly he raised his hand; twisting her black hair in his fist, he dealt her a stinging blow across the lips half-opened to scream, then flung her away so violently that she nearly sprawled from her chair.

The scream died in her throat; dazed by the blow, she dropped her head to the table, while sobs of pain and fear shook her. Coherent thought had departed, and she knew only that her lips stung, that her clear, active little mind was caught in a mesh of befuddlement. She couldn't think; she could only sob in the haze of dizziness that encompassed her. After a long interval, she raised her head, opened her eyes upon a swaying, unsteady world, and faced her companion, who had silently resumed his seat.

"Nicholas Devine," she said slowly, speaking as if each word were an effort, "I hate you!"

"Ah!" he said and was again silent.

She forced her eyes to focus on his face, while his features danced vaguely as if smoke flowed between the two of them. It was as if there were smoke in her mind as well; she made a great effort to rise above the clouds that bemused her thoughts.

"Take me home," she said. "Nicholas, I want to go home."

"Why should I?" he asked impassively. "The experiment is hardly begun."

"Experiment?" she echoed dully. "Oh, yes—experiment. I'm an experiment."

"An experiment in evil," he said.

"Yes—in evil. And I hate you! That's evil enough, isn't it?"

He reached down, lifted the bottle to the table, and methodically poured himself a drink of the liquor. He raised it, watching the oily swirls in the light, then tipped the fluid to his lips while the girl gazed at him with a sullen set to her own lips. A tiny crimson spot had appeared in the corner of her mouth; at its sting, she raised her hand and brushed it away. She stared as if in unbelief at the small red smear it left on her fingers.

"Nicholas," she said pleadingly, "won't you take me home? Please, Nicholas, I want to leave here."

"Do you hate me?" he asked, a queer twisting smile appearing on his lips.

"If you'll take me home I won't" said Pat, snatching through the rising clouds of dizziness at a straw of logic. "You're going to take me home, aren't you?"

"Let me hear you say you hate me!" he demanded, rising again. The girl cringed away with a little whimper as he approached. "You hate me, don't you?"

He twisted his hand again in her ebony hair, drawing her face back so that he stared down at it.

"There's blood on your lips," he said as if gloating. "Blood on your lips!"

He clutched her hair more tightly; abruptly he bent over her, pressing his mouth to hers. Her bruised lips burned with pain at the fierce pressure of his; she felt a sharp anguish at the impingement of his teeth. Yet the cloudy pall of dizziness about her was unbroken; she was too frightened and bewildered for resistance.

"Blood on your lips!" he repeated exultingly. "Now is the beauty of evil!"

"Nicholas," she said wearily, clinging desperately to a remnant of logic, "what do you want of me? Tell me what you want and then let me go home."

"I want to show you the face of evil," he said. "I want you to know the glory of evil, the loveliness of supreme evil!"

He dragged his chair around the table, placing it beside her. Seated, he drew her into his arms, where she lay passive, too limp and befuddled to resist. With a sudden movement, he turned her so that her back rested across his knees, her face gazing up into his. He stared intently down at her, and the light, shining at an angle into his eyes, suddenly struck out the red glow that lingered in them.

"I want you to know the power of evil," he murmured. "The irresistible, incomprehensible fascination of it, and the unspeakable pleasures of indulgence in it."

Pat scarcely heard him; she was struggling now in vain against the overwhelming fumes of the alcohol she had consumed. The room was wavering around her, and behind her despair and terror, a curious elation was thrusting itself into her consciousness.

"Evil," she echoed vaguely.

"Blood on your lips!" he muttered, peering down at her. "Taste the unutterable pleasure of kisses on bloody lips; drain the sweet anguish of pain, the fierce delight of suffering!"

He bent down; again his lips pressed upon hers, but this time she felt herself responding. Some still sane portion of her brain rebelled, but the intoxication of sense and alcohol was dominant. Suddenly she was clinging to him, returning his kisses, glorying in the pain of her lacerated lips. A red mist suffused her; she had no consciousness of anything save the exquisite pain of the kiss, that somehow contrived to transform itself into an ecstasy of delight. She lay gasping as the other withdrew his lips.

"You see!" he gloated. "You understand! Evil is open to us, and all the unutterable pleasures of the damned, who cry out in transports of joy at the bite of the flames of Hell. Do you see?"

The girl made no answer, sobbing in a chaotic mingling of pain and excruciating pleasure. She was incapable of speech or connected thought; the alcohol beat against her brain with a persistence that defied resistance. After a moment, she stirred, struggling erect to a sitting posture.

"Evil!" she said dizzily. "Evil and good—what's difference? All in a lifetime!"

She felt a surge of tipsy elation, and then the muffled music of the mechanical piano, drifting through the closed door, penetrated her befuddled consciousness.

"I want to dance!" she cried. "I'm drunk and I want to dance! Am I drunk?" she appealed to her companion.

"Yes," he said.

"I am not! I just want to dance, only it's hot in here. Dance with me, Nicholas—show me an evil dance! I want to dance with the Devil, and I will! You're the Devil, name and all! I want to dance with Old Nick himself!"

She rose unsteadily from her chair; instantly the room reeled crazily about her and she fell sprawling. She felt the grasp of arms beneath her shoulders, raising her erect; she leaned against the wall and heard herself laughing wildly.

"Funny room!" she said. "Evil room—on pivots!"

"You're still to learn," came the toneless voice of Nicholas Devine. "Do you want to see the face of evil?"

"Sure!" she said. "Got a good memory for faces!"

She realized that he was fumbling with the catch of her dress on her left shoulder; again some remnant, some vestige of sanity deep in her brain warned her.

"Mustn't," she said vaguely.

Then suddenly the catch was open; the dress dropped away around her, crumpling to a shapeless blob of cloth about her diminutive feet. She covered her face with her hands, fighting to hold that last, vanishing vestige of sobriety, while she stood swaying drunkenly against the wall.

Then Nicholas Devine's arms were about her again; she felt the sharp sting of his kisses on her throat. He swung her about, bent her backwards across the low table; she was conscious of a bewildered sensation of helplessness and of little else.

"Now the supreme glory of evil!" he was muttering in her ear. She felt his hands on her bare shoulders as he pressed her backward.

Then, abruptly, he paused, releasing her. She sat dizzily erect, following the direction of his gaze. In the half open door stood the nondescript bartender leering in at them.

10. Rescue from Abaddon

Pat slid dizzily from her perch on the table and sank heavily to a chair. The interruption of the mustached keeper of this den of contradictions struck her as extremely humorous; she giggled hysterically as her wavering gaze perceived the consternation in his sharp little face. Some forlorn shred of modesty asserted itself, and she dragged a corner of the red-checked table cloth across her knees.

"Get out!" said Nicholas Devine in that voice of rasping metal. "Get out!" he repeated in unchanging tones.

The other made no move to leave. "Yeah?" he said. "Listen, Bud—this place is respectable, see? You want to pull something like this, you go upstairs, see? And pay for your room."

"Get out!" There was no variation in the voice.

"*You* get out! The both of you, see?"

Nicholas Devine stepped slowly toward him; his back, as he advanced upon the bartender, was toward Pat, yet through the haze of intoxication, she had an impression of evil red eyes in a chill, impassive face. "Get out!"

The other had no stomach for such an adversary. He backed out of the door, closing it as he vanished. His voice floated in from the hall.

"I'm telling you!" he called. "Clear out!"

Nicholas Devine turned back toward the girl. He surveyed her sitting in her chair; she had dropped her chin to her hand to steady the whirling of her head.

"We'll go," he said. "Come on."

"I just want to sit here," she said. "Just let me sit here. I'm tired."

"Come on," he repeated.

"Why?" she muttered petulantly. "I'm tired."

"I want no interruptions. We'll go elsewhere."

"Must dress!" she murmured dazedly, "can't go on street without dress."

Nicholas Devine swept her frock from its place in the corner,

55

gathered her wrap from the chair, and flung them over his arm. He grasped her wrist, tugging her to an unsteady standing position.

"Come on," he said.

"Dress!"

He snatched the red checked table cloth from its place, precipitating bottles, ash-tray, and glasses into an indiscriminate pile, and threw the stained and odorous fabric across her shoulders. She gathered it about her like a toga; it hung at most points barely below her waist, but it satisfied the urge of her muddled mind for a covering of some sort.

"We'll go through the rear," her companion said. "Into the alley. I want no trouble with that rat in the bar—yet!"

He still held Pat's wrist; she stumbled after him as he dragged her into the darkness of the hall. They moved through it blindly to a door at the far end; Nicholas swung it open upon a dim corridor flanked by buildings on either side, with a strip of star-sprinkled sky above.

Pat's legs were somehow incapable of their usual lithe grace; she failed to negotiate the single step, and crashed heavily to the concrete paving. The shock and the cooler air of the open steadied her momentarily; she felt no pain from her bruised knees, but a temporary rift in the fog that bound her mind. She gathered the red-checked cloth more closely about her shoulders as her companion, still clutching her wrist, jerked her violently to her feet.

They moved into the gulch of the alley, and here she found difficulty in following. Her tiny high-heeled pumps slipped at every step on the uneven cobbles of the paving, and the unsteady footing made her lurch and stumble until the dusty stretch of the alley was a writhing panorama of shadows and lighted windows and stars. Nicholas Devine turned an impatient glare on her, and here in the semi-darkness, his face was again the face of the red-eyed demon. She dragged him to a halt, laughing strangely.

"There it is!" she cried, pointing at him with her free hand. He turned again, staring at her with grim features.

"What?"

"There! Your face—the face of evil!" Again she laughed hysterically.

The other stepped to her side; the disturbing eyes were inches

56

from her own. He raised his hand as she laughed, slapped her sharply, so that her head reeled. He seized her shoulders, shaking her until the checkered cloth billowed like a flag in a wind.

"Now come!" he muttered.

But the girl, laughing no longer, leaned pale and weak again a low board fence. Her limbs seemed paralyzed, and movement was quite impossible. She was conscious of neither the blow nor the shaking, but only of a devastating nausea and an all-encompassing weakening. She bent over the fence; she was violently ill.

Then the nausea had vanished, and weariness, a strange lassitude, was all that remained. Nicholas Devine stood over her; suddenly he pressed her body to him in a convulsive embrace, so that her head dropped back, and his face loomed above her, obliterating the stars.

"Ah!" he said. He seemed about to kiss her when a sound—voices—filtered out of somewhere in the maze of dark courts and littered yards along the alley. He released her, seized her wrist, and once more she was stumbling wretchedly behind him over the uneven surface of the cobblestones.

A numbness had come over her; consciousness burned very low as she wavered doggedly along through the darkness. She perceived dimly that they were approaching the end of the alley; the brighter glow of the street loomed before them, and a passing motor car cut momentary parallel shafts of luminescence across the opening.

Nicholas Devine slowed his pace, still clutching her wrist in a cold grip; he paused, moving cautiously toward the corner of the building. He peered around the edge of the structure, surveying the now deserted street, while Pat stood dully behind him, incapable alike of thought or voluntary movement, clutching desperately at the dirty cloth that hung about her shoulders.

Her companion finished his survey; apparently satisfied that progress was safe, he dragged her after him, turning toward the corner beyond which his car was parked. The girl staggered behind him with diminishing vigor; consciousness was very nearly at the point of disappearance, and her steps were wavering unsteadily, and doggedly slow. She dragged heavily on his arm; he gave a gesture of impatience at her weakness.

"Come on!" he growled. "We're just going to the corner." His voice rose slightly in pitch, still sounding harsh as rasping metals. "There still remains the ultimate evil!" he said. "There is still a depth of beauty unplumbed, a pain whose exquisite pleasure is yet to find!"

They approached the corner; abruptly Nicholas Devine drew back as two figures came unexpectedly into view from beyond it. He turned back toward the alleyway, dragging the girl in a dizzy circle. He took a few rapid steps.

But Pat was through, exhausted. At his first step she stumbled and sprawled, dragging prone behind him. He released her hand and turned defiantly to face the approaching men, while the girl lying on the pavement struggled to a sitting posture with her back against the wall. She turned dull, indifferent eyes on the scene, then was roused to a somewhat higher pitch of interest by the sound of a familiar voice.

"There he is! I told you it was his car."

Dr. Horker! She struggled for clarity of thought; she realized dimly that she ought to feel relief, happiness—but all she could summon was a faint quickening of interest, or rather, a diminution of the lassitude that held her. She drew the rag of a table cloth about her and huddled against the wall, watching. The Doctor and some strange man, burly and massive in the darkness, dashed upon them, while Nicholas Devine waited, his red-orbed face a demoniac picture of cold contempt. Then the Doctor glanced at her huddled, bedraggled figure; she saw his face aghast, incredulous, as he perceived the condition of her clothing.

"Pat! My God, girl! What's happened? Where've you been?"

She found a hidden reserve somewhere within her. Her voice rose, shrill and hysterical.

"We've been in Hell!" she said. "You came to take me back, didn't you? Orpheus and Eurydice!" She laughed. "Dr. Orpheus Horker!"

The Doctor flashed her another incredulous glance and a grim and very terrible expression flamed in his face. He turned toward Nicholas Devine, his hands clenching, his mouth twisting without utterance, with no sound save a half-audible snarl. Then he spoke, a low, grating phrase flung at his thick-set companion.

"Bring the car," was all he said. The man lumbered away toward the corner, and he turned again toward Nicholas Devine, who faced him impassively. Suddenly his fist shot out; he struck the youth or demon squarely between the red eyes, sending him reeling back against the building. Then the Doctor turned, bending over Pat; she felt the pressure of his arms beneath knees and shoulders. He was carrying her toward a car that drew up at the curb; he was placing her gently in the back seat. Then, without a glance at the figure still leaning against the building, he swept from the sidewalk the dark mass that was Pat's dress and her wrap, and re-entered the car beside her.

"Shall I turn him in?" asked the man in the front seat.

"We can't afford the publicity," said the Doctor, adding grimly, "I'll settle with him later."

"Pat's head lurched as the car started; she was losing consciousness, and realized it vaguely, but she retained one impression as the vehicle swung into motion. She perceived that the face of the lone figure learning against the building, a face staring at her with horror and unbelief, was no longer the visage of the demon of the evening, but that of her own Nick.

11. Wreckage

Pat opened her eyes reluctantly, with the impression that something unpleasant awaited her return to full consciousness. Something, as yet she could not recall just what, had happened to her; she was not even sure where she was awakening.

However, her eyes surveyed her own familiar room; there opposite the bed grinned the jade Buddha on his stand on the mantel—the one that Nick had—Nick! A mass of troubled, terrible recollections thrust themselves suddenly into consciousness. She visioned a medley of disturbing pictures, as yet disconnected, unassorted, but waiting only the return of complete wakefulness. And she realized abruptly that her head ached miserably, that her mouth was parched, that twinges of pain were making themselves evident in various portions of her anatomy. She turned her head and caught a glimpse of a figure at the bedside; her startled glance revealed Dr. Horker, sitting quietly watching her.

"Hello, Doctor," she said, wincing as her smile brought a sharp pain from her lips. "Or should I say, Good morning, Judge?"

"Pat!" he rumbled, his growling tones oddly gentle. "Little Pat! How do you feel, child?"

"Fair," she said. "Just fair. Dr. Carl, what happened to me last night? I can't seem to remember—Oh!"

A flash of recollection pierced the obscure muddle. She remembered now—not all of the events of that ghastly evening, but enough. Too much!

"Oh!" she murmured faintly. "Oh, Dr. Carl!"

"Yes," he nodded. "'Oh!'—and would you mind very much telling me what that 'Oh' of yours implies?"

"Why—". She paused shuddering, as one by one the events of that sequence of horrors reassembled themselves. "Yes, I'd mind very much," she continued. "It was nothing—" She turned to him abruptly. "Oh, it was, though, Dr. Carl! It was horrible, unspeakable, incomprehensible!—But I can't talk about it! I can't!"

"Perhaps you're right," said the Doctor mildly. "Don't you really want to discuss it?"

"I do want to," admitted the girl after a moment's reflection. "I want to—but I can't. I'm afraid to think of all of it."

"But what in Heaven's name did you do?"

"We just started out to go dancing," she said hesitatingly. "Then, on the way to town, Nick—changed. He said someone was following us."

"Someone was," said Horker. "*I* was, with Mueller. That Nick of yours has the Devil's own cleverness!"

"Yes," the girl echoed soberly. "The Devil's own!—Who's Mueller, Dr. Carl?"

"He's a plain-clothes man, friend of mine. I treated him once. What do you mean by changed?"

"His eyes," she said. "And his mouth. His eyes got reddish and terrible, and his mouth got straight and grim. And his voice turned sort of—harsh."

"Ever happen before, that you know of?"

"Once. When—" She paused.

"Yes. Last Wednesday night, when you came over to ask those questions about pure science. What happened then?"

"We went to a place to dance."

"And that's the reason, I suppose," rumbled the Doctor sardonically, "that I found you wandering about the streets in a table cloth, step-ins, and a pair of hose! That's why I found you on the verge of passing out from rotten liquor, and looking like the loser of a battle with an airplane propeller! What happened to your face?"

"My face? What's wrong with it?"

The Doctor rose from his chair and seized the hand-mirror from her dressing table.

"Look at it!" he commanded, passing her the glass.

Pat gazed incredulously at the reflection the surface presented; a dark bruise colored her cheek, her lips were swollen and discolored, and her chin bore a jagged scratch. She stared at the injuries in horror.

"Your knees are skinned, too," said Horker. "Both of them."

Pat slipped one pajamaed limb from the covers, drawing the pants-leg up for inspection. She gasped in startled fright at the great red stain on her knee.

"That's mercurochrome," said the Doctor. "I put it there."

"You put it there. How did I get home last night, Dr. Carl? How did I get to bed?"

"I'm responsible for that, too. I put you to bed." He leaned forward. "Listen, child—your mother knows nothing about this as yet. She wasn't home when I brought you in, and she's not awake yet this morning. We'll tell her you had an automobile accident; explain away those bruises.—And now, how did you get them?"

"I fell, I guess. Two or three times."

"That bruise on your cheek isn't from falling."

The girl shuddered. Now in the calm light of morning, the events of last night seemed doubly horrible; she doubted her ability to believe them, so incredible did they seem. She was at a loss to explain even her own actions, and those of Nicholas Devine were simply beyond comprehension, a chapter from some dark and blasphemous book of ancient times—the Kabala or the Necronomicon.

"What happened, Pat?" queried the Doctor gently. "Tell me," he urged her.

"I—can't explain it," she said doubtfully. "He took me to that place, but drinking the liquor was my own fault. I did it out of spite because I saw he didn't—care for me. And then—" She fell silent.

"Yes? And then?"

"Well—he began to talk about the beauty of evil, the delights of evil, and his eyes glared at me, and—I don't understand it at all, Dr. Carl, but all of a sudden I was—yielding. Do you see?"

"I see," he said gently, soberly.

"Suddenly I seemed to comprehend what he meant—all that about the supreme pleasure of evil. And I was sort of—swept away. The dress—was his fault, but I—somehow I'd lost the power to resist. I guess I was drunk."

"And the bruises? And your cut lips?" queried the Doctor grimly.

"Yes," she said in a low voice. "He—struck me. After a while I didn't care. He could have—would have done other things, only we were interrupted, and had to leave. And that's all, Dr. Carl."

"Isn't that enough?" he groaned. "Pat, I should have killed the fiend there!"

"I'm glad you didn't."

"Do you mean to say you'd care?"

"I—don't know."

"Are you intimating that you still love him?"

"No," she said thoughtfully. "No, I don't love him, but—Dr. Carl, there's something inexplicable about this. There's something I don't understand, but I'm certain of one thing!"

"What's that?"

"That it wasn't Nick—not my Nick—who did those things to me last night. It wasn't, Dr. Carl!"

"Pat, you're being a fool!"

"I know it. But I'm sure of it, Dr. Carl. I know Nick; I loved him, and I know he couldn't have done—that. Not the same gentle Nick that I had to beg to kiss me!"

"Pat," said the Doctor gently, "I'm a psychiatrist; it's my business to know all the rottenness that can hide in a human being. My office is the scene of a parade of misfits, failures, potential criminals, lunatics, and mental incompetents. It's a nasty, bitter side I see of life, but I know that side—and I tell you this fellow is dangerous!"

"Do you understand this, Dr. Carl?"

He reached over, taking her hand in his great palm with its long, curious delicate fingers. "I have my theory, Pat. The man's a sadist, a lover of cruelty, and there's enough masochism in any woman to make him terribly dangerous. I want your promise."

"About what?"

"I want you to promise never to see him again."

The girl turned serious eyes on his face; he noted with a shock of sympathy that they were filled with tears.

"You warned me I'd get burned playing with fire," she said. "You did, didn't you?"

"I'm an old fool, honey. If I'd believed my own advice, I'd have seen that this never happened to you." He patted her hand. "Have I your promise?"

She averted her eyes. "Yes," she murmured. He winced as he perceived that the tears were on her cheeks.

"So!" he said, rising. "The patient can get out of bed when she feels like it—and don't forget that little fib we've arranged for your mother's peace of mind."

She stared up at him, still clinging to his hand.

"Dr. Carl," she said, "are you sure—quite sure—you're right

63

about him? Couldn't there be a chance that you're mistaken—that it's something your psychiatry has overlooked or never heard of?"

"Small chance, Pat dear."

"But a chance?"

"Well, neither I nor any reputable medic claims to know everything, and the human mind's a subtle sort of thing."

12. Letter from Lucifer

"I'm glad!" Pat told herself. I'm glad it's over, and I'm glad I promised Dr. Carl—I guess I was mighty close to the brink of disaster that time." She examined the injuries on her face, carefully powdered to conceal the worst effects from her mother. The trick had worked, too; Mrs. Lane had delivered herself of an excited lecture on the dangers of the gasoline age, and then thanked Heaven it was no worse. Well, Pat reflected, she had good old Dr. Carl to thank for the success of the subterfuge; he had broken the news very skillfully, set the stage for her appearance, and calmed her mother's apprehensions of scars. And Pat, surveying her image in the glass above her dressing table, could see for herself the minor nature of the hurts.

"Scars—pooh!" she observed. "A bruised cheek, a split lip, a skinned chin. All I need is a black eye, and I guess I'd have had that in five minutes more, and perhaps a cauliflower ear into the bargain."

But her mood was anything but flippant; she was fighting off the time when her thoughts had of necessity to face the unpleasant, disturbing facts of the affair. She didn't want to think of the thing at all; she wanted to laugh it off and forget it, yet she knew that for an impossibility. The very desire to forget she recognized as a coward's wish, and she resented the idea that she was cowardly.

"Forget the wise-cracks," she advised her image. "Face the thing and argue it out; that's the only way to be satisfied."

She rose with a little grimace of pain at the twinge from her bruised knees, and crossed to the chaise lounge beside the far window. She settled herself in it and resumed her cogitations. She was feeling more or less herself again; the headache of the morning had nearly vanished, and aside from the various aches and a listless fagged-out sensation, she approximated her normal self. Physically, that is; the shadow of that other catastrophe, the one she hesitated to face, was another matter.

"I'm lucky to get off this easily," she assured herself, "after going on a bust like that one, like a lumberjack with his pay in his pocket." She shook her head in mournful amazement. "And I'm Patricia Lane, the girl whom Billy dubbed 'Pat the Impeccable'! Impeccable! Wandering through alleys in step-ins and a table cloth—getting beaten up in a drunken brawl—passing out on rot-gut liquor—being carried home and put to bed! Not impeccable; incapable's the word! I belong to Dr. Carl's parade of incompetents."

She continued her rueful reflections. "Well, item one is, I don't love Nick any more. I couldn't now!" she flung at the smiling green Buddha on the mantel. "That's over; I've promised."

Somehow there was not satisfaction in the memory of that promise. It was logical, of course; there wasn't anything else to do now, but still—

"That *wasn't* Nick!" she told herself. "That wasn't *my* Nick. I guess Dr. Carl is right, and he's a depressed whatever-it-was; but if he's crazy, so am I! He had me convinced last night; I understood what he meant, and I felt what he wanted me to feel. If he's crazy, I am too; a fine couple we are!"

She continued. "But it wasn't Nick! I saw his face when we drove off, and it had changed again, and that was Nick's face, not the other. And he was sorry; I could see he was sorry, and the other could never have regretted it—not ever! The other isn't—quite human, but Nick is."

She paused, considering the idea. "Of course," she resumed, "I might have imagined that change at the end. I was hazy and quivery, and it's the last thing I *do* remember; that must have been just before I passed out."

And then, replying to her own objection, "But I *didn't* imagine it! I saw it happen once before, that other night when—Well, what difference does it make, anyway? It's over, and I've given my promise."

But she was unable to dismiss the matter as easily as that. There was some uncanny, elusive element in it that fascinated her. Cruel, terrible, demoniac, he might have been; he had also been kind, lovable, and gentle. Yet Dr. Carl had told her that split personalities could contain no characteristics that were not present in the original, normal character. Was cruelty, then, a part of kindness? Was cruelty merely the lack of kindness, or, cynical thought, was kindness but the lack of cruelty? Which qualities were positive in the antagonistic phases of Nicholas Devine's individuality, and which negative? Was the gentle, lovable, but indubitably weaker character the split, and the demon of last evening his normal self? Or vice-versa? Or were both of these fragmentary entities, portions of some greater personality as yet unapparent to her?

The whole matter was a mystery; she shrugged in helpless perplexity.

"I don't think Dr. Carl knows as much about it as he says," she mused. "I don't think psychiatry or any other science knows that much about the human soul. Dr. Carl doesn't even believe in a soul; how could he know anything about it, then?" She frowned in puzzlement and gave up the attempt to solve the mystery.

The hours she had spent in her room, at her mother's insistence, began to pall; she didn't feel particularly ill—it was more of a languor, a depressed, worn-out feeling. Her mother, of course, was out somewhere; she felt a desire for human companionship, and wondered if the Doctor might by some chance drop in. It seemed improbable; he had his regular Sunday afternoon routine of golf at the Club, and it took a real catastrophe to keep him away from that. She sighed, stretched her legs, rose from her position on the chase lounge, and wandered toward the kitchen where Magda was doubtless to be found.

It was in the dusk of the rear hall that the first sense of her loss came over her. Heretofore her renunciation of Nicholas Devine was a rational thing, a promise given but not felt; but now it was suddenly a poignant reality. Nick was gone, she realized; he was out of her world, irrevocably sundered from her. She paused at the top of the rear flight of stairs, considering the matter.

"He's gone! I won't see him ever again." The thought was appalling; she felt already a premonition of loneliness to come, of an emptiness in her world, a lack that nothing could replace.

"I shouldn't have promised Dr. Carl," she mused, knowing that even without that promise her course must still have been the same. "I shouldn't have, not until I'd talked to Nick—my own Nick."

And still, she reflected forlornly, what difference did it make? She had to give him up; she couldn't continue to see him not knowing at what instant that terrible caricature of him might appear to torment her. But he might have explained, she argued miserably, answering her own objection at once—he's said he couldn't explain, didn't understand. The thing was at an impasse.

She shook her shining black head despondently, and descended the dusky well of the stairs to the kitchen. Magda was there clattering among her pots and pans; Pat entered quietly and perched on the high stool by the long table. Old Magda, who had warmed her babyhood milk and measured out her formula, gave her a single glance and continued her work.

"Sorry about the accident, I was," she said without looking up.

"Thanks," responded the girl. "I'm all right again."

"You don't look it."

"I feel all right."

She watched the mysterious, alchemistic mixing of a pastry, and thought of the vast array of them that had come from Magda's hands. As far back as she could remember she had perched on this stool observing the same mystic culinary rites.

Suddenly another memory rose out of the grave of forgetfulness and went gibbering across her world. She remembered the stories Magda used to tell her, frightening stories of witchcraft and the evil eye, tales out of an older region and a more credulous age.

"Magda," she asked, "did you ever see a devil?"

"Not I, but I've talked with them that had."

"Didn't you ever see one?"

"No." The woman slid a pan into the oven. "I saw a man once, when I was a tot, possessed by a devil."

"You did? How did he look?"

"He screamed terrible, then he said queer things. Then he fell down and foam came out of his mouth."

"Like a fit?"

"The Priest, he said it was a devil. He came and prayed over him, and after a while he was real quiet, and then he was all right."

"Possessed by a devil," said Pat thoughtfully. "What happened to him?"

"Dunno."

"What queer things did he say?"

"Wicked things, the Priest said. I couldn't tell! I was a tot."

"Possessed by a devil!" Pat repeated musingly. She sat immersed in thoughts on the high stool while Magda clattered busily about. The woman paused finally, turning her face to the girl.

"What you so quiet about, Miss Pat?"

"I was just thinking."

"You get your letter?"

"Letter? What letter? Today's Sunday."

"Special delivery. The girl, she put it in the hall."

"I didn't know anything about it. Who'd write me a special?"

She slipped off the high stool and proceeded to the front hall. The letter was there, solitary on the salver that always held the mail. She picked it up, examining the envelope in sudden startled amazement and more than a trace of illogical exultation.

For the letter, postmarked that same morning, was addressed in the irregular script of Nicholas Devine!

13. Indecision

Pat turned the envelope dubiously in her hands, while a maze of chaotic thoughts assailed her. She felt almost a sensation of guilt as if she were in some manner violating the promise given to Dr. Horker; she felt a tinge of indignation that Nicholas Devine should dare communicate with her at all, and she felt too that queer exultation, an inexplicable pleasure, a feeling of secret triumph. She slipped the letter in the pocket of her robe and padded quietly up the stairs to her own room. Strangely, her loneliness had vanished. The great house, empty now save for herself and Magda in the distant kitchen, was no longer a place of solitude; the discovery of the letter, whatever its contents, had changed the deserted rooms into chambers teeming with her own excitements, trepidations, doubts, and hopes. Even hopes, she admitted to herself, though hopes of what nature she was quite unable to say.

What *could* Nick write that had the power to change things? Apologies? Pleas? Promises? None of these could alter the naked, horrible facts of the predicament. Nevertheless, she was almost a-tremble with expectation as she skipped hastily into her own room, carefully closed the door, and settled herself by the west windows. She drew the letter from her pocket, and then, with a tightening of her throat, tore open the envelope, slipping out the several pages of scrawled paper. Avidly she began to read.

> *I don't know whether you'll ever see this and I'll not blame you, Pat dear, if you do return it unopened. There's nothing you can do that wouldn't be justified, nor can you think worse of me than I do of myself. And that's a statement so meaningless that even as I wrote it, I could anticipate its effect on you.*
>
> *Pat—How am I going to convince you that I'm sincere? Will you believe me when I write that I love you? Can you believe that I love you tenderly, worshipfully—reverently?*
>
> *You can't; I know you can't after that catastrophe of last night.*

But it's true, Pat, though the logic of a Spinoza might fail to convince you of it.

I don't know how to write you this. I don't know whether you want to hear what I could say, but I know that I must try to say it. Not apologies, Pat—I shouldn't dare approach you for so poor a reason as that—but a sort of explanation. You more than any one in the world are entitled to that explanation, if you want to hear it.

I can't write it to you, Pat; it's something I can only make you believe by telling you—something dark and rather terrible. But please, Dear, believe that I mean you no harm, and that I plan no subterfuge, when I suggest that you see me. It will be, I think, for the last time.

Tonight, and tomorrow night, and as many nights to follow as I can, I'll sit on a bench in the park near the place where I kissed you that first time. There will be people passing there, and cars driving by; you need fear nothing from me. I choose the place to bridle my own actions, Pat; nothing can happen while we sit there in the view of the world.

To write you more than this is futile. If you come, I'll be there; if you don't, I'll understand.

I love you.

The letter was signed merely 'Nick'. She stared at the signature with feelings so confused that she forebore any attempt to analyze them.

"But I can't go," she mused soberly. "I've promised Dr. Carl. Or at least, I can't go without telling him."

That last thought, she realized, was a concession. Heretofore she hadn't let herself consider the possibility of seeing Nicholas Devine again, and now suddenly she was weakening, arguing with herself about the ethics of seeing him. She shook her head decisively.

"Won't do, Patricia Lane!" she told herself. "Next thing, you'll be slipping away without a word to anybody, and coming home with two black eyes and a broken nose. Won't do at all!"

She dropped her eyes to the letter. "Explanations", she reflected. "I guess Dr. Carl would give up a hole-in-one to hear that explanation. And I'd give more than that." She shook her head regretfully. "Nothing to do about it, though. I promised."

The sun was slanting through the west windows; she sat watching the shadows lengthen in the room, and tried to turn her thoughts into more profitable channels. This was the first Sunday in many months that she had spent alone in the house; it was a custom for herself and her mother to spend the afternoon at the club. The evening too, as a rule; there was invariably bridge for Mrs. Lane, and Pat was always the center of a circle of the younger members. She wondered dreamily what the crowd thought of her non-appearance, reflecting that her mother had doubtless enlarged on Dr. Carl's story of an accident. Dr. Carl wouldn't say much, simply that he'd ordered her to stay at home. But sooner or later, Nick would hear the accident story; she wondered what he'd think of it.

She caught herself up sharply. "My ideas wander in circles," she thought petulantly. "No matter where I start, they curve around back to Nick. It won't do; I've got to stop it."

Nearly time for the evening meal, she mused, watching the sun as it dropped behind Dr. Horker's house. She didn't feel much like eating; there was still a remnant of the exhausted, dragged-out sensation, though the headache that had accompanied her awakening this morning had disappeared.

"I know what the morning after feels like, anyway," she reflected with a wry little smile. "Everybody ought to experience it once, I suppose. I wonder how Nick—"

She broke off abruptly, with a shrug of disgust. She slipped the letter back into its envelope, rose and deposited it in the drawer of the night-table. She glanced at the clock ticking on its shiny top.

"Six o'clock," she murmured. Nick would be sitting in the park in another two hours or so. She had a twinge of sympathy at the thought of his lone vigil; she could visualize the harried expression on his face when the hours passed without her arrival.

"Can't be helped," she told herself. "He's no right to ask for anything of me after last night. He knows that; he said so in his letter."

She suppressed an impulse to re-read that letter, and trotted deliberately out of the room and down the stairs. Magda had set the table in the breakfast room; it was far cozier than the great dining room, especially without her mother's company. And the maid was away; the breakfast room simplified serving, as well.

She tried valorously to eat what Magda supplied, but the food

72

failed to tempt her. It wasn't so much her physical condition, either; it was—She clenched her jaws firmly; was the memory of Nicholas Devine to haunt her forever?

"Pat Lane," she said in admonition, "you're a crack-brained fool! Just because a man kicks you all over the place is no reason to let him become an obsession."

She drank her coffee, feeling the sting of its heat on her injured lips. She left the table, tramped firmly to her room, and began defiantly to read. The effort was useless; half a dozen times she forced her attention to the page only to find herself staring vaguely into space a moment or two later. She closed the book finally with an irritable bang, and vented her restlessness in pacing back and forth.

"This house is unbearable!" she snapped. "I'm not going to stay shut up here like a jail-bird in solitary confinement. A walk in the open is what I need, and that's what I'll have."

She glanced at the clock; seven-thirty. She tore off her robe pettishly, flung out of her pajamas, and began to dress with angry determination. She refused to think of a lonely figure that might even now be sitting disconsolately on a bench in the nearby park.

She disguised her bruised cheek as best she could, dabbed a little powder on the abrasion on her chin, and tramped militantly down the stairs. She caught up her wrap, still lying where the Doctor had tossed it last night, and moved toward the door, opening it and nearly colliding with the massive figure of Dr. Horker!

"Well!" boomed the Doctor as she started back in surprise. "You're pretty spry for a patient. Think you were going out?"

"Yes," said Pat defiantly.

"Not tonight, child! I left the Club early to take a look at you."

"I am perfectly all right. I want to go for a walk."

"No walk. Doctor's orders."

"I'm of legal age!" she snapped. "I want to go for a walk. Do I go?"

"You do not." The Doctor placed his great form squarely in the doorway. "Not unless you can lick me, my girl, and I'm pretty tough. I put you to bed last night, and I can do as much tonight. Shall I?"

Pat backed into the hall. "You don't have to", she said sullenly. "I'm going there myself." She flung her wrap angrily to a chair and stalked up the stairs.

73

"Goodnight, spit-fire," he called after her. "I'll read down here until your mother comes home."

The girl stormed into her room in anger that she knew to be illogical.

"I won't be watched like a problem child!" she told herself viciously. "I know damn well what he thought—and I wasn't going to meet Nick! I wasn't at all!"

She calmed suddenly, sat on the edge of her bed and kicked off her pumps. It had occurred to her that Nick had written his intention to wait for her in the park tomorrow night as well, and Dr. Horker's interference had confirmed her in a determination to meet him.

14. Bizarre Explanation

"I won't be bullied!" Pat told herself, examining her features in the mirror. The two day interval had faded the discoloration of her cheek to negligible proportions, and all that remained as evidence of the violence of Saturday night was the diminishing mark on her chin. Of course, her knees—but they were covered; most of the time, at least. She gave herself a final inspection, and somewhere below a clock boomed.

"Eight o'clock," she remarked to her image. "Time to be leaving, and it serves Dr. Carl right for his highhanded actions last night. I won't be bullied by anybody." She checked herself as her mind had almost added, "Except Nick." True or not, she didn't relish the thought; the recent recollections it roused were too disturbing.

She tossed a stray wisp of black hair from her forehead and turned to the door. She heard her mother's voice as she descended the stairs.

"Are you going out, Patricia? Do you think it wise?"

"I am perfectly all right. I want to go for a walk."

"I know, Dear; it was largely your appearance I meant." She surveyed the girl with a critical eye. "Nice enough, except for that little spot on your chin, and will you never learn to keep your hair away from that side of your forehead? One can never do a bob right; why don't you let it grow out like the other girls?"

"Makes me individual," replied Pat, moving toward the outer door. "I won't be late at all," she added.

On the porch she cast a cautious glance at Dr. Horker's windows, but his great figure was nowhere evident. Only a light burning in the library evinced his presence. She gave a sigh of relief, and tiptoed down the steps to the sidewalk, and moved hastily away from the range of his watchful eyes.

No sooner had she sighted the park than doubts began to torment her. Suppose this were some trick of Nicholas Devine's, to trap her into some such situation as that of Saturday night. Even

75

suppose that she found him the sweet personality that she had loved, might that also be a trick? Mightn't he be trusting to his ability to win her over, to the charm she had confessed to him that he held for her? Couldn't he be putting his faith in his own amorous skill, planning some specious explanation to win her forgiveness only to use her once more as the material for some horrible experiment? And if he were, would she be able to prevent herself from yielding?

"Forewarned is fore-armed," she told herself. "I'll not put up such a feeble resistance this time, knowing what I now know. And it's only fair of me to listen to his explanation, if he really has one."

She was reassured by the sight of the crowded park; groups strolled along the walks, and an endless procession of car-headlights marked the course of the roadway. Nothing could happen in such an environment; they'd be fortunate even to have an opportunity for confidential talk. She waited for the traffic lights, straining her eyes to locate Nicholas Devine; at the click of the signal she darted across the street.

She moved toward the lake; here was the spot, she was sure. She glanced about with eagerness unexpected even to herself, peering through the shadow-shot dusk. He wasn't there, she concluded, with a curious sense of disappointment; her failure to appear last night had disheartened him; he had abandoned his attempt.

Then she saw him. He sat on a bench isolated from the rest in a treeless area overlooking the lake. She saw his disconsolate figure, his chin on his hand, staring moodily over the waters. A tremor ran through her, she halted deliberately, waiting until every trace of emotion had vanished, then she advanced, standing coolly beside him.

For a moment he was unaware of her presence; he sat maintaining his dejected attitude without glancing at her. Suddenly some slight movement, the flutter of her skirt, drew his attention; he turned sharply, gazing directly into her face.

"Pat!" He sprang to his feet. "Pat! Is it you—truly you? Or are you one of these visions that have been plaguing me for hours?"

"I'm real," she said, returning his gaze with a studied coolness in her face. She made no other move; her cold composure disconcerted him, and he winced, flushed, and moved nervously aside as she seated herself. He dropped beside her; he made no attempt to touch her, but sat watching her in silence for so long a time that she felt her composure ebbing. There was a hungry, defeated look about him; there was a wistfulness, a frustration, in his eyes that seemed about to tug tears from her own eyes. Abruptly she dropped her gaze from his face.

"Well?" she said finally in a small voice, and as he made no reply, "I'm here."

"Are you really, Pat? Are you truly here?" he murmured, still watching her avidly. "I—I still don't believe it. I waited here for hours and hours last night, and I'd given up hope for tonight, or any night. But I would have come again and again."

She started as he bent suddenly toward her, but he was merely examining her face. She saw the gleam of horror in his expression as his eyes surveyed the faintly visible bruise on her cheek, the red mark on her chin.

"Oh my God, Pat!" His words were barely audible. "Oh my God!" he repeated, drawing away from her and resuming the attitude of desolation in which her arrival had found him. "I've hoped it wasn't true!"

"What wasn't?" She was keeping her voice carefully casual; this miserable contrition of Nick's was tugging at her rather too powerfully for complete safety.

"What I remembered. What I saw just now."

"You hoped it wasn't true?" she queried in surprise. "But you did it."

"*I* did it, Pat? Do you think I could have done it?"

"But you did!" Her voice had taken on a chill inflection; the memory of those indignities came to steel her against him.

"Pat, do you think I could assault your daintiness, or maltreat the beauty I worship? Didn't anything occur to you? Didn't anything seem queer about—about that ghastly evening?"

"Queer! That's certainly a mild word to use, isn't it?"

"But I mean—hadn't you any idea of what had happened? Didn't you think anything of it except that I had suddenly gone mad? Or that I'd grown to hate you?"

"What was I to think?" she countered, trying to control the tremor that had crept into her voice.

"But did you think that?"

"No," the girl confessed after a pause. "At first, when you started with that drink, I thought you were looking for material for your work. That's what you said—an experiment. Didn't you?"

"I guess so," he groaned.

"But after that, after I'd swallowed that horrible stuff, but before everything went hazy, I—thought differently."

"But what, Pat? What did you think?"

"Why, then I realized that it wasn't you—not the real you. I could feel the—well, the presence of the person I knew; this presence that was tormenting me was another person, a terrible, cold, inhuman stranger."

"Pat!" There was a note almost of relief in his voice. "Did you really feel that?"

"Yes. Does it help matters, my sensing that? I can't see how."

His eyes, which had been fixed on hers, dropped suddenly. "No," he muttered, all the relief gone out of his tones, "no, it doesn't help, does it? Except that it's a meager consolation to me to know that you felt it."

Pat struggled to suppress an impulse to reach out her hand, to stroke his hair. She caught herself sharply; this was the very danger against which she had warned herself—this was the very attitude she had anticipated in Nicholas Devine, the lure which might bait a trap. Yet he looked so forlorn, so wistful! It was an effort to forbear from touching him; her fingers fairly ached to brush his cheek.

"Only a fool walks twice into the same trap," she told herself. Aloud she said, "You promised me an explanation. If you've any excuse, I'd like to hear it." Her voice had resumed its coolness.

"I haven't any excuse," he responded gloomily, "and the explanation is perhaps too bizarre, too fantastic for belief. *I* don't believe it entirely; I suppose you couldn't believe it at all."

"You promised," she repeated. The carefully assumed composure of her voice threatened to crack; this wistfulness of his was a powerful weapon against her defense.

"Oh, I'll give you the explanation," he said miserably. "I just wanted to warn you you'd not believe me." He gave her a despondent glance. "Pat, as I love you I swear that what I tell you is the truth. Do you think you can believe me?"

"Yes," she murmured. The tremor had reappeared in her voice despite her efforts.

Nicholas Devine turned his eyes toward the lake and began to speak.

15. A Modern Mr. Hyde

"I don 't remember when I first noticed it," began Nick in a low voice, "but I'm two people. I'm me, the person who's talking to you now, and I'm—another."

Pat, looking very pale and serious in the dusky light, said nothing at all. She simply gazed at him silently, without the slightest trace of surprise in her wide dark eyes.

"This is the real me," proceeded Nick miserably. "The other is an outsider, that has somehow contrived to grow into me. He is different; cold, cruel, utterly selfish, and not exactly—human. Do you understand?"

"Y—Yes," said the girl, fighting to control her voice. "Sort of."

"This is a struggle that has continued for a long time," he pursued. "There were times in childhood when I remember punishments for offenses I never committed, for nasty little meannesses he perpetrated. My mother, and after her death, my tutoress, thought I was lying when I tried to explain; they thought I was trying to evade responsibility. After a while I learned not to explain; I learned to accept my punishments doggedly, and to fight this other when he sought dominance."

"And could you?" asked Pat, her voice frankly quivery. "Could you fight him?"

"I was the stronger; I could win—usually. He slipped into consciousness as willful, mean little impulses, nasty moods, unreasoning hates and such unpleasant things. But I was always the stronger: I learned to drive him into the background."

"You said you were the stronger," she mused. "What does that mean, Nick?"

"I've always been the stronger; I am now. But recently, Pat— I think it's since I fell in love with you—the struggle has been on evener terms. I've weakened or he's gained. I have to guard against him constantly; in any moment of weakness he may slip in, as on our ride last week, when we had that near accident. And again Saturday." He turned appealing eyes on the girl. "Pat, do you believe me?"

"I guess I'll have to," she said unhappily. "It—makes things rather hopeless, doesn't it?"

He nodded dejectedly. "Yes. I've always felt that sooner or later I'd win, and drive him away permanently. I've felt on the verge of complete victory more than once, but now—" He shook his head doubtfully. "He had never dominated me so entirely until Saturday night—Pat, you don't know what Hell is like until you're forced as I was to watch the violation of the being you worship, to stand helpless while a desecration is committed. I'd rather die than suffer it again!"

"Oh!" said the girl faintly. She was thinking of the sorry picture she must have presented as she reeled half-clothed through the alley. "Can you see what—he sees?"

"Of course, and think his thoughts. But only when he's dominant. I don't know what evil he's planning now, else I could forestall him, I would have warned you if I could have known."

"Where is he now?"

"Here," said Nick somberly. "Here listening to us, knowing what I'm thinking and feeling, laughing at my unhappiness."

"Oh!" gasped Pat again. She watched her companion doubtfully. Then the memory of Dr. Horker's diagnosis came to her, and set her wondering. Was this story the figment of an unsettled mind? Was this irrational tale of a fiendish intruder merely evidence that the Doctor was right in his opinion? She was in a maze of uncertainty.

"Nick," she said, "did you ever try medical help? Did you ever go to a doctor about it?"

"Of course, Pat! Two years ago I went to a famous psychiatrist in New York—you'd know the name if I mentioned it—and told him about the—the case. And he studied me, and he treated me, and psychoanalyzed me, and the net result was just nothing. And finally he dismissed me with the opinion that 'the whole thing is just a fixed delusion, fortunately harmless! Harmless! Bah! But it wasn't I that did those things, Pat; I had to stand by in horror and watch. It was enough to drive me crazy, but it didn't—quite."

"But—Oh, Nick, what is it? What is this—this outsider? Can't we fight it somehow?"

"How can anyone except me fight it?"

"Oh, I don't know!" she wailed miserably. "There must be a way. Doctors claim to know pretty nearly everything; there must be something to do."

"But there isn't," he retorted gloomily. "I don't know any more than you what that thing is, but it's beyond your doctors. I've got to fight it out alone."

"Nick—" Her voice was suddenly tense. "Are you sure it isn't some kind of madness? Something tangible like that could perhaps be treated."

"It's no kind your doctors can treat, Pat. Did you ever hear of a madman who stood aside and rationally watched the working of his own insanity? And that's what I'm forced to do. And yet—this other isn't insane either. Were its actions insane?"

Pat shuddered. "I—don't know," she said in low tones. "I guess not."

"No. Horrible, cruel, bestial, devilishly cunning, evil—but not insane. I don't know what it is, Pat. I know that the fight has to be made by me alone. There's nothing, nobody in the world, that can help."

"Nick!" she wailed.

"I'm sorry, Pat dear. You understand now why I was so reluctant to fall in love with you. I was afraid to love you; now I know I was right."

"Nick!" she cried, then paused hopelessly. After a moment she continued, "Yesterday I was determined to forget you, and now—now I don't care if this whole tale of yours is a mesh of fantastic lies, I love you! I'd love you even if your real self were that—that other creature, and even if I knew that this was just a trap. I'd love you anyway."

"Pat," he said seriously, "don't you believe me? Why should I offer to give you up if this were—what you said? Wouldn't I be pleading for another chance, making promises, finding excuses?"

"Oh, I believe you, Nick! It isn't that; I was just thinking how strange it is that I could hate you so two nights past and love you so tonight."

"Oh God, Pat! Even you can't know how much I love you; and to win you and then be forced to give you up—" He groaned.

The girl reached out her hand and covered his; it was the first time during the evening that she had touched him, and the feel of his flesh sent a tingle through her. She was miserably distraught.

"Honey," she murmured brokenly. "Nick, honey."

He looked at her. "Do you suppose there's a chance to beat the thing?" he asked. "I'd not ask you to wait, Pat, but if I only glimpsed a chance——"

"I'll wait. I don't think I could do anything else but wait for you."

"If I only knew what I had to fight!" he whispered. "If I only knew that!"

A sudden memory leaped into Pat's mind. "Nick," she said huskily, "I think I know."

"What do you mean, Pat?"

"It's something Magda—the cook—said to me. It's foolish, superstitious, but Nick, what else can it be?"

"Tell me!"

"Well, she was talking to me yesterday, and she said that when she was a child in the old country, she had seen a man once——" she hesitated—"a man who was possessed by a devil. Nick, I think you're possessed by a devil!"

He stared at her. "Pat," he said hoarsely, "that's—an impossibility!"

"I know, but what else can it be?"

"Out of the Dark Ages," he muttered. "An echo of the Black Mass and witchcraft, but——"

"What did they do," asked the girl, "to people they thought were possessed?"

"Exorcism!" he whispered.

"And how did they—exorcise?"

"I don't know," he said in a low voice. "Pat, that's an impossible idea, but—I don't know!" he ended.

"We'll try," she murmured, still covering his hand with her own. "What else can we do, Nick?"

"What's done I'll do alone, Pat."

"But I want to help!"

"I'll not let you, Dear. I won't have you exposed to a repetition of those indignities, or perhaps worse!"

"I'm not afraid."

"Then I am, Pat! I won't have it!"

"But what'll you do?"

"I'll go away. I'll battle the thing through once for all, and I'll either come back free of it or—" He paused and the girl did not question him further, but sat staring at him with troubled eyes.

"I won't write you, Pat," he continued. "If you should receive a letter from me, burn it—don't read it. It might be from—the other, a trap or a lure of some sort. Promise me! You'll promise that, won't you?"

She nodded; there was a glint of tears in her eyes.

"And I don't want you to wait, Pat," he proceeded. "I don't want you to feel that you have any obligations to me—God knows you've nothing to thank me for! When—If I come back and you haven't changed, then we'll try again."

"Nick," she said in a small voice, "how do you know the—the other won't come back here? How can you promise for—it?"

"I'm still master!" he said grimly. "I won't be dominated long enough at any time for that to happen. I'll fight it down."

"Then—it's goodbye?"

He nodded. "But not for always—I hope."

"Nick," she murmured, "will you kiss me?" She felt a tear on her cheek. "I'll stand losing you a little better if I can have a—last kiss—to remember." Her voice was faltering.

His arms were about her. She yielded herself completely to his caress; the park, the crowd passing a few yards away, the people on nearby benches, were all forgotten, and once more she felt herself alone with Nicholas Devine in a vast empty cosmos.

An insistent voice penetrated her consciousness; she realized that it had been calling her name for some seconds.

"Miss Lane," she heard, and again, "Miss Lane." A hand tapped her shoulder; with a sudden start, she tore her lips away, and looked up into a face unrecognized for a moment. Then she placed it. It was the visage of Mueller, Dr. Horker's companion on that disastrous Saturday night.

16. Possessed

Pat stared at the intruder in a mingling of embarrassment, perplexity, and indignation. She felt her cheeks reddening as the latter emotion gained the dominance of her mood. "Well!" she snapped. "What do you want?"

"I thought I'd walk home with you," Mueller said amiably.

"Walk home with me! Please explain that!" She grasped the arm of Nicholas Devine, who had risen angrily at the interruption. "Sit down, Nick, I know the fellow."

"So should he," said Mueller. "Sure; I'll explain. I'm on a job for Dr. Horker."

"Spying on me for him, I suppose!" taunted the girl.

"No. Not on you."

"He means on me," said Nick soberly. "You can't blame him, Pat. And perhaps you had better go home; we've finished here. There's nothing more we can do or say."

"Very well," she said, her voice suddenly softer. "In a moment, Nick." She turned to Mueller. "Would you mind telling me why you waited until now to interfere? We've been here two hours, you know."

"Sure I'll tell you. I got no orders to interfere, that's why."

"Then why did you?" queried Pat tartly.

"I didn't until I saw him there"—he nodded at Nick—"put his arms around you. Then I figured, having no orders, it was time to use my own judgment."

"If any!" sniffed the girl. She turned again to Nick; her face softened, became very tender. "Honey," she murmured huskily, "I guess it's goodbye now. I'll be fighting with you; you know that."

"I know that," he echoed, looking down into her eyes. "I'm almost happy, Pat."

"When'll you go?" she whispered in tones inaudible to Mueller.

"I don't know," he answered, his voice unchanged. "I'll have to make some sort of preparations—and I don't want you to know."

She nodded. She gazed at him a moment longer with tear-bright eyes. "Goodbye, Nick," she whispered.

She rose on tiptoe, and kissed him very lightly on his lips, then turned and walked quickly away, with Mueller following behind.

She walked on, ignoring him until he halted beside her at the crossing of the Drive. Then she gave him a cold glance.

"Why is Dr. Carl having him watched?" she asked.

Mueller shrugged. "The ins and outs of this case are too much for me," he said. "I do what I'm paid to do."

"You're not watching him now."

"Nope. Seemed like the Doctor would think it was more important to get you home."

"You're wasting your time," she said irritably as the lights changed and they stepped into the street. "I was going home anyway."

"Well, now you got company all the way." Mueller's voice was placid.

The girl sniffed contemptuously, and strode silently along. The other's presence irritated her; she wanted time and solitude to consider the amazing story Nicholas Devine had given her. She wanted to analyze her own feelings, and most of all she wanted just a place of privacy to cry out her misery. For now the loss of Nicholas Devine had changed from a fortunate escape to a tragedy, and liar, madman, or devil, she wanted him terribly, with all the power of her tense little heart. So she moved as swiftly as she could, ignoring the silent companionship of Mueller.

They reached her home; the light in the living room window was evidence that the bridge game was still in progress. She mounted the steps, Mueller watching her silently from the walk; she fumbled for her key.

Suddenly she snapped her hand-bag shut; she couldn't face her mother and the two spinster Brocks and elderly, inquisitive Carter Henderson. They'd suggest that she cut into the game, and they'd argue if she refused, and she couldn't play bridge now! She glanced at the impassive Mueller, turned and crossed the strip of lawn to Dr. Horker's residence, where the light still glowed in the library, and rang the bell. She saw the figure on the sidewalk move away as the shadow of the Doctor appeared on the lighted square of the door.

"Hello," boomed the Doctor amiably. "Come in."

Pat stalked into the library and threw herself angrily into Dr. Horker's particular chair. The other grinned, and chose another place.

"Well," he said, "What touched off the fuse this time?"

"Why are you spying on my friends?" snapped the girl. "By what right?"

"So he's spotted Mueller, eh? That lad's diabolically clever, Pat—and I mean diabolic."

"That's no answer!"

"So it isn't," agreed the Doctor. "Say it's because I'm acting *in loco parentis*."

"And in loco is as far as you'll get, Dr. Carl, if you're going to spy on me!"

"On you?" he said mildly. "Who's spying on you?"

"On us, then!"

"Or on us?" queried the Doctor. "I set Mueller to watch the Devine lad. Have you by some mischance broken your promise to me?"

Pat flushed. She had forgotten that broken promise; the recollection of it suddenly took the wind from her sails, placed her on the defensive.

"All right," she said defiantly. "I did; I admit it. Does that excuse you?"

"Perhaps it helps to explain my actions, Pat. Don't you understand that I'm trying to protect you? Do you think I hired Mueller out of morbid curiosity, or professional interest in the case? Times aren't so good that I can throw money away on such whims."

"I don't need any protection. I can take care of myself!"

"So I noticed," said the Doctor dryly. "You gave convincing evidence of it night before last."

"Oh!" said the girl in exasperation. "You would say that!"

"It's true, isn't it?"

"Suppose it is! I don't have to learn the same lesson twice."

"Well, apparently once wasn't enough," observed the other amiably. "You walked into the same danger tonight."

"I wasn't in any danger tonight!" Suddenly her mood changed as she recalled the circumstances of her parting with Nicholas Devine. "Dr. Carl," she said, her voice dropping, "I'm terribly unhappy."

"Lord!" he exclaimed staring at her. "Pat, your moods are as changeable as my golf game! You're as mercurial as your Devine lad! A moment ago you were snapping at me, and now I'm suddenly acceptable again." He perceived the misery in her face. "All right, child; I'm listening."

"He's going away," she said mournfully.

"Don't you think that's best for everybody concerned? I commend his judgment."

"But I don't want him to!"

"You do, Pat. You can't continue seeing him, and his absence will make it easier for you."

"It'll never be easier for me, Dr. Carl." She felt her eyes fill. "I guess I'm—just a fool about him."

"You still feel that way, after the experience you went through?"

"Yes. Yes, I do."

"Then you are a fool about him, Pat. He's not worth such devotion."

"How do you know what he's worth? I'm the only one to judge that."

"I have eyes," said the Doctor. "What happened tonight to change your attitude so suddenly? You were amenable to reason yesterday."

"I didn't know yesterday what I know now."

"So he told a story, eh?" The Doctor watched her serious, troubled features, "Would you mind telling me, honey? I'm interested in the defense mechanisms these psychopathic cases erect to explain their own impulses to themselves."

"No, I won't tell you!" snapped Pat indignantly. "Psychopathic cases! We're all just cases to you. I'm a case and he's another, and all you want is our symptoms!"

Doctor Horker smiled placatingly into her face. "Pat dear," he said earnestly, "don't you see I'd give my eyes to help you? Don't take my flippancies too seriously, honey; look once in a while at the intentions behind them." He continued his earnest gaze.

The girl returned his look; her face softened. "I'm sorry," she said contritely. "I never doubted it, Dr. Carl—it's only that I'm so—so torn to pieces by all this that I get snappy and irritable." She paused. "Of course I'll tell you."

"I'd like to hear it."

"Well," she began hesitantly, "he said he was two personalities—one the character I knew, and one the character that we saw Saturday night. And the first one is—well, dominant, and fights the other one. He says the other has been growing stronger; until lately he could suppress it. And he says—Oh, it sounds ridiculous, the way I tell it, but it's true! I'm sure it's true!" She leaned toward the Doctor. "Did you ever hear of anything like it? Did you, Dr. Carl?"

"No." He shook his head, still watching her seriously. "Not exactly like that, honey. Don't you think he might possibly have lied to you, Pat? To excuse himself for the responsibility of Saturday night, for instance?"

"No, I don't," she said defiantly.

"Then you have an idea yourself what the trouble is? I judge you have."

"Yes," she said in low tones. "I have an idea."

"What is it?"

"I think he's possessed by a devil!" said the girl flatly.

A quizzical expression came into the Doctor's face. "Well, of all the queer ideas that harum-scarum mind of yours has ever produced, that's the queerest!" He broke into a chuckle.

"Queer, is it?" flared Pat. "I don't think you and your mind-doctors know as much as a Swahili medicine man with a mask!"

She leaped angrily to her feet, stamped viciously into the hall.

"Devil and all," she repeated, "I love him!"

"Pat!" called the Doctor anxiously. "Pat! Where are you going, child?"

"Where do devils live?" Her voice floated tauntingly back from the front door. "Hell, of course!"

17. Witch-Doctor

Pat had no intentions, however, of following the famous high-way that evening. She stamped angrily down the Doctor's steps, swished her way through the break in the hedge with small regard to the safety of her sheer hose, and mounted to her own porch. She found her key, opened the door and entered.

As she ascended the stairs, her fit of temper at the Doctor passed, and she felt lonely, weary, and unutterably miserable. She sank to a seat on the topmost step and gave herself over to bitter reflections.

Nick was gone! The realization came poignantly at last; there would be no more evening rides, no more conversations whose range was limited only by the scope of the universe, no more breath-taking kisses, the sweeter for his reluctance. She sat mournfully silent, and considered the miserable situation in which she found herself.

In love with a madman! Or worse—in love with a demon! With a being half of whose nature worshiped her while the other half was bent on her destruction! Was any one, she asked herself— was any one, anywhere, ever in a more hopeless predicament?

What could she do? Nothing, she realized, save sit helplessly aside while Nick battled the thing to a finish. Or possibly—the only alternative—take him as he was, chance the vicissitudes of his unstable nature, lay herself open to the horrors she had glimpsed so recently, and pray for her fortunes to point the way of salvation. And in the mood in which she now found herself, that seemed infinitely the preferable solution. Yet rationally she knew it was impossible; she shook her head despondently, and leaned against the wall in abject misery.

Then, thin and sharp sounded the shrill summons of the door bell, and a moment later, the patter of the maid's footsteps in the hall below. She listened idly to distract herself from the chain of despondency that was her thoughts, and was mildly startled to recognize the booming drums of Dr. Horker's voice. She heard his greeting and the muffled reply from the group, and then a phrase understandable because of his sonorous tones.

"Where's Pat?" The words drifted up the well of the stairs, followed by a scarcely audible reply from her mother. Heavy footfalls on the carpeted steps, and then his figure bulked on the landing below her. She cupped her chin on her hands, and stared down at him while he ascended to her side, sprawling his great figure beside her.

"Pat, honey," he rumbled, "you're beginning to get me worried!"

"Am I?" Her voice was weary, dull. "I've had myself like that for a long time."

"Poor kid! Are you really so miserable over this Nick problem of yours?"

"I love him."

"Yes." He looked at her with sympathy and calculation mingling in his expression. "I believe you do. I'm sorry, honey; I didn't realize until now what he means to you."

"You don't realize now," she murmured, still with the weary intonation.

"Perhaps not, Pat, but I'm learning. If you're in this thing as deeply as all that, I'm in too—to the finish. Want me?"

She reached out her hand, plucking at his coat-sleeve. Abruptly she leaned toward him, burying her face against the rough tweed of his suit; she sobbed a little, while he patted her gently with his great, delicately fingered hand. "I'm sorry, honey," he rumbled. "I'm sorry."

The girl drew herself erect and leaned back against the wall, shaking her head to drive the tears from her eyes. She gave the Doctor a wan little smile.

"Well?" she asked.

"I'll return your compliment of the other night," said Horker briskly. "I'll ask a few questions—purely professional, of course."

"Fire away, Dr. Carl."

"Good. Now, when our friend has one of these—uh—attacks, is he rational? Do his utterances seem to follow a logical thought sequence?"

"I—think so."

"In what way does he differ from his normal self?"

"Oh, every way," she said with a tremor. "Nick's kind and gentle and sensitive and—and naive, and this—other—is cruel, harsh, gross, crafty, and horrible. You can't imagine a greater difference."

"Um. Is the difference recognizable instantly? Could you ever be in doubt as to which phase you were encountering?"

"Oh, no! I can—well, sort of dominate Nick, but the other—Lord!" She shuddered again. "I felt like a terrified child in the presence of some powerful, evil god."

"Humph! Perhaps the god's name was Priapus. Well, we'll discount your feelings, Pat, because you weren't exactly in the best condition for—let's say sober judgment. Now about this story of his. What happens to his own personality when this other phase is dominant? Did he say?"

"Yes. He said his own self was compelled to sort of stand by while the—the intruder used his voice and body. He knew the thoughts of the other, but only when it was dominant. The rest of the time he couldn't tell its thoughts."

"And how long has he suffered from these—intrusions?"

"As long as he can remember. As a child he was blamed for the other's mischief, and when he tried to explain, people thought he was lying to escape punishment."

"Well," observed the Doctor, "I can see how they might think that."

"Don't you believe it?"

"I don't exactly disbelieve it, honey. The human mind plays queer tricks sometimes, and this may be one of its little jokes. It's a psychiatrist's business to investigate such things, and to painlessly remove the point of the joke."

"Oh, if you only can, Dr. Carl! If you only can!"

"We'll see." He patted her hand comfortingly.

"Now, you say the kind, gentle, and all that, phase is the normal one. Is that usually dominant?"

"Yes. Nick can master the other, or could until recently. He says this last—attack—is the worst he's ever had; the other has been gaining strength."

"Strange!" mused the Doctor. "Well," he said with a smile of encouragement, "I'll have a look at him."

"Do you think you can help?" Pat asked anxiously. "Have you any idea what it is."

"It isn't a devil, at any rate," he smiled.

"But have you any idea?"

"Naturally I have, but I can't diagnose at second hand. I'll have to talk to him."

"But what do you think it is?" she persisted.

"I think it's a fixation of an idea gained in childhood, honey. I had a patient once—" He smiled at the reminiscence—"who had a fixed delusion of that sort. He was perfectly rational on every point save one—he believed that a pig with a pink ribbon was following him everywhere! Down town, into elevators and offices, home to bed—everywhere he went this pink-ribboned prize porker pursued him!"

"And did you cure him?"

"Well, he recovered," said the Doctor noncommittally. "We got rid of the pig. And it might be something of that nature that's troubling your boyfriend. Your description doesn't sound like a praecox or a manic depressive, as I thought originally."

"Oh," said Pat abruptly. "I forgot. He went to a doctor in New York, a very great doctor."

"Muenster?"

"He didn't say whom. But this doctor studied him a long time, and finally came out with this fixed idea theory of yours. Only he couldn't cure him."

"Um." Horker grunted thoughtfully.

"Do fixed ideas do things like that to people?" queried the girl. "Things like the pig and what happened to Nick?"

"They might."

"Then they're devils!" she announced with an air of finality. "They're just your scientific jargon for exactly what Magda means when she says a person's possessed by a devil. So I'm right anyway!"

"That's good orthodox theology, Pat," chuckled the Doctor. "We'll try a little exorcism on your devil, then." He rose to his feet. "Bring your boyfriend around, will you?"

"Oh, Dr. Carl!" she cried. "He's leaving! I'll have to call him tonight!"

"Not tonight, honey. Mueller would let me know if anything of that sort were happening. Tomorrow's time enough."

The girl stood erect, mounting to the top step to bring her head level with the Doctor's. She threw her arms about him, burying her face in his massive shoulder.

"Dr. Carl," she murmured, "I'm a nasty, ill-tempered, vicious little shrew, and I'm sorry, and I apologize. You know I'm crazy about you, and," she whispered in his ear, "so's mother!"

18. Vanished

He doesn't answer! I'm too late, thought Pat disconsolately as she replaced the telephone. The cheerfulness with which she had awakened vanished like a patch of spring sunshine. Now, with the failure of her third attempt in as many hours to communicate with Nicholas Devine, she was ready to confess defeat. She had waited too long. Despite Dr. Horker's confidence in Mueller, she should have called last night—at once.

"He's gone!" she murmured distractedly. She realized now the impossibility of finding him. His solitary habits, his dearth of friends, his lonely existence, left her without the least idea of how to commence a search. She knew, actually, so little about him—not even the source of the apparently sufficient income on which he subsisted. She felt herself completely at a loss, puzzled, lonesome, and disheartened. The futile buzzing of the telephone signal symbolized her frustration.

Perhaps, she thought, Dr. Horker might suggest something to do; perhaps, even, Mueller had reported Nick's whereabouts. She seized the hope eagerly. A glance at her wrist-watch revealed the time as ten-thirty; squarely in the midst of the Doctor's morning office hours, but no matter. If he were busy she could wait. She rose, bounding hastily down the stairs.

She glimpsed her mother opening mail in the library, and paused momentarily at the door. Mrs. Lane glanced up as she appeared.

"Hello," said the mother. "You've been on the telephone all morning, and what did Carl want of you last night?"

"Argument," responded Pat briefly.

"Carl's a gem! He's been of inestimable assistance in developing you into a very charming and clever daughter, and Heaven knows what I'd have raised without him!"

"Cain, probably," suggested Pat. She passed into the hall and out the door, blinking in the brilliant August sunshine. She crossed the strip of turf, picked her way through the break in the hedge, and approached the Doctor's door. It was open; it often was in summer time, especially during his brief office hours. She entered and went into the chamber used as waiting room.

His office door was closed; the faint hum of his voice sounded. She sat impatiently in a chair and forced herself to wait.

Fortunately, the delay was nominal; it was but a few minutes when the door opened and an opulent, middle-aged lady swept past her and away. Pat recognized her as Mrs. Lowry, some sort of cousin of the Brock pair.

"Good morning!" boomed the Doctor. "Professional call, I take it, since you're here during office hours." He settled his great form in a chair beside her.

"He's gone!" said Pat plaintively. "I can't reach him."

"Humph!" grunted Horker helpfully.

"I've tried all morning—he's always home in the morning."

"Listen, you little scatterbrain!" rumbled the Doctor. "Why didn't you tell me Mueller brought you home last night? I thought he was on the job."

"I didn't think of it," she wailed. "Nick said he'd have to make some preparations, and I never dreamed he'd skip away like this."

"He must have gone home directly after you left him, and skipped out immediately," said the Doctor ruminatively. "Mueller never caught up with him."

"But what'll we do?" she cried desperately.

"He can't have gone far with no more preparation than this," soothed Horker. "He'll write you in a day or two."

"He won't! He said he wouldn't. He doesn't want me to know where he is!" She was on the verge of tears.

"Now, now," said the Doctor still in his soothing tones. "It isn't as bad as all that."

"Take off your bedside manner!" she snapped, blinking to keep back the tears. "It's worse! What ever can we do? Dr. Carl," she changed to a pleading tone, "can't you think of something?"

"Of course, Pat! I can think of several things to do if you'll quiet down for a moment or so."

"I'm sorry, Dr. Carl—but what can we do?"

"First, perhaps Mueller can trace him. That's his business, you know."

"But suppose he can't—what then?"

95

"Well, I'd suggest you write him a letter."

"But I don't know where to write!" she wailed. "I don't know his address!"

"Be still a moment, scatterbrain! Address it to his last residence; you know that, don't you? Of course you do. Now, don't you suppose he'll leave a forwarding address? He must receive some sort of mail about his income, or estate, or whatever he lives on. Your letter'll find him, honey; don't you doubt it."

"Oh, do you think so?" she asked, suddenly hopeful. "Do you really think so?"

"I really think so. You would too if you didn't fly into a panic every time some little difficulty confronts you. Sometimes even my psychiatry is puzzled to explain how you can be so clever and so stupid, so self-reliant and so dependent, so capable and so helpless—all at one and the same time. Your Nick can't be as much of a paradox as you are!"

"I wonder if a letter *will* reach him," she said eagerly, ignoring the Doctor's remarks. "I'll try. I'll try immediately."

"I sort of had a feeling you would," said Horker amiably. "I hope you succeed; and not only for your sake, Pat, because God knows how this thing will work out. But I'm anxious to examine this youngster of yours on my own account; he must be a remarkable specimen to account for all the perturbation he's managed to cause you. And this Jekyll and Hyde angle sounds interesting, too."

"Jekyll and Hyde!" echoed Pat. "Dr. Carl, is that possible?"

"Not literally," chuckled the other, "though in a sense, Stevenson anticipated Freud in his thesis that liberating the evil serves also to release the good."

"But it was a drug that caused that change in the story, wasn't it?"

"Well? Do you suspect your friend of being addicted to some mysterious drug? Is that the latest hypothesis?"

"*Is* there such a drug? One that could change a person's character?"

"*All* alkaloids do that, honey. Some of them stimulate, some depress, some breed frenzies, and some give visions of delight—but all of them influence one's mental and emotional organization, which you call character. So for that matter, does a square meal, or a cup of coffee, or even a rainy day."

"But isn't there a drug that can separate good qualities from evil, like the story?"

"Emphatically not, Pat! That's not the trouble with this pesky boyfriend of yours."

"Well," said the girl doubtfully, "I only wish I had as much faith in your psychologies as you have. If you brain-doctors know it all, why do you switch theories every year?"

"We don't know it all. On the other hand, there are a few things to be said in our favor."

"What are they?"

"For one," replied the Doctor, "we do cure people occasionally. You'll admit that."

"Sure," said Pat. "So did the Salem witches—occasionally." She gave him a suddenly worried look. "Oh, Dr. Carl, don't think I'm not grateful! You know how much I'm hoping for your help, but I'm miserably anxious over all this."

"Never mind, honey. You're not the first one to point out the shortcomings of the medical profession. That's a game played by plenty of physicians too." He paused at the sound of footsteps on the porch, followed by the buzz of the doorbell. "Run along and write your letter, dear—here comes that Tuesday hypochondriac of mine, and he's rich enough for my careful attention."

Pat flashed him a quick smile of farewell and slipped quietly into the hall. At the door she passed the Doctor's patient—a lean, elderly gentleman of woebegone visage—and returned to her own home.

Her spirits, mercurial to a degree, had risen again. She was suddenly positive that the Doctor's scheme would bring results, and she darted into the house almost buoyantly. Her mother had abandoned the desk, and she ensconced herself before it, finding paper and pen, and staring thoughtfully at the blank sheet. Finally she wrote:

Dear Nick—

Something has happened, favorable, I think, to us. I believe I have found the help we need.

Will you come if you can, or if that's not possible, break that self-given promise of yours, and communicate with me?

I love you.

She signed it simply *Pat*, placed it in an envelope, addressed it hastily, and hurried out to post it. On her return she spied the Doctor's hypochondriac in the act of leaving. He walked past her with his lean, worry-smitten face like a study of Hogarth, and she heard him mumbling to himself. The elation went out of her; she mounted the steps very soberly, and went miserably inside.

19. Man or Monster

Pat suffered Wednesday through somehow, knowing that any such early response to her letter was impossible. Still, that impossibility did not deter her from starting at the sound of the telephone, and sorting through the mail with an eagerness that drew a casual attention from her mother.

"Good Heavens, Patricia! You're like a child watching for an answer to his note to Santa Claus!"

"That's what I am, I guess," responded the girl ruefully. "Maybe I expect too much from Santa Claus."

Late in the afternoon she drifted over to Dr. Horker's residence, to be informed that he was out. For distraction, she went in anyway, and spent a while browsing among the books in the library. She blundered into Kraft-Ebing, and read a few pages in growing indignation.

"I'm ashamed to be human!" she muttered disgustedly to herself, slamming shut the *Psychopathia Sexualis*. "I wouldn't be a doctor, or have a child of mine become one, if I were positively certain he'd turn into Lord Lister himself! Nick was right when he said doctors live on people's troubles."

She wondered how Dr. Horker could remain so human, so kindly and understanding, when as he said himself his world was a parade of misfits, incompetents, and all the nastiness of mortals. He was nice; she felt no embarrassment in confiding in him even when she might hesitate to bare her feelings to her own mother. Or was it simply the natural thing to do to tell one's troubles to a doctor?

Not, of course, that the situation reflected any discredit on her mother. Mrs. Lane was a very precious sort of parent, she mused, young as Pat in spirit, appreciative and enthusiastically fond of her daughter. That she trusted Pat, that she permitted her to do entirely as she pleased, was exactly as the girl would have it; it argued no lack of affection that each of them had their separate interests, and if the girl occasionally found herself in unpleasantness such as this, that too was her own fault.

And yet, she reflected, it was a bitter thing to have no one to whom to turn. If it weren't for Dr. Carl and his jovial willingness to commit any sin up to malpractice to help her, she might have felt differently. But there always *was* Dr. Carl, and that, she concluded, was that.

She wandered back to her own side of the hedge, missing for the first time in many weeks the companionship of the old crowd. There hadn't been many idle afternoons heretofore during the summer; there'd always been some of the collegiate vacationing in town, and Pat had never needed other lure than her own piquant vivacity to assure herself of ample attention. Now, of course, it was different; she had so definitely tagged herself with the same Nicholas Devine that even the most ardent of the group had taken the warning.

"And I don't regret it either!" she told herself as she entered the house. "Trouble, mystery, suffering and all—I don't regret it! I've had my compensations too."

She sighed and trudged upstairs to prepare for dinner.

Morning found Pat in a fair frenzy of trepidation. She kept repeating to herself that two days wasn't enough, that more time might be required, that even had Nicholas Devine received her letter, he might not have answered at once. Yet she was quivering as she darted into the hall to examine the mail.

It was there! She spied a fragment of the irregular handwriting and seized the envelope from beneath a clutter of notes, bills, and advertisements. She glanced at the postmark. Chicago! He hadn't left the city, trusting perhaps to the anonymity conferred by its colossal swarm of humanity. Indeed, she thought as she stared at the missive, he might have moved around the corner, and save for the chance of a fortuitous meeting she'd never know it.

She tore open the envelope and scanned the several scrawled lines.

No heading, no salutation, not even a signature, just 'Thursday evening at our place in the park.' No more; she studied the few words intently, as if she could read into their bald phrasing the moods and hidden emotions of the writer.

A single phrase, but sufficient. The day was suddenly brighter, and the hope which had glowed so dimly yesterday was abruptly

almost more than a hope—a certainty. All her doubts of Dr. Horker's abilities were forgotten; already the solution of this uncanny
mystery seemed assured, and the restoration of romance imminent.
She carried the letter to her own room and tucked it carefully by the
other in the drawer of the night-table.

Thursday evening—this evening! Many hours intervened between now and a reasonable time for the meeting, but they loomed
no longer drab, dull, and hopeless. She lay on her bed and dreamed.

She could meet Nick as early as possible; perhaps at eight-thirty,
and bring him directly to the Doctor's residence. No use wasting a
moment, she mused; the sooner some light could be thrown on the
affliction, the sooner they could lay the devil—exorcise it. Demon,
fixed idea, mental aberration, or whatever Dr. Carl chose to call it,
it had to be met and vanquished once and forever. And it could be
vanquished; in her present mood she didn't doubt it. Then—after
that—there was the prospect of her own Nick regained, and the
sweet vistas opened by that reflection.

She lunched in an abstracted manner. In the afternoon, when
the phone rang, she jumped in a startled manner, then relaxed with
a shrug.

But this time it was for her. She darted into the hall to take the
call on the lower phone; she was hardly surprised but thoroughly
excited to recognize the voice of Nicholas Devine.

"Pat?"

"Nick! Oh, Nick, honey! What is it?"

"My note to you." Even across the wire she sensed the strain in
his tense tones. "You've read it?"

"Of course, Nick! I'll be there."

"No." His voice was trembling. "You won't come, Pat. Promise
you won't!"

"But why? Why not, Nick? Oh, it's terribly important that I
see you!"

"You're not to come, Pat!"

"But—" An idea was struggling to her consciousness. "Nick,
was it—?"

"Yes. You know now."

"But, honey, what difference does it make? You come. You
must, Nick!"

"I won't meet you, I tell you!" She could hear his voice rising excitedly in pitch, she could feel the intensity of the struggle across unknown miles of lifeless copper wire.

"Nick," she said, "I'm going to be there, and you're going to meet me."

There was silence at the other end.

"Nick!" she cried anxiously. "Do you hear me? I'll be there. Will you?"

His voice sounded again, now flat and toneless.

"Yes," he said. "I'll be there."

The receiver clicked at the far end of the wire; there was only a futile buzzing in Pat's ears. She replaced the instrument and sat staring dubiously at it.

Had that been Nick, really her Nick, or—? Suppose she went to that meeting and found—the other? Was she willing to face another evening of indignities and terrors like those still fresh in her memory?

Still, she argued, what harm could come to her on that bench, exposed as it was to the gaze of thousands who wandered through the park on summer evenings? Suppose it was the other who met her; there was no way to force her into a situation such as that of Saturday night. Nick himself had chosen that very spot for their other meeting, and for that very reason.

"There's no risk in it," she told herself, "Nothing can possibly happen. I'll simply go there and bring Nick back to Dr. Carl's, along a lighted, busy street, the whole two blocks. What's there to be afraid of?"

Nothing at all, she answered herself. But suppose—She shuddered and deliberately abandoned her chain of thought as she rose and rejoined her mother.

20. The Assignation

Pat was by no means as buoyant as she had been in the morning. She approached the appointed meeting place with a feeling of trepidation that all her arguments could not subdue.

She surveyed the crowded walks of the park with relief; she felt confirmed in her assumption that nothing unpleasant could occur with so many onlookers. So she approached the bench with somewhat greater self-assurance than when she had left the house.

She saw the seat with its lone occupant, and hastened her steps. Nicholas Devine was sitting exactly as he had on that other occasion, chin cupped on his hands, eyes turned moodily toward the vast lake that coruscated now with the reflection of stars and many lights. As before, she moved close to his side before he looked up, but here the similarity of the two occasions vanished. Her fears were realized; she was looking into the red-gleaming eyes and expressionless features of his other self—the demon of Saturday evening!

"Sit down!" he said as a sardonic half-smile twisted his lips. "Aren't you pleased? Aren't you thrilled to the very core of your being?"

Pat stood irresolute; she controlled an impulse to break into sudden, abandoned flight. The imminence of the crowded walks again reassured her, and she seated herself gingerly on the extreme edge of the bench, staring at her companion with coolly inimical eyes. He returned her gaze with features as immobile as carven stone; only his red eyes gave evidence of the obscene, uncanny life behind the mask.

"Well?" said Pat in as frigid a voice as she could muster.

"Yes," said the other surveying her. "You are quite as I recalled you. Very pretty, almost beautiful, save for a certain irregularity in your features. Not unpleasant, however." His eyes traveled over her body; automatically she drew back, shrinking away from him. "You have a seductive body," he continued. "A most seductive body; I regret that circumstances prevented our full enjoyment of it. But that will come. Yes, that will come!"

"Oh!" said Pat faintly. It took all her determination to remain seated by the side of the horror.

"You were extremely attractive as I attired you Saturday," the other proceeded. His lips took on a curious sensual leer. "I could have done better with more time; I would have stripped you somewhat more completely. Everything, I think, except your legs; I am pleased by the sight of long, straight, silk-clad legs, and should perhaps have received some pleasure by running these hands along them—scratching at proper intervals for the aesthetic effect of blood. But that too will come."

The girl sprang erect, gasping and speechless in outraged anger. She turned abruptly; nothing remained of her determination now. She felt only an urge to escape from the sneering tormentor who had lost in her mind all connection with her own Nicholas Devine. She took a sudden step.

"Sit down!" She heard the tones of the entity behind her, flat, unchanged. "Sit down, else I'll drag you here!"

She paused in sheer surprise, turning a startled face on the other.

"You wouldn't dare!" she said, amazed at the bald effrontery of the threat. "You won't dare touch me here!"

The other laughed. "Won't I? What have I to risk? He'll suffer for any deed of mine! You'll call for aid against me and only loose the hounds on him."

Pat stared blankly at the evil face. She had no answer; for once her ready tongue found no retort.

"Sit down!" reiterated the other, and she dropped dazedly to her position on the bench. She turned dark questioning eyes on him.

"Do you see," he sneered, "how weakening an influence is this love of yours? To protect him you are obeying me; this is my authority over you—this body I share with him!"

She made no reply; she was making a desperate effort to lash her mind into activity, to formulate some means of combating the being who tortured her.

"It has weakened him, too," the other proceeded. "This disturbed love of his has taken away the mastery which birth gave him, and his enfeeblement has given that mastery to me. He knows now the reason for his weakness; I tell it to him too late to harm me."

Pat struggled for composure. The very presence of the cold

demon tore at the roots of her self-control, and she suppressed a fierce desire to break into hysterical laughter. Ridiculous, hopeless, incomprehensible situation! She forced her quivering throat to husky speech.

"What—what are you?" she stammered.

"Synapse! I'm a question of synapses," jeered the other. "Simple! Very simple! Ask your friend the Doctor!"

"I think," said the girl, a measure of control returning to her voice, "that you're a devil. You're some sort of a fiend that has managed to attach itself to Nick, and you're not human. That's what I think!"

"Think what you please," said the other. "We're wasting time here," he said abruptly. "Come."

"Where?" Pat was startled; she felt a recurrence of fright.

"No matter where. Come."

"I won't! Why do you want me?"

"To complete the business of Saturday night," he said. "Your lips have healed; they bleed no longer, but that is easy to remedy. Come."

"I won't!" exclaimed the girl in sudden panic. "I won't!" She moved as if to rise.

"You forget," intoned the being beside her. "You forget the authority vested in me by virtue of this love of yours. Let me convince you." He stretched forth a thin hand. "Move and you condemn your sweetheart to the punishment you threaten me."

He seized her arm, pinching the flesh brutally, his nails breaking the smooth skin. Pat felt her face turn ashy pale; she closed her eyes and bit her nearly-healed lips at the excruciating pain, but she made not the slightest sound nor the faintest movement. She simply sat and suffered.

"You see!" sneered the other, releasing her, "Thank my kindly nature that I marked your arm instead of your face. Shall we go?"

A scarcely audible whimper of pain came from the girl's lips. She sat palled and unmoving, with her eyes still closed.

"No," she murmured faintly at last. "No. I won't go with you."

"Shall I drag you?"

"Yes. Drag me if you dare."

His hand closed on her wrist; she felt herself jerked violently to her feet, so roughly that it wrenched her shoulder. A startled, frightened little cry broke from her lips, and then she closed them firmly at the sight of several by-passers turning curious eyes on them.

"I'll come," she murmured. The glimmering of an idea had risen in her chaotic mind.

She followed him in grim, bitter silence across the clipped turf to the limit of the park. She recognized Nick's modest automobile standing in the line of cars along the street; her companion, or captor, moved directly towards it, opened the door and clambered in without a single backward glance. He turned about and watched her as she paused with one diminutive foot on the running board, and rubbed her hand over her aching arm.

"Get in!" he ordered coldly.

She made no move. "I want to know where you intend to take me."

"It doesn't matter. To a place where we can complete that unfinished experiment of ours. Aren't you happy at the prospect?"

"Do you think," she said unsteadily, "that I'd consent to that even to save Nick from disgrace and punishment? Do you think I'm fool enough for that?"

"We'll soon see." He extended his hand. "Scream—fight—struggle!" he jeered. "Call them down on your sweetheart!"

He had closed his hand on her wrist; she jerked it convulsively from his grasp.

"I'll bargain with you!" she gasped. She needed a moment's respite to clarify a thought that had been growing in her mind.

"Bargain? What have you to offer?"

"As much as you!"

"Ah, but I have a threat—the threat to your sweetheart! And I'm offering too the lure of that evil whose face so charmed you recently. Have you forgotten how nearly I won you to the worship of that principle? Have you forgotten the ecstasy of that pain?"

His terrible, bloodshot eyes were approaching her face; and strangely, the girl felt a curious recurrence of that illogical desire to yield that had swept over her on that disastrous night of Saturday. There had been an ecstasy; there had been a wild, ungodly, unhallowed pleasure in his blows, in the searing pain of his kisses on her lacerated lips. She realized vaguely that she was staring blankly, dazedly, into the red eyes, and that somewhere within her, some insane brain-cells were urging her to clamber to the seat beside him.

She tore her eyes away. She rubbed her bruised shoulder, and the pain of her own touch restored her vanishing logical faculties. She returned her gaze to the face of the other, meeting his gaze now coolly.

"Nick!" she said earnestly, as if calling him from a distance. "Nick!"

There was, she fancied, the faintest gleam of concern apparent in the features opposite her. She continued.

"Nick!" she repeated. "You can hear me, honey. Come to the house as soon as you are able. Come tonight, or any time; I'll wait until you do. You'll come, honey; you must!"

She backed away from the car; the other made no move to halt her. She circled the vehicle and dashed recklessly across the street. From the safety of the opposite walk she glanced back; the red-eyed visage was regarding her steadily through the glass of the window.

21. A Question of Synapses

Pat almost ran the few blocks to her home. She hastened along in a near panic, regardless of the glances of pedestrians she chanced to pass. With the disappearance of the immediate urge, the composure for which she had struggled had deserted her, and she felt shaken, terrified, and weak. Her arm ached miserably, and her wrenched shoulder pained at each movement. It was not until she attained her own doorstep that she paused, panting and quivering, to consider the events of the evening.

"I can't stand any more of this!" she muttered wretchedly to herself. "I'll just have to give up, I guess; I can't pit myself another time against—that thing."

She leaned wearily against the railing of the porch, rubbing her injured arm.

"Dr. Carl was right," she thought. "Nick was right; it's dangerous. There was a moment there at the end when he—or it—almost had me. I'm frightened," she admitted. "Lord only knows what might have happened had I been a little weaker. If the Lord does know," she added.

She found her latch-key and entered the house. Only a dim light burned in the hall; her mother, of course, was at the Club, and the maid and Magda were far away in their chambers on the third floor. She tossed her wrap on a chair, switched on a brighter light, and examined the painful spot on her arm, a red mark already beginning to turn a nasty blue, with two tiny specks of drying blood. She shuddered, and trudged wearily up the stairs to her room.

The empty silence of the house oppressed her. She wanted human companionship—safe, trustworthy, friendly company, anyone to distract her thoughts from the eerie, disturbing direction they were taking. She was still in somewhat of a panic, and suppressed with difficulty a desire to peep fearfully under the bed.

"Coward!" she chided herself. "You knew what to expect."

Suddenly the recollection of her parting words recurred to her.

108

She had told Nick—if Nick had indeed heard—to come to the house, to come at once, tonight, if he could. A tremor of apprehension ran through her. Suppose he came; suppose he came as her own Nick, and she admitted him, and then—or suppose that other came, and managed by some trick to enter, or suppose that unholy fascination of his prevailed on her—she shivered, and brushed her hand distractedly across her eyes.

"I can't stand it!" she moaned. "I'll have to give up, even if it means never seeing Nick again. I'll have to!" She shook her head miserably as if to deny the picture that had risen in her mind of herself and that horror alone in the house.

"I won't stay here!" she decided. She peeped out of the west windows at the Doctor's residence, and felt a surge of relief at the sight of his iron-gray hair framed in the library window below. He was reading; she could see the book on his knees. There was her refuge; she ran hastily down the stairs and out of the door.

With an apprehensive glance along the street she crossed to his door and rang the bell. She waited nervously for his coming, and, with a sudden impulse, pulled her vanity-case from her bag and dabbed a film of powder over the mark on her arm. Then his ponderous footsteps sounded and the door opened.

"Hello," he said genially. "These late evening visits of yours are becoming quite customary—and see if I care!"

"May I come in a while?" asked Pat meekly.

"Have I ever turned you away?" He followed her into the library, pushed a chair forward for her, and dropped quickly into his own with an air of having snatched it from her just in time.

"I didn't want your old armchair," she remarked, occupying the other.

"And what's the trouble tonight?" he queried.

"I—well, I was just nervous. I didn't want to stay in the house alone."

"You?" His tone was skeptical. "You were nervous? That hardly sounds reasonable, coming from an independent little spitfire like you."

"I was, though. I was scared."

"And of what—or whom?"

"Of haunts and devils."

"Oh." He nodded. "I see you've had results from your letter-writing."

"Well, sort of."

"I'm used to your circumlocutions, Pat. Suppose you come directly to the point for once. What happened?"

"Why, I wrote Nick to get in touch with me, and I got a reply. He said to meet him in the park at a place we knew. This evening."

"And you did, of course."

"Yes, but before that, this afternoon, he called up and told me not to, but I insisted and we did."

"Told you not to, eh? And was his warning justified?"

"Yes. Oh, yes! When I came to the place, it was—the other."

"So! Well, he could hardly manhandle you in a public park."

Pat thought of her wrenched shoulder and bruised arm. She shuddered.

"He's horrible!" she said. "Inhuman! He kept referring to Saturday night, and he threatened that if I moved or made a disturbance he'd let Nick suffer the consequences. So I kept still while he insulted me."

"You nitwit!" There was more than a trace of anger in the Doctor's voice. "I want to see that pup of yours! We'll soon find out what this thing is—a mania or simply lack of a good licking!"

"What it is?" echoed Pat. "Oh—it told me! Dr. Carl, what's a synopsis?"

"A synopsis! You know perfectly well."

"I mean applied to physiology or psychology or something. It—he told me he was a question of synopsis."

"This devil of yours said that?"

"Yes."

"Hum!" The Doctor's voice was musing. He frowned perplexedly, then looked up abruptly. "Was it—did he by any chance say synapses? Not synopsis—synapses?"

"That's it!" exclaimed the girl. "He said he was a question of synapses. Does that explain him? Do you know what he is?"

"Doesn't explain a damn thing!" snapped Horker. "A synapse is a juncture, or the meeting of two nerves. It's why you can develop automatic motions and habits, like playing piano, or dancing. When you form a habit, the synapses of the nerves involved are sort of

110

worn thin, so the nerves themselves are, in a sense, short-circuited. You go through motions without the need of your brain intervening, which is all a habit amounts to. Understand?"

"Not very well," confessed Pat.

"Humph! It doesn't matter anyway. I can't see that it helps to analyze your devil."

"I don't care if it's never analyzed," said Pat with a return of despondency. "Dr. Carl, I can't face that evil thing again. I can't do it, not even if it means never seeing Nick!"

"Sensible," said the Doctor approvingly. "I'd like to have a chance at him, but not enough to keep you in this state of jitters. Although," he added, "a lot of this mystery is the product of your own harum-scarum mind. You can be sure of that, honey."

"You would say so," responded the girl wearily. "You've never seen that—change. If it's my imagination, then I'm the one that needs your treatments, not Nick."

"It isn't all imagination, most likely," said Horker defensively. "I know these introverted types with their hysterias, megalomanias, and defense mechanisms! They've paraded through my office there for a good many years, Pat; they've provided the lion's share of my practice. But this young psychopathic of yours seems to have it bad—abnormally so, and that's why I'm so interested, apart from helping you, of course."

"I don't care," said Pat apathetically, repressing a desire to rub her injured arm. "I'm through. I'm scared out of the affair. Another week like this last one and I would be one of your patients."

"Best drop it, then," said Horker, eyeing her seriously. "Nothing's worth upsetting yourself like this, Pat."

"Nick's worth it," she murmured. "He's worth it—only I just haven't the strength. I haven't the courage. I can't do it!"

"Never mind, honey," the Doctor muttered, regarding her with an expression of concern. "You're probably well out of the mess. I know damn well you haven't told me everything about this affair—notably, how you acquired that ugly mark on your arm that's so carefully powdered over. So, all in all, I guess you're well out of it."

"I suppose I am." Her voice was still weary. Suddenly the glare of headlights drew her attention to the window; a car was stopping before her home. "There's Mother," she said. "I'll go on back now, Dr. Carl, and thanks for entertaining a lonesome and depressed lady."

She rose with a casual glance through the window, then halted in frozen astonishment and a trace of terror.

"Oh!" she gasped. The car was the modest coupe of Nicholas Devine.

She peered through the window; the Doctor rose and stared over her shoulder. "I told him to come," she whispered. "I told him to come when he was able. He heard me, he or—the other."

A figure alighted from the vehicle. Even in the dusk she could perceive the exhaustion, the weariness in its movements. She pressed her face to the pane, surveying the form with fascinated intentness. It turned, supporting itself against the car and gazing steadily at her own door. With the movement the radiance of a street-light illuminated its features.

"It's Nick!" she cried with such eagerness that the Doctor was startled. "It's *my* Nick!"

22. Doctor and Devil

Pat rushed to the door, out upon the porch, and down to the street. Dr. Horker followed her to the entrance and stood watching her as she darted toward the dejected figure beside the car.

"Nick!" she cried. "I'm here, honey. You heard me, didn't you?"

She flung herself into his arms; he held her eagerly, pressing a hasty, tender kiss on her lips. "You heard me!" she murmured.

"Yes." His voice was husky, strained. "What is it, Pat? Tell me quickly—God knows how much time we have!"

"It's Dr. Carl. He'll help us, Nick."

"Help us! No one can help us, dear. No one!"

"He'll try. It can't do any harm, honey. Come in with me. Now!"

"It's useless, I tell you!"

"But come," she pleaded. "Come anyway!"

"Pat, I tell you this battle has to be fought out by me alone. I'm the only one who can do anything at all and," he lowered his voice, "Pat, I'm losing!"

"Nick!"

"That's why I came tonight. I was too cowardly to make our last meeting—Monday evening in the park—a definite farewell. I wanted to, but I weakened. So tonight, Pat, it's a final goodbye, and you thank Heaven for it!"

"Oh, Nick dear!"

"It was touch and go whether I came at all tonight. It was a struggle, Pat; he is as strong as I am now. Or stronger."

The girl gazed searchingly into his worn, weary face. He looked miserably ill, she thought; he seemed as exhausted as one who had been engaged in a physical battle.

"Nick," she said insistently, "I don't care what you say, you're coming with me. Only for a little while."

She tugged at his hand, dragging him reluctantly after her. He followed her to the porch where the open door still framed the great figure of the Doctor.

"You know Dr. Carl," she said.

"Come inside," growled Horker. Pat noticed the gruffness of his voice, his lack of any cordiality, but she said nothing as she pulled her reluctant companion through the door and into the library.

The Doctor drew up another chair, and Pat, more accustomed to his devices, observed that he placed it in such position that the lamp cast a stream of radiance on Nick's face. She sank into her own chair and waited silently for developments.

"Well," said Horker, turning his shrewd old eyes on Nick's countenance, "let's get down to cases. Pat's told me what she knows; we can take that much for granted. Is there anything more you might want to tell?"

"No, sir," responded the youth wearily. "I've told Pat all I know."

"Humph! Maybe I can ask some leading questions, then. Will you answer them?"

"Of course, any that I can."

"All right. Now," the Doctor's voice took on a cool professional edge, "you've had these—uh—attacks as long as you can remember. Is that right?"

"Yes."

"But they've been more severe of late?"

"Much worse, sir!"

"Since when?"

"Since—about as long as I've known Pat. Four or five weeks,"

"M-m," droned the Doctor. "You've no idea of the cause for this increase in the malignancy of the attacks?"

"No sir," said Nick, after a barely perceptible hesitation.

"You don't think the cause could be in any way connected with, let us say, the emotional disturbances attending your acquaintance with Pat here?"

"No, sir," said the youth flatly.

"All right," said Horker. "Let that angle go for the present. Are there any after effects from these spells?"

"Yes. There's always a splitting headache." He closed his eyes. "I have one of them now."

"Localized?"

"Sir?"

"Is the pain in any particular region? Forehead, temples, eyes, or so forth?"

"No. Just a nasty headache."

"But no other after-effects?"

"I can't think of any others. Except, perhaps, a feeling of exhaustion after I've gone through what I've just finished." He closed his eyes as if to shut out the recollection.

"Well," mused the Doctor, "we'll forget the physical symptoms. What happens to your individuality, your own consciousness, while you're suffering an attack?"

"Nothing happens to it," said Nick with a suppressed shudder. "I watch and hear, but what he does is beyond my control. It's terrifying—horrible!" he burst out suddenly.

"Doubtless," responded Horker smoothly. "What about the other? Does that one stand by while you're in the saddle?"

"I don't know," muttered Nick dully. "Of course he does!" he added abruptly. "I can feel his presence at all times—even now. He's always lurking, waiting to spring forth, as soon as I relax!"

"Humph!" ejaculated the Doctor. "How do you manage to sleep?"

"By waiting for exhaustion," said Nick wearily. "By waiting until I can stay awake no longer."

"And can you bring this other personality into dominance? Can you change controls, so to speak, at will?"

"Why—yes," the youth answered, hesitating as if puzzled. "Yes, I suppose I could."

"Let's see you, then."

"But—" Horror was in his voice.

"No, Dr. Carl!" Pat interjected in fright. "I won't let him!"

"I thought you declared yourself out of this," said Horker with a shrewd glance at the girl.

"Then I'm back in it! I won't let him do what you want—anyway, not that!"

"Pat," said the Doctor with an air of patience, "you want me to treat this affliction, don't you? Isn't that what both of you want?"

The girl murmured a scarcely audible assent.

115

"Very well, then," he proceeded. "Do you expect me to treat the thing blindly—in the dark? Do you think I can guess at the cause without observing the effect?"

"No," said Pat faintly.

"Now then," he turned to Nick, "Let's see this transformation."

"Must I?" asked the youth reluctantly.

"If you want my help."

"All right," he agreed with another tremor. He sat passively staring at the Doctor; a moment passed. Horker heard Pat's nervous breathing; other than that, the room was in silence. Nicholas Devine closed his eyes, brushed his hand across his forehead. A moment more and he opened them to gaze perplexedly at the Doctor.

"He won't!" he muttered in astonishment. "He won't do it!"

"Humph!" snapped Horker, ignoring Pat's murmur of relief. "Finicky devil, isn't he? Likes to pick company he can bully!"

"I don't understand it!" Nick's face was blank. "He's been tormenting me until just now!" He looked at the Doctor. "You don't think I'm lying about it, do you, Dr. Horker?"

"Not consciously," replied the other coolly. "If I thought you were responsible for a few of the indignities perpetrated on Pat here, I'd waste no time in questions, young man. I'd be relieving myself of certain violent impulses instead."

"I couldn't harm Pat!"

"You gave a passable imitation of it, then! However, that's beside the point; as I say, I don't hold you responsible for aberrations which I believe are beyond your control. The main thing is a diagnosis."

"Do you know what it is?" cut in Pat eagerly.

"Not yet—at least, not for certain. There's only one real method available; these questions will get us nowhere. We'll have to psychoanalyze you, young man."

"I don't care what you do, if you can offer any hope!" he declared vehemently. "Let's get it over!"

"Not as easy as all that!" rumbled Horker. "It takes time; and besides, it can't be successful with the subject in a hectic mood such as yours." He glanced at his watch. "Moreover, it's after midnight."

He turned to Nicholas Devine. "We'll make it Saturday evening," he said. "Meanwhile, young man, you're not to see Pat. Not at all—understand? You can see her here when you come."

116

"That's infinitely more than I'd planned for myself," said the youth in a low voice. "I'd abandoned the hope of seeing her."

He rose and moved toward the door, and the others followed. At the entrance he paused; he leaned down to plant a brief, tender kiss on the girl's lips, and moved wordlessly out of the door. Pat watched him enter his car, and followed the vehicle with her eyes until it disappeared. Then she turned to Horker.

"Do you really know anything about it?" she queried. "Have you any theory at all?"

"He's not lying," said the Doctor thoughtfully. "I watched him closely; he believes he's telling the truth."

"He is. I know what I saw!"

"He hasn't the signs of praecox or depressive," mused the Doctor. "It's puzzling; it's one of those functional aberrations, or a fixed delusion of some kind. We'll find out just what it is."

"It's the devil," declared Pat positively. "I don't care what sort of scientific tag you give it—that's what it is. You doctors can hide a lot of ignorance under a long name."

Horker paid no attention to her remarks. "We'll see what the psychoanalysis brings out," he said. "I shouldn't be surprised if the whole thing were the result of a defense mechanism erected by a timid child in an effort to evade responsibility. That's what it sounds like."

"It's a devil!" reiterated Pat.

"Well," said the Doctor, "if it is, it has one thing in common with every spook or devil I ever heard of."

"What's that?"

"It refuses to appear under any conditions where one has a chance to examine it. It's like one of these temperamental mediums trying to perform under a spotlight."

23. Werewolf

Pat awoke in rather better spirits. Somehow, the actual entrance of Dr. Horker into the case gave her a feeling of security, and her natural optimistic nature rode the pendulum back from despair to hope. Even the painful black-and-blue mark on her arm, as she examined it ruefully, failed to shake her buoyant mood.

Her mood held most of the day; it was only at evening that a recurrence of doubt assailed her. She sat in the dim living room waiting the arrival of her mother's guests, and wondered whether, after all, the predicament was as easily solvable as she had assumed.

She watched the play of lights and shadows across the ceiling, patterns cast through the windows by moving headlights in the street, and wondered anew whether her faith in Dr. Carl's abilities was justified. Science! She had the faith of her generation in its omnipotence, but here in the dusk, the outworn superstitions of childhood became appalling realities, and some of Magda's stories, forgotten now for years, rose out of their graves and went squeaking and maundering like sheeted ghosts in a ghastly parade across the universe of her mind. The meaningless taunts she habitually flung at Dr. Carl's science became suddenly pregnant with truth; his patient, hard-learned science seemed in fact no more than the frenzies of a witch-doctor dancing in the heart of a Rhodesian swamp.

What was it worth—this array of medical facts—if it failed to cure? Was medicine falling into the state of Chinese science—a vast collection of good rules for which the reasons were either unknown or long forgotten? She sighed; it was with a feeling of profound relief that she heard the voices of the Brocks outside; she played miserable bridge the whole evening, but it was less of an affliction than the solitude of her own thoughts.

Saturday morning, cloudy and threatening though it was, found the pendulum once more at the other end of the arc. She found herself, if not buoyantly cheerful, at least no longer prey to the inchoate doubts and fears of the preceding evening. She couldn't even recall their nature; they had been apart from the cool, daytime logic that preached a common-sense reliance on accepted practices. They had been, she concluded, no more than childish nightmares induced by darkness and the play of shadows.

She dressed and ate a late breakfast; her mother was already *en route* to the Club for her bridge luncheon. Thereafter, she wandered into the kitchen for the company of Magda, whom she found with massive arms immersed in dish water. Pat perched on her particular stool beside the kitchen table and watched her at her work.

"Magda," she said finally.

"I'm listening, Miss Pat."

"Do you remember a story you told me a long time ago? Oh, years and years ago, about a man in your town who could change into something—some fierce animal. A wolf, or something like that."

"Oh, him!" said Magda, knitting her heavy brows. "You mean the werewolf."

"That's it! The werewolf. I remember it now—how frightened I was after I went to bed. I wasn't more than eight years old, was I?"

"I couldn't remember. It was years ago, though, for sure."

"What was the story?" queried Pat. "Do you remember that?"

"Why, it was the time the sheep were being missed," said the woman, punctuating her words with the clatter of dishes on the drain board. "Then there was a child gone, and another, and then tales of this great wolf about the country. I didn't see him; us little ones stayed under roof by darkness after that."

"That wasn't all of it," said Pat. "You told me more than that."

"Well," continued Magda, "there was my uncle, who was best hand with a rifle in the village. He and others went after the creature, and my uncle, he came back telling how he'd seen it plain against the sky, and how he'd fired at it. He couldn't miss, he was that close, but the wolf gave him a look and ran away."

"And then what?"

"Then the Priest came, and he said it wasn't a natural wolf. He melted up a silver coin and cast a bullet, and he gave it to my uncle, he being the best shot in the village. And the next night he went out once more."

"Did he get it?" asked Pat. "I don't remember."

"He did. He came upon it by the pasture, and he aimed his gun. The creature looked straight at him with its evil red eyes, and he shot it. When he came to it, there wasn't a wolf at all, but this man—his name I forget—with a hole in his head. And then the Priest, he said he was a werewolf, and only a silver bullet could kill him. But my uncle, he said those evil red eyes kept staring at him for many nights."

"Evil red eyes!" said Pat suddenly. "Magda," she asked in a faint voice, "could he change any time he wanted to?"

"Only by night, the Priest said. By sunrise he had to be back."

"Only by night!" mused the girl. Another idea was forming in her active little mind, another conception, disturbing, impossible to phrase. "Is that worse than being possessed by a devil, Magda?"

"Sure it's worse! The Priest, he could cast out the devil, but I never heard no cure for being a werewolf."

Pat said nothing further, but slid from her high perch to the floor and went soberly out of the kitchen. The fears of last night had come to life again, and now the overcast skies outside seemed a fitting symbol to her mood. She stared thoughtfully out of the living room windows, and the sudden splash of raindrops against the pane lent a final touch to the whole desolate ensemble.

"I'm just a superstitious little idiot!" she told herself. "I laugh at Mother because she always likes to play North and South, and here I'm letting myself worry over superstitions that were discarded before there was any such thing as a game called contract bridge."

But her arguments failed to carry conviction. The memory of the terrible eyes of that *other* had clicked to aptly to Magda's phrase. She couldn't subdue the picture that haunted her, and she couldn't cast off the apprehensiveness of her mood. She recalled gloomily that Dr. Horker was at the Club—wouldn't be home before evening, else she'd have gladly availed herself of his solid, matter-of-fact company.

She thought of Nick's appointment with the Doctor for that evening. Suppose his psychoanalysis brought to light some such horror as these fears of hers—that would forever destroy any possibility of happiness for her and Nick. Even though the Doctor refused to recognize it, called it by some polysyllabic scientific name, the thing would be there to sever them.

She wandered restlessly into the hall. The morning mail, unexamined, lay in its brazen receptacle, she moved over, fingering it idly. Abruptly she paused in astonishment—a letter in familiar script had flashed at her. She pulled it out; it was! It was a letter from Nicholas Devine!

She tore it open nervously, wondering whether he had reverted to his original refusal of Dr. Horker's aid, whether he was unable to come, whether that had happened. But only a single unfolded sheet slipped from the envelope, inscribed with a few brief lines of poetry.

"*The grief that is too faint for tears,*
And scarcely breathes of pain,
May linger on a hundred years
Ere it creep forth again.
But I, who love you now too well
To suffer your disdain,
Must try tonight that love to quell—
And try in vain!"

24. The Dark Other

It was early in the evening, not yet eight o'clock, when Pat saw the car of Nicholas Devine draw up before the house. She had already been watching half an hour, sitting cross-legged in the deep window seat, like her jade Buddha. That equivocal poem of his had disturbed her, lent an added strength to the moods and doubts already implanted by Magda's mystical tale, and it was with a feeling of trepidation that she watched him emerge wearily from his vehicle and stare in indecision first at her window and then at the Horker residence. The waning daylight was still sufficient to delineate his worn features; she could see them, pale, harried, but indubitably the mild features of her own Nick.

While he hesitated, she darted to the door and out upon the porch. He gave her a wan smile of greeting, advanced to the foot of the steps, and halted there.

"The Doctor's not home yet," she called to him. He stood motionless below her.

"Come up on the porch," she invited, as he made no move. She uttered the words with a curious feeling of apprehension; for even as she ached for his presence, the uncertain state of affairs was frightening. She thought fearfully that what had happened before might happen again. Still, there on the open porch, in practically full daylight, and for so brief a time—Dr. Carl would be coming very shortly, she reasoned.

"I can't," said Nick, staring wistfully at her. "You know I can't."

"Why not?"

"I promised. You remember—I promised Dr. Horker I'd not see you except in his presence."

"So you did," said Pat doubtfully. The promise offered escape from a distressing situation, she thought, and yet—somehow, seeing Nick standing pathetically there, she couldn't imagine anything harmful emanating from him. There had been many and many evenings in his company that had passed delightfully, enjoyably, safely.

She felt a wave of pity for him; after all, the affliction was his, most of the suffering was his.

"We needn't take it so literally," she said almost reluctantly. "He'll be home very soon now."

"I know," said Nick soberly, "but it was a promise, and besides, I'm afraid."

"Never mind, honey," she said, after a momentary hesitation. "Come up and sit here on the steps, then—here beside me. We can talk just as well as there on the settee."

He climbed the steps and seated himself, watching Pat with longing eyes. He made no move to touch her, nor did she suggest a kiss.

"I read your poem, honey," she said finally. "It worried me."

"I'm sorry, Pat. I couldn't sleep. I kept wandering around the house, and at last I wrote it and took it out and mailed it. It was a vent, a relief from the things I'd been thinking."

"What things, honey?"

"A way, mostly," he answered gloomily, "of removing myself from your life. A permanent way."

"Nick!"

"I didn't, as you see, Pat. I was too cowardly, I suppose. Or perhaps it was because of this forlorn hope of ours. There's always hope, Pat; even the condemned man with his foot on the step to the gallows feels it."

"Nick dear!" she cried, her voice quavering in pity. "Nick, you mustn't think of those things! It might weaken you—make it easier for him!"

"It can't. If it frightens him, I'm glad."

"Honey," she said soothingly, "we'll give Dr. Carl a chance. Promise me you'll let him try, won't you?"

"Of course I will. Is there anything I'd refuse to promise you, Pat? Even," he added bitterly, "when reason tells me it's a futile promise."

"Don't say it!" she urged fiercely. "We've got to help him. We've got to believe—There he comes!" she finished with sudden relief.

The Doctor's car turned up the driveway beyond his residence. Pat saw his face regarding them as he disappeared behind the building.

"Come on, honey," she said. "Let's get at the business."

They moved slowly over to the Doctor's door, waiting there until his ponderous footsteps sounded. A light flashed in the hall, and his broad shadow filled the door for a moment before it opened.

"Come in," he rumbled jovially. "Fine evening we're spoiling, isn't it?"

"It could be," said Pat as they followed him into the library, "only it'll probably rain some more."

"Hah!" snorted the Doctor, frowning at the mention of rain. "The course was soft. Couldn't get any distance, and it added six strokes to my score. At least six!"

Pat chuckled commiseratingly. "You ought to lay out a course in Greenland," she suggested. "They say anyone can drive a ball a quarter of a mile on smooth ice."

"Humph!" The Doctor waved toward a great, low chair. "Suppose you sit over there, young man, and we'll get about our business. And don't look so woebegone about it."

Nick settled himself nervously in the designated chair; the Doctor seated himself at a little distance to the side, and Pat sat tensely in her usual place beside the hearth. She waited in strained impatience for the black magic of psychoanalysis to commence.

"Now," said Horker, "I want you to keep quiet, Pat—if possible. And you, young man, are to relax, compose yourself, get yourself into as passive a state as possible. Do you understand?"

"Yes, sir," The youth leaned back in the great chair, closing his eyes.

"So! Now, think back to your childhood, your earliest memories. Let your thoughts wander at random, and speak whatever comes to your mind."

Nick sat a moment in silence. "That's hard to do, sir," he said finally.

"Yes. It will take practice, weeks of it, perhaps. You'll have to acquire the knack of it, but to do that, we'll have to start."

"Yes, sir." He sat with closed eyes. "My mother," he murmured, "was kind. I remember her a little, just a little. She was very gentle, not apt to blame me. She could understand. Made excuses to my father. He was hard, not cruel—strict. Couldn't understand. Blamed me when I wasn't to blame. Other did it. I wasn't mischievous,

124

but got the blame. Couldn't explain, he wouldn't believe me." He paused uncertainly.

"Go on," said Horker quietly, while Pat strained her ears to listen.

"Mrs. Stevens," he continued. "Governess after Mother died. Strict like Father, got punished when I wasn't to blame. Just as bad after Father died. Always blamed. Couldn't explain, nobody believed me. Other threw cat in window, I had to go to bed. Put salt in bird seed, broke leg of chair to make it fall. Punished—I couldn't explain." His voice droned into silence; he opened his eyes. "That all," he said nervously.

"Good enough for the first time," said the Doctor briskly. "Wait a few weeks; we'll have your life's history out of you. It takes practice."

"Is that all?" queried Pat in astonishment.

"All for the first time. Later we'll let him talk half an hour at a stretch, but it takes practice, as I've mentioned. You run along home now," he said to Nick.

"But it's early!" objected Pat.

"Early or not," said the Doctor, "I'm tired, and you two aren't to see each other except here. You remember that."

Nick rose from his seat in the depths of the great chair. "Thank you, sir," he said. "I don't know why, but I feel easier in your presence. The—the struggle disappears while I'm here."

"Well," said Horker with a smile, "I like patients with confidence in me. Goodnight."

At the door Nick paused, turning wistful eyes on Pat. "Good night," he said, leaning to give her a light kiss. A rush of some emotion twisted his features; he stared strangely at the girl. "I'd better go," he said abruptly, and vanished through the door.

"Well?" said Pat questioningly, turning to the Doctor. "Did you learn anything from that?"

"Not much," the other admitted, yawning. "However, the results bear out my theory."

"How?"

"Did you notice how he harped on the undeserved punishment theme? He was punished for another's mischief?"

"Yes. What of that?"

"Well, picture him as a timid, sensitive child, rather afraid of being punished. Afraid, say, of being locked up in a dark closet. Now, when he inadvertently commits a mischief, as all children do, he tries desperately to divert the blame from himself. But there's no one else to blame! So what does he do?"

"What?"

"He invents this other, the mischievous one, and blames him. And now the other has grown to the proportions of a delusion, haunting him, driving him to commit acts apart from his normal inclinations. Understand? Because I'm off to bed whether you do or not."

"I understand all right," murmured Pat uncertainly as she moved to the door. "But somehow, it doesn't sound reasonable."

"It will," said the Doctor. "Goodnight."

Pat wandered slowly down the steps and through the break in the hedge, musing over Doctor Horker's expression of opinion. Then, according to him, the devil was nothing more than an invention of Nick's mind, the trick of a cowardly child to evade just punishment. She shook her head; it didn't sound like Nick at all. For all his gentleness and sensitivity, he wasn't the one to hide behind a fabrication. He wasn't a coward; she was certain of that. And she was as sure as she could ever be that he hated, feared, loathed this personality that afflicted him; he couldn't have created it.

She sighed, mounted the steps, and fumbled for her key. The sound of a movement behind her brought a faint gasp of astonishment. She turned to see a figure materializing from the shadows of the porch. The light from the hall fell across its features, and she drew back as she recognized Nicholas Devine—not the being she had just kissed good night, but in the guise of her tormentor, the red-eyed demon!

126

25. The Demon Lover

Pat drew back, leaning against the door, and her key tinkled on the concrete of the porch. She was startled, shocked, but not as completely terrified as she might have expected. After all, she thought rapidly, they were standing in full view of a public street, and Dr. Carl's residence was but a few feet distant. She could summon his help by screaming.

"Well!" she exclaimed, eyeing the figure inimically. "Your appearances and disappearances are beginning to remind me of the Cheshire Cat."

"Except for the grin," said the other in his cold tones.

"What do you want?" snapped Pat.

"You know what I want."

"You'll not get it," said the girl angrily. "You—you're doomed to extinction, anyway! Go away!"

"Suppose," said the other with a strange, cold, twisted smile, "it were *he* that's doomed to extinction—what then?"

"It isn't!" cried Pat. "It isn't!" she repeated, while a quiver of uncertainty shook her. "He's the stronger," she said defiantly.

"Then where is he now?"

"Dr. Carl will help us!"

"Doctor!" sneered the other. "He and his clever theory! Am I an illusion?" he queried sardonically, thrusting his red-glinting eyes toward her. "Am I the product of his puerile, vacillating nature? Bah! I gave you the clue, and your Doctor hasn't the intelligence to follow it!"

"Go away!" murmured Pat faintly. The approach of his face had unnerved her, and she felt terror beginning to stir within her. "Go away!" she said again. "Why do you have to torment me? Anyone would serve your purpose—any woman!"

"You have an aesthetic appeal, as I've told you before," replied the other in that toneless voice of his. "There is a pleasure in the defacement of black hair and pale skin, and your body is seductive,

127

most seductive. Another might afford me less enjoyment, and besides, you hate me. Don't you hate me?" He peered evilly at her.

"Oh, God—yes!" The girl was shuddering.

"Say it, then! Say you hate me!"

"I hate you!" the girl cried vehemently. "Will you go away now?"

"With you!"

"I'll scream if you come any closer. You don't dare touch me; I'll call Dr. Horker."

"You'll only damage *him*—your lover."

"Then I'll do it! He'll understand."

"Yes," said the other reflectively. "He's fool enough to forgive you. He'll forgive you anything—the weakling!"

"Go away! Get away from here!"

The other stared at her out of blood-shot eyes. "Very well," he said in his flat tones. "This time the victory is yours."

He backed slowly toward the steps. Pat watched him as he moved, feeling a surge of profound relief. As his shadow shifted, her key gleamed silver at her feet, and she stooped to retrieve it.

There was a rush of motion as her eyes left the form of her antagonist. A hand was clamped violently over her mouth, an arm passed with steel-like rigidity about her body. Nicholas Devine was dragging her toward the steps; she was half-way down before she recovered her wits enough to struggle.

She writhed and twisted in his grasp. She drove her elbow into his body with all her power, and kicked with the strength of desperation at his legs. She bit into the palm across her mouth—and suddenly, with a subdued grunt of pain, he released her so abruptly that her own struggles sent her spinning blindly into the bushes of the hedge.

She turned gasping, unable for the moment to summon sufficient breath to scream. The other stood facing her with his eyes gleaming terribly into her own; then they ranged slowly from her diminutive feet to the rumpled ebony of her hair that she was brushing back with her hands from her pallid, frightened face.

"Obstinate," he observed, rubbing his injured palm. "Obstinate and unbroken—but worth the trouble. Well worth it!" He reached out a swift hand, seizing her wrist as she backed against the bushes.

Pat twisted around, gazing frantically at Doctor Horker's house, where a light had only now flashed on in the upper windows. Her breath flowed back into her lungs with a strengthening rush.

"Dr. Carl!" she screamed. "Dr. Carl! Help me!"

The other spun her violently about. She had a momentary glimpse of a horribly evil countenance, then he drew back his arm and shot a clenched fist to her chin.

The world reeled into a blaze of spinning lights that faded quickly to darkness. She felt her knees buckling beneath her, and realized that she was crumpling forward toward the figure before her. Then for a moment she was aware of nothing.

She didn't quite lose consciousness, or at least for no more than a moment. She was suddenly aware that she was gazing down at a moving pavement, at her own arms dangling helplessly toward it. She perceived that she was lying limply across Nicholas Devine's shoulder with his arms clenched about her knees. And then, still unable to make the slightest resistance, she was bundled roughly into the seat of his coupe; he was beside her, and the car was purring into motion.

She summoned what remained of her strength. She drew herself erect, fumbling at the handle of the door with a frantic idea of casting herself out of the car to the street. The creature beside her jerked her violently back; as she reeled into the seat, he struck her again with the side of his fist. It was a random blow, delivered with scarcely a glance at her; it caught her on the forehead, snapping her head with an audible thump against the wall of the vehicle. She swayed for a moment with closing eyes, then collapsed limply against him, this time in complete unconsciousness.

That lapse too must have been brief. She opened dazed eyes on a vista of moving street lights; they were still in the car, passing now along some unrecognized thoroughfare lined with dark old homes. She lay for some moments uncomprehending; she was completely unaware of her situation.

It dawned on her slowly. She moaned, struggled away from the shoulder against which she had been leaning, and huddled miserably in the far corner of the seat. Nicholas Devine gave her a single glance with his unpleasant eyes, and turned them again on the street.

The girl was helpless, unable to put forth the strength even for another attempt to open the door. She was still only half aware of her position, and realized only that something appalling was occurring to her. She lay in passive misery against the cushions of the seat as the other turned suddenly up a dark driveway and into the open door of a small garage. He snapped off the engine, extinguished the headlights, and left them in a horrible, smothering, silent darkness.

She heard him open the door on his side; after an apparently interminable interval, she heard the creak of the hinges on her own side. She huddled terrified, voiceless, and immobile.

He reached in, fumbling against her in the darkness. He found her arm, and dragged her from the car. Again, as on that other occasion, she found herself reeling helplessly behind him through the dark as he tugged at her wrist. He paused at a door in the building adjacent to the garage, searching in his pocket with his free hand.

"I won't go in there!" she muttered dazedly. The other made no reply, but inserted a key in the lock, turned it, and swung open the door.

He stepped through it, dragging her after him. With a sudden access of desperate strength, she caught the frame of the door, jerked violently on her prisoned wrist, and was unexpectedly free. She reeled away, turned toward the street, and took a few faltering steps down the driveway.

Almost instantly her tormentor was upon her, and his hand closed again on her arm. Pat had no further strength; she sank to the pavement and crouched there, disregarding the insistent tugging on her arm.

"Come on," he growled. "You only delay the inevitable. Must I drag you?"

She made no reply. He tugged violently at her wrist, dragging her a few inches along the pavement. Then he stooped over her, raised her in his arms, and bore her toward the dark opening of the door. He crowded her roughly through it, disregarding the painful bumping of her shoulders and knees. She heard the slam of the door as he kicked it closed, and she realized that they were mounting a flight of stairs, moving somewhere into the oppressive threatening darkness.

Then they were moving along a level floor, and her arm was

bruised against another door. There was a moment of stillness, and then she was released, dropped indifferently to the surface of a bed or couch. A moment later a light flashed on.

The girl was conscious at first only of the gaze of the red eyes. They held her own in a fascinating, unbreakable, trance-like spell. Then, in a wave of dizziness, she closed her own eyes.

"Where are we?" she murmured. "In Hell?"

"You should call it Heaven," came the sardonic voice. "It's the home of your sweetheart. His home—and mine!"

26. The Depths

"Heaven and hell always were the same place," said Nicholas Devine, his red eyes glaring down at the girl. "We'll demonstrate the fact."

Pat shifted wearily, and sat erect, passing her hand dazedly across her face. She brushed the tangled strands of black hair from before her eyes, and stared dully at the room in which she found herself.

It had some of the aspects of a study, and some of a laboratory, or perhaps a doctor's office. There was a case of dusty books on the wall opposite, and another crystal-fronted cabinet containing glassware, bottles, little round boxes suggestive of drugs or pharmaceuticals. There was a paper-littered table too; she gave a convulsive shudder at the sight of a bald, varnished death's head, its lower jaw articulated, that reposed on a pile of papers and grinned at her.

"Where—" she began faintly.

"This was the room of your sweetheart's father," said the other. "His and my mutual father. He was an experimenter, a researcher, and so, in another sense, am I!" He leered evilly at her. "He used this chamber to further his experiments, and I for mine—the carrying on of a noble family tradition!"

The girl scarcely heard his words; the expressionless tone carried no meaning to the chaos which was her mind. She felt only an inchoate horror and a vague but all-encompassing fear, and her head was aching from the blows he had dealt her.

"What do you want?" she asked dully.

"Why, there is an unfinished experiment. You must remember our interrupted proceedings of a week ago! Have you already forgotten the early steps of our experiment in evil?"

Pat cringed at the cold, sardonic tones of the other. "Let me go," she whimpered. "Please!" she appealed. "Let me go!"

"In due time," he responded. "You lack gratitude," he continued. "Last time, out of the kindness that is my soul, I permitted you to dull your senses with alcohol, but you failed, apparently, to appreciate my indulgence. But this time"—His eyes lit up queer-ly—"this time you approach the consummation of our experiment with undimmed mind!"

He approached her. She drew her knees up, huddling back on the couch, and summoned the final vestiges of her strength.

"I'll kick you!" she muttered desperately. "Keep back from me!"

He paused just beyond her reach. "I had hoped," he said ironi-cally, "if not for your cooperation, at least for no further active resistance. It's quite useless; I told you days ago that this time would come."

He advanced cautiously; Pat thrust out her foot, driving it with all her power. Instantly he drew back, catching her ankle in his hand. He jerked her leg sharply upwards, and she was precipitated violently to the couch. Again he advanced.

The girl writhed away from him. She slipped from the foot of the couch and darted in a circle around him, turning in an attempt to gain the room's single exit—the door by which they had en-tered. He moved quickly to intercept her; he closed the door as she backed despairingly away, retreating to the far end of the room. Once more he faced her, his malicious eyes gleaming, and moved deliberately toward her.

She drew back until the table halted her; she pressed herself against it as if to force her way still further. The other moved at un-altered pace. Suddenly her hand pressed over some smooth, round, hard object; she grasped it and flung the grinning skull at the more terrible face that approached her. He dodged; there was a crash of glass as the gruesome missile shattered the pane of the cabinet of drugs. And inexorably, Nicholas Devine approached once more.

She moved along the edge of the table, squeezed herself between it and the wall. Behind her was one of the room's two windows, curtainless, with drawn shades. She found the cord, jerked it, and let the blind coil upward with an abrupt snap.

"I'll throw myself through the window!" she announced with a sort of desperate calm. "Don't dare move a step closer!"

The demon paused once more in his deliberate advance. "You will, of course," he said as if considering. "Given the opportunity. Your body torn and broken, spotted with blood—that might be a pleasure second only to that I plan."

"You'll suffer for it!" said the girl hysterically. "I'll be glad to do it, knowing you'll suffer!"

"Not I—your sweetheart."

"I don't care! I can't stand it!"

The other smiled his demoniac smile, and resumed his advance. She watched him in terror that had now reached the ultimate degree; her mind could bear no more. She turned suddenly, raised her arm, and beat her fist against the pane of the window.

With the surprising resistance glass sometimes displays, it shook at her blow but did not shatter. She drew back for a second attempt, and her upraised arm was caught in a rigid grip, and she was dragged backward to the center of the room, thrown heavily to the floor. She sat dazedly looking up at the form standing over her.

"Must I render you helpless again?" queried the flat voice of the other. "Are you not yet broken, convinced of the uselessness of this struggle?"

She made no answer, staring dully at his immobile features.

"Are you going to fight me further?" As she was still silent, he repeated, "Are you?"

She shook her head vaguely. "No," she muttered. She had reached the point of utter indifference; nothing at all was important enough now to struggle for.

"Stand up!" ordered the being above her.

She pulled herself wearily to her feet, leaning against the wall. She closed her eyes for a moment, then opened them dully as the other moved.

"What—are you—are you going to do?" she murmured.

"First," said the demon coldly, "I shall disrobe you somewhat more completely than on our other occasion. Thereafter we will proceed to the consummation of our experiment."

She watched him indifferently, uncomprehendingly, as he crooked a thin finger in the neck of her frock. She felt the pressure as he pulled, heard the rip of the fabric, and the pop of buttons, but she was conscious of no particular sensation as the garment cascaded into a black and red pool at her feet. She stood passive as he hooked his finger in the strap of her vest, and that too joined the little mound of cloth. She shivered slightly as she stood bared to the waist, but gave no other sign.

Again the thin hand moved toward her; from somewhere in her tormented spirit a final shred of resistance arose, and she pushed the questing member feebly to one side. She heard a low, sardonic laugh from her oppressor.

"Look at me!" he commanded.

She raised her eyes wearily; she drew her arm about her in a forlorn gesture of concealment. Her eyes met the strange orbs of the other, and a faint thrill of horror stirred; other than this, she felt nothing. Then his eyes were approaching her; she was conscious of the illusion that they were expanding, filling all the space in front of her. Their weird glow filled the world, dominated everything.

"Will you yield?" he queried.

The eyes commanded. "Yes," she said dully.

She felt his hands icy cold on her bare shoulders. They traveled like a shudder about her body, and suddenly she was pressed close to him.

"Are you mine?" he demanded. For the first time there was a tinge of expression in the toneless voice, a trace of eagerness. She made no answer; her eyes, held by his, stared like the eyes of a person in a trance, unwinking, fascinated.

"Are you mine?" he repeated, his breath hissing on her cheek.

"Yes." She heard her own voice in automatic reply.

"Mine—for the delights of evil?"

"Yours!" she murmured. The eyes had blotted out everything.

"And do you hate me?"

"No."

The arms about her tightened into crushing bands. The pressure stopped her breath; her very bones seemed to give under their fierce compression.

"Do you hate me?" he muttered.

"Yes!" she gasped. "Yes! I hate you!"

"Ah!" He twisted his hand in her black hair, wrenching it roughly back. "Are you ready now for the consummation? To look upon the face of evil?"

She made no reply. Her eyes, as glassy as those of a sleep-walker, stared into his.

"Are you ready?"

"Yes," she said.

He pressed his mouth to hers. The fierceness of the kiss bruised her lips, the pull of his hand in her hair was a searing pain, the pressure of his arm about her body was a suffocation. Yet—somehow—there was again the dawning of that unholy pleasure—the same degraded delight that had risen in her on that other occasion, in the room of the red-checked table cloth. Through some hellish alchemy, the leaden pain was transmuting itself into the garish gold of a horrible, abnormal pleasure. She found her crushed lips attempting a feeble, painful response.

At her movement, she felt herself swung abruptly from her feet. With his lips still crushing hers, he raised her in his arms; she felt herself borne across the room. He paused; there was a sudden release, and she crashed to the hard surface of the couch, whose rough covering scratched the bare flesh of her back. Nicholas Devine bent over her; she saw his hand stretch toward her single remaining garment. And again, from somewhere in her harassed soul, a spark of resistance flashed.

"Nick!" she moaned. "Oh, Nick! Help me!"

"Call him!" said the other, a sneer on his face. "Call him! He hears; it adds to his torment!"

She covered her eyes with her hands. She felt his hand slip coldly between her skin and the elastic about her waist.

"Nick!" she moaned again. "Nick! Oh, my God! Nick!"

27. Two in Hell

The cold hand against Pat was still; she felt it rigid and stiff on her flesh. She lay passive with closed eyes; having voiced her final appeal, she was through. The words torn from her misery represented the final iota of spirit remaining to her; and her bruised body and battered mind had nothing further to give.

The hand quivered and withdrew. For a moment more she lay motionless with her arms clutched about her, then she opened her eyes, gazing dully, hopelessly at the demon standing over her. He was watching her with a curious abstracted frown; as she stirred, the scowl intensified, and he drew back a step.

His face contorted suddenly in a spasm of some unguessable emotion. His fists clenched; a low unintelligible mutter broke from his lips. "Strange!" she heard him say, and after a moment, "I'm still master here!"

He was master; in a moment the emotion vanished, and he was again standing over her, his face the same impassive demoniac mask. She watched him in a dull stupor of despair that was too deep for even a whimper of pain as he wrenched at the elastic about her waist, and it cut into her flesh and parted. He tore the garment away, and the red eyes bored down with a wild elation in their depths.

"Mine!" the being muttered, a new hoarseness in his voice. "Are you mine?" Pat made no answer; his voice croaked in more insistent tones. "Are you mine?"

She could not reply. She felt his fingers bite into the flesh of her shoulder. She was shaken roughly, violently, and the question came again, fiercely. The eyes flamed in command, and she felt through her languor and weakness, the stirring of that strange and unholy fascination that he held over her.

"Answer!" he croaked. "Are you mine?"

The torture of his searing grip on her shoulder wrung an answer from her.

"Yes," she murmured faintly. "Yours."

137

She closed her eyes again in helpless resignation. She felt the hand withdrawn, and she lay passive, waiting, on the verge of unconsciousness, numb, spirit-broken, and beaten.

Nothing happened. After a long interval she opened her eyes, and saw the other standing again with clenched fists and contorted countenance. His features were writhing in the intensity of his struggle; a strange low snarl came from his lips. He backed away from her, step by step; he leaned against the bookshelves, and beads of perspiration formed on his scowling face.

He was no longer master! She saw the change; imperceptibly the evil vanished from his features, and suddenly they were no longer his, but the weary, horror-stricken visage of her Nick! The red eyes were no longer Satanic, but only the blood-shot, troubled, gentle eyes of her sweetheart, and the lips had lost their grimness, and gasped and quivered and trembled. He reeled against the wall, staggered to the chair at the table, and sank weakly into it.

Pat was far too exhausted, far too dazed, to feel anything but the faintest sensation of relief. She realized only dimly that tears were welling from her eyes, and that sharp sobs were shaking her. She was for the moment unable to stir, but it was not long before the being at the table turned stricken eyes on her and she moved. Then she drew her knees up before her, as if to hide her body behind their slim, chiffon-clad grace.

Nick rose from the table, approaching her with weary, hesitant tread. He seized a cover of some sort that was folded over the foot of the couch, shook it out and cast it over her. She clutched it about her body, sat erect and leaned back against the wall in utter exhaustion. Many minutes passed with no word from either of the occupants of the unholy chamber. It was Nick who broke the long silence.

"Pat," he murmured in low tones. "Pat—Dear. Are you—all right?"

She stared at him dazedly without answer.

"Honey!" he said. "Honey! Tell me you're all right!"

"All right?" she repeated uncomprehendingly. "Yes. I guess I'm all right."

"Then go, Pat! Get away from here before he—before anything happens! Put your clothes on and hurry away!"

"I can't!" she faintly. "I—can't!"

"You must, Honey!"

"I'm just—not able to. I will soon, Nick—honest. When I—when I get my breath back."

"Pat!" There was anguish in the cry. "Oh, God—Pat! We mustn't ever be together again—not ever!"

"No," she said. A bit of sanity was returning to her; comprehension of her position sent a shudder through her. "No, we mustn't."

"I couldn't bear another night like this—watching! I'd go mad!"

"Oh!" she choked, tears starting. "If you hadn't come back, Nick!"

"I conquered him," he said. "I don't think I could do it again. It was your call that gave me the strength, Pat." He shook his head as if bewildered. "He thought it was being in love with you that weakened me, but in the end it was that which gave me the strength to subdue him."

"I'm scared!" said the girl suddenly. "Oh, Nick! I'm frightened!"

"You'd better go. You'd better dress and leave at once, Honey. Here." He gathered her clothes from the floor, depositing them beside her on the couch. "There are pins in the tray on the table, Pat. Fix yourself up as well as you can, dear—and hurry out of here!"

He turned toward the door as if to leave, and a shock of terror shook her.

"Nick!" she cried. "Don't go away! I'm more afraid when I can't see you—afraid that he—" She broke off sobbing.

"All right, Honey. I'll turn my back."

She slipped out from under the blanket, found the pins, and repaired her ruined costume. The frock was torn, crushed and bedraggled; she pinned it together at the throat, though her trembling fingers made the task difficult. She pulled it on and took a tentative step toward the door.

"Nick!" she called as a wave of dizziness sent her swaying against the wall.

"What's the matter, Honey?" He turned anxiously at her cry.

"I'm dizzy," she moaned. "My head aches, and—I'm scared!"

"Pat, darling! You can't go out alone like this—and," he added miserably, "I can't take you!" He slipped his arm around her tenderly, supporting her to the couch. "Honey, what'll we do?"

"I'll be—all right," she murmured. "I'll go in a moment." The dizziness was leaving her; strength was returning.

"You must!" he said dolefully. "What a parting, Pat! Never to see you again, and then having this to remember as farewell!"

"I know, Nick. You see, I love you too." She turned her dark, troubled eyes on him. "Honey, kiss me goodbye! We'll have that to remember, anyway!" Tears were again on her cheeks.

"Do I dare?" he asked despondently. "After the things these lips of mine have said, and what these arms have done to you?"

"But you didn't, Nick! Could I blame you for—that *other*?"

"God! You're kind, Pat! Honey, if ever I win out in this battle, if ever I know I'm the final victor, I'll—No," he said his tones dropping abruptly. "I'll never come back to you, Pat. It's far too dangerous, and—can I ever be certain? Can I?"

"I don't know, Nick. Can you?"

"I can't be, Pat! I'll never be sure that he isn't just dormant, as he was before, waiting for my weakness to betray me! I'll never be certain, Honey! It has to be goodbye!"

"Then kiss me!"

She clung to him; the room that had been so recently a chamber of horrors was transformed. As she held him, as her lips were pressed to his, she thought suddenly of the words of the demon, that Heaven and Hell were always the same place. They had taken on a new meaning, those words; she drew away from Nick and turned her tear-bright eyes tenderly on his.

"Honey," she murmured, "I don't want you to leave me. I don't want you to go!"

"Nor do I want to, Pat! But I must."

"You mustn't! You're to stay, and we'll fight it out together—be married, or any way that permits us to fight it through together."

"Pat! Do you think I'd consent to that?"

"Nick," she said. "Nick darling—It's worth it to me! I'm realizing it now; I thought it wasn't—but it is! I can't lose you, Nick—anything, even that *other*, is better than losing you."

"You're sweet, Pat! You know I'd trade my very soul for that, but—No. I can't do it! And don't torture me by suggesting it again."

"But I will, Nick!" She was speaking softly, earnestly. "You're

140

worth anything to me! If he should kill me, you'd still be worth it!" She gazed tenderly at him. "I'd want to die anyway without you!"

"No more than I without you," he muttered brokenly. "But I won't do it, Pat! I won't do that to you!"

"I love you, Nick!" she said in a low voice. "I don't want to live without you. Do you understand me, dear? I don't want to live without you!"

He stared at her somberly. "I've thought of that too," he said. "Pat—if I only believed that we'd be together after, together anywhere, I'd say yes. If only I believed there were an afterwards!"

"Doesn't he prove that by his very existence?"

"Your Doctor would deny that."

"Doctor Carl never saw him, Nick. And anyway, even oblivion together would be better than being separated, and far better than this!"

He gazed at her silently. She spoke again. "That doesn't frighten me, Nick. It's only losing you that frightens me, especially the fear of losing you to him."

He continued his silent gaze. Suddenly he drew her close to him, held her in a tight, tender embrace.

28. Lunar Omen

After a considerable interval, during which Nick held the girl tightly and silently in his arms, he released her, sat with his head resting on his cupped palms in an attitude of deep study. Pat, beside him, fell mechanically to re-pinning the throat of her frock, which had opened during the moments of the embrace. He rose to his feet, pacing nervously before her.

"It isn't a thing to do on the impulse of a moment, Pat," he muttered, pausing at her side. "You must see that."

"It isn't the impulse of a moment."

"But one doesn't abandon everything, the whole world, so easily, Honey. One doesn't cast away a last hope, however forlorn a hope it may be!"

"Is there a hope, Nick?" she asked gently. "Is there a chance left to us?"

"I don't know! Before God—I—don't know!"

"If there's a chance, the very slightest shadow of the specter of a chance, we'll take it, won't we? Because the other way is always open to us, Nick."

"Yes. It's always open."

"But we won't take that chance," she continued defiantly, "if it involves my losing you, Honey. I meant what I said, Nick: I don't want to live without you!"

"What chance have we?" he queried somberly. "Those are our alternatives—life apart, death together."

"Then you know my choice!" she cried desperately. "Nick, Honey—don't let's draw it out in futile talking! I can't stand it!"

He moved his hand in a gesture of bewilderment and frustration, and turned away, striding nervously toward the window whose blind she had raised. He leaned his hands on the table, peering dejectedly out upon the street below.

"What time," he asked irrelevantly in a queer voice, "did the Doctor say the moon rose? Do you remember?"

"No," she said tensely. "Oh, Honey! Please—don't stand there with your back to me now, when I'm half crazy!"

"I'm thinking," he responded. "It rises a little earlier each night—or is it later? No matter; come here, Pat."

She rose wearily and joined him; he slipped his arm about her, and drew her against him.

"Look there," he said, indicating the night-dark vista beyond the window.

She looked out upon a dim-lit street or court, at the blind end of which the house was apparently situated. Far off at the open end, across a distant highway where even at this hour passed a constant stream of traffic, flashed a narrow strip of lake; and above it, rising gigantic from the coruscating moon-path, lifted the satellite. She watched the remote flickering of the waves as they tossed back the broken bits of the light strewn along the path. Then she turned puzzled eyes on her companion.

"That's Heaven," he said pointing a finger at the great flowing lunar disk. "There's a world that never caught the planet-cancer called Life, or if it ever suffered, it's cured. It's clean—burned clean by the sun and scoured clean by the airless zero of space. A dead world, and therefore not an unhappy one."

The girl stared at him without comprehension. She murmured, "I don't understand, Nick."

"Don't you, Pat?" He pointed again at the moon. "That's Heaven, the dead world, and this is Hell, the living one. Heaven and Hell swinging forever about their common center!" He gestured toward the sparkling moon-path on the water. "Look, Pat! The dead world strews flowers on the grave of the living one!"

Some of his bitter ecstasy caught the girl; she felt his somber mood of exaltation.

"I love you, Nick!" she whispered, pressing closely to him.

"What difference does it make—our actions?" he queried. "There's the omen, that lifeless globe in the sky. Where we go, all humanity now living will follow before a century, and in a million years, the human race as well! What if we go a year or a million years before the rest? Will it make any difference in the end?" He looked down at her. "All we've been valuing here is hope. To the devil with hope! Let's have peace instead!"

"I'm not afraid, Nick."

"Nor I. And if we go, he goes, and he's mortally afraid of death!"

"Can he—prevent you?"

"Not now! I'm the stronger now. For this time, I'm master."

He turned again to stare at the glowing satellite as it rose imperceptibly from the horizon. "There's nothing to regret," he murmured, "except one thing—the loss of beauty. Beauty like that—and like you, Pat. That's bitterly hard to foreswear!" He leaned forward toward the remote disk of the moon; he spoke as if addressing it, in tones so low that the girl, pressed close to him, had to quiet the sound of her own breath to listen. He said:

"Long miles above cloud-bank and blast,
And many miles above the sea,
I watch you rise majestically
Feeling your chilly light at last—
Cold beauty in the way you cast
Split silver fragments on the waves,
As if this planet's life were past,
And all men peaceful in their graves."

Pat was silent for a moment as he paused, then she murmured a low phrase. "Oh, I love you, Nick!" she said.

"And I you, dear," he responded. "Have we decided anything? Are we—going through with it?"

"I've not faltered," she said soberly. "I meant it, Nick. Without you, life would be as empty as that airless void you speak of. I'm not afraid. What's there to be afraid of?"

"Only the transition, Pat. That and the unknown—but no situation could possibly be more terrible than our present one. It couldn't be! Oblivion, annihilation—they're preferable, aren't they?"

"Oh, yes! Nothing I can imagine could be other than a change for the better."

"Then let's face it!" His voice took on a note of determination. "I've thought to face it a dozen times before this, and each time I've hesitated. The hesitation of a coward, Pat."

"You're no coward, dear. It was that illusion of hope; that always weakens one. No one's strong who hasn't given up hope."

"Then," he repeated, "let's face it!"

"How, Nick?"

144

"My father has left us the means. There in the cabinet are a hundred deaths—swift ones, lingering ones, painful, and easy! I don't know one from the other; our choice must be blind." He strode over to the case, sending slivers of glass from the shattered front glistening along the floor. "I'd choose an easy one, Dear, if I knew, for your sake. Euthanasia!"

He stared hesitantly at the files of mysterious drugs with their incomprehensible labels.

Suddenly the scene appeared humorous to the girl, queerly funny, in some unnatural horrible fashion. Her nerves, overstrained for hours, were on the verge of breaking; without realization of it, she had come to the border of hysteria.

"Shopping for death!" she choked, trying to suppress the wild laughter that beat in her throat. "Which one's most suitable? Which one's most becoming? Which one"—an hysterical laughing sob shook her—"will wear the longest?"

He turned, gazing at her with an illogical concern in his face.

"What's the difference?" she cried wildly. "I don't care—painful or pleasant, it all ends in the same grave! Close your eyes and choose!"

Suddenly he was holding her in his arms again, and she was sobbing, clinging to him frantically. She was miserably unstrung; her body shook under the impact of her gasping breath. Then gradually, she quieted, and was silent against him.

"We've been mad!" he murmured. "It's been an insane idea—for me to inflict this on you, Pat. Do you think I could consider the destruction of your beauty, Dear? I've been lying to myself, stifling my judgment with poetic imagery, when all the while it was just that I'm afraid to face the thing alone!"

"No," she murmured, burying her face against his shoulder. "I'm the coward, Nick. I'm the one that's frightened, and I'm the one that broke down! It's just been—too much, this evening; I'm all right now."

"But we'll not go through with this, Pat!"

"But we will! It's better than life without you, dear. We've argued and argued, and at last forgotten the one truth, the one thing I'll never retract: I can't face living without you, Nick! I can't!"

He brushed his hand wearily before his eyes. "Back at the starting point," he muttered. "All right, Honey. So be it!"

He strode again to the cabinet. "Corrosive sublimate." he murmured. "Cyanide of Potassium. They're both deadly, but I think the second is rapid, and therefore less painful. Cyanide let it be!"

He extracted two small beakers from the glassware on the shelf. He filled them with water from a carafe on the table, and, while the girl watched him with fascinated eyes, he deliberately tilted a spoonful or so of white crystals into each of them. The mixture swirled a moment, then settled clear and colorless, and the crystals began to shrink as they passed swiftly into solution.

"There it is," he announced grimly. "There's peace, oblivion, forgetfulness, and annihilation for you, for me, and—for him! Beyond all doubt, the logical course for us, isn't it? Do we take it?"

"Please," she said faintly. "Kiss me first, Honey. Isn't that the proper course for lovers in this situation?" She felt a faint touch of astonishment at her own irony; the circumstances had ceased to have any reality to her, and had become merely a dramatic sequence like the happenings in a play.

He gathered her again into his arms and pressed his lips to hers. It was a long, tender, wistful kiss; when at last it ended, Pat found her eyes again filled with tears, but not this time the tears of hysteria. "Nick!" she murmured. "Nick, darling!" He gave her a deep, somber, but very tender smile, and reached for one of the deadly beakers, "To another meeting!" he said as his fingers closed on it.

Suddenly, amazingly, the strident ring of a doorbell sounded, the more surprising since they had all but forgotten the existence of a world about them. Interruption! It meant only the going through once more of all that they had just passed.

"Drink it!" exclaimed Pat impulsively, seizing the remaining beaker.

29. Scopolamine for Satan

The glass was struck from Pat's hand, and the water-clear contents streamed into pools and darkening blots over the table and its litter of papers. She stared unseeingly at the mess, without realizing that it was Nick who had dashed the draught from her very lips. She felt neither anger nor relief, but only a numbness, and a sense of anticlimax. Somewhere below the bell was ringing again, and a door was resounding to violent blows, but she only continued her bewildered, questioning gaze. "I can't let you, Pat!" he muttered, answering her unspoken query.

"But Nick—why?"

"There's somebody at the door, isn't there? Mustn't we find out who?"

"What difference can it make?" she asked wearily.

"I don't know. I want to find out."

"It's that illusion of hope again," she murmured. "That's all it is, Nick—and it means now that it's all to do over again! The whole thing, from the beginning—and we were so near—the end!"

"I know," he said miserably. "I know all that, but—" He paused as the insistent racket below was redoubled. "I'm going to answer that bell," he ended.

He moved away from her, vanishing through the room's single door. She watched his disappearance without moving, but no sooner had he passed from sight than a curious feeling of fear oppressed her. She cast off the numbness and languor, and darted after him into the darkness of the hall.

"Nick!" she called. Somewhere ahead a light flashed on; she saw the well of a staircase, and heard his footsteps descending. She followed in frantic haste, gaining the top step just as the pounding below ceased. She heard the click of the door, and paused suddenly at the sound of a familiar voice.

"Where's Pat?" The words drifted up in low, rumbling, ominous tones.

147

"Dr. Carl!" she shrieked. She ran swiftly down the stairs to Nick's side, where he stood facing the great figure of the Doctor. "Dr. Carl! How'd you find me?"

The newcomer gave her a long, narrow-eyed, speculative survey. "I spent nearly the whole night doing it," he growled at last. "It took me hours to locate Mueller and get this address from him." He stepped forward, taking the girl's arm. "Come on!" he said gruffly, without a glance at Nick standing silently beside her. "I'm taking you home!"

She held back. "But why?"

"Why? Because I don't like the company you keep. Is that reason enough?"

She still resisted his insistent tug. "Nick hasn't done anything," she said defiantly, with a side glance at the youth's flushed, unhappy features.

"He hasn't? Look at yourself, girl! Look at your clothes, and your forehead! What's more, I saw enough from my window; I saw him bundle you into that car!" His eyes were flashing angrily, and his grip on her arm tightened, while his free hand clenched into an enormous fist.

"That wasn't Nick!"

"No. It was your devil, I suppose!" said Horker sarcastically. "Anyway, Pat, you're coming with me before I do violence to what remains of your devil!"

Nick spoke for the first time since the Doctor's entrance. "Please do, Pat," he said softly. "Please go with him."

"I won't!" she snapped. The sudden shifts of situation during the long hours of that terrible evening were irritating her. She had alternated so rapidly between horror and hope and despair that her frayed nerves had seized now at the same reality of anger.

Her mind, so long overstrained, was now deliberately forgetting her swing from the pit of terror to the verge of death. "You come up like a hero to the rescue!" she taunted the doctor. "Hairbreadth Horker!"

"You little fool!" growled the Doctor. "A fine reception, after losing a night's sleep! I'll drag you home, if I have to!" He moved ponderously toward the door; she gave a violent wrench and freed her arm from his grasp.

"If you can, you mean!" she jeered. She looked at his exasperated face, and suddenly, with one of her abrupt changes of mood, she softened. "Dr. Carl, Honey," she said in apologetic tones, "I'm sorry. You're very sweet, and I'm really grateful, but I can't leave Nick now." Her eyes turned troubled. "Not now."

"Why, Pat?" Mollified by the change in her mien, his voice rumbled in sympathetic notes.

"I can't," she repeated. "It's—it's getting worse."

"Bah!"

"So it's 'Bah'!" she flared. "Well, if you're so contemptuous of the thing, why don't you cure it? What good did your psychoanalysis do? You don't even know what it is!"

"What do you expect?" roared the Doctor. "Can I diagnose it by absent treatment? I haven't had a chance to see the condition active yet!"

"All right!" said Pat, her strained nerves driving her to impatience. "You're here and Nick's here! Go on with your diagnosis; get it over with, and let's see what you can do. You ought at least to be able to name the condition—the outstanding authority in the Middle West on neural and mental pathology!" Her tone was sardonic.

"Listen, Pat," said Horker with exaggerated patience, in the manner of one addressing a stupid child, "I've explained before that I can't get at the root of a mental aberration when the subject's as unstrung as your young man here seems to be. Psychoanalysis just won't work unless the subject is calm, composed, and not in a nervous state. Can you comprehend that?"

"Just dimly!" she snapped. "You ought to know another way— you, the outstanding authority—"

"Be still!" he interrupted gruffly. "Of course I know another way, if I wanted to drag all of us back to my office, where I have the equipment!—which I won't do tonight," he finished grimly.

"Then do it here."

"I haven't what I need."

"There's everything upstairs," said Pat. "It's all there, all Nick's father's equipment."

"Not tonight! That's final."

The girl's manner changed again. She turned troubled, imploring eyes on Horker. "Dr. Carl," she said plaintively, "I can't leave Nick now." She seized the arm of the silent, dejected youth, who had been standing passively by. "I can't leave him, really. I'd not be sure of seeing him again, ever. Please, Dr. Carl!"

"If these frenzies of yours," rumbled Horker, "are so violent and malicious, you ought to be confined. Do you know that, young man?"

"Yes, sir," mumbled Nick wretchedly.

"And I've thought of it," continued the Doctor. "I've thought of it!"

"Please!" cried Pat imploringly. "Won't you try, Dr. Carl?"

"The devil!" he growled. "All right, then."

He followed the girl up the stairs, while Nick trailed disconsolately behind. She led him back into the chamber they had quitted, where a curious odor of peach pits seemed to scent the air. Horker sniffed suspiciously, then seized the remaining beaker, raising it cautiously to his nostrils.

"Damnation!" he exploded. "Prussic acid—or cyanide! What in—" He caught sight of Pat's tragic eyes, and suddenly replaced the container. "Pat!" he groaned. "Pat, Honey!" He drew her into the circle of his great arm. "I'll help you, dear! All I can, with all my heart, since it means that much to you!" He groaned again under his breath. "Oh, my God!"

He held her a moment, patting her tousled black head with his massive, delicate fingered hand. Then he released her, turning to Nick.

"This the stuff?" he asked, brusquely, indicating the cabinet of bottles, with its splintered front.

Nick nodded. Pat sank to the chair beside the table and watched Horker as he scanned the array of containers. He pulled out a tiny wooden case and snapped it open to reveal a number of steel needles that glinted brightly in the yellow light. He grunted in satisfaction and continued his inspection.

"Atropine," he muttered, reading the labeled boxes. "Cocaine, daturine, hyoscine, hyoscyamine—won't do!"

"What do you need?" the girl queried faintly.

"A mild hypnotic," said the Doctor abstractedly, still searching. "Pretty good substitutes for psychoanalysis—certain drugs. Dulls the conscious mind, but not to complete unconsciousness. Good means of getting at the subconscious. See?"

"Sort of," said Pat. "If it only works!"

"Oh, it'll work if we can find—ah!" He seized a tiny cardboard box. "Scopolamine! This'll do the work."

He extracted a tiny glassy something from one or other of the boxes he held, and frowned down at it. He seized the carafe of water, plunged something pointed and shiny into it.

"Antiseptic," he muttered thoughtfully. He seized a brown bottle from the case, held it toward the light, and shook it. "Peroxide's gone flat," he growled. "Nothing but water."

He pulled a silver cigar-lighter from his pocket and snapped a yellow flame to it. He passed the point of the hypodermic rapidly back and forth through the little spear of fire. Finally he turned to Nick.

"Take off your coat," he ordered. "Roll up your shirt sleeve—the left one. And sit over there." He indicated the couch along the wall.

The youth obeyed without a word. The only indication of emotion was a long, miserable, wistful look at Pat as he seated himself impassively on the spot that the girl had so recently occupied.

"Now!" said the Doctor briskly, approaching the youth. "This will make you drowsy, sleepy. That's all it'll do. Don't fight the effect. Just relax, let the thing take its course, and I'll see what I can get out of you."

Pat gasped and Nick winced as he drove the needle into the bared arm.

"So!" he said. "Now relax. Lean back and close your eyes."

He stepped to the door, dragged in a battered chair from the hall, and occupied it. He sat beside Pat, watching the pale features of the youth, who sat quietly with closed eyes, breathing slowly, heavily.

"Long enough," muttered Horker. He raised his voice. "Can you hear me?" he called to the motionless figure on the couch. There was no response, but Pat fancied she saw a slight change in Nick's expression.

"Can you hear me?" repeated Horker in louder tones.

"Yes, I can hear you," came in icy tones from the figure on the couch. Pat started violently as the voice sounded. The eyes opened, and she saw in sudden terror the ruddy orbs of the demon!

30. The Demon Free

Pat emitted a small, startled shriek, and heard it echoed by a surprised grunt from Dr. Horker.

"Queer!" he muttered. "The stuff must be mislabeled. Scopolamine doesn't act like this; it's a narcotic."

"He's—the other!" gasped Pat, while the being on the couch grinned sardonically.

"Eh? An attack? Can't be!" The Doctor shook his head emphatically.

"It's not Nick!" cried the girl in panic. "You're not, are you?" she appealed to the grim entity.

"Not your sweetheart?" queried the creature, still with his mocking leer. "A few hours ago you were lying here all but naked, confessing you were mine. Have you forgotten?"

She shuddered at the reference, and shrank back in her chair. She heard the Doctor's ominous, angry rumble, and the evil tittering chuckle of the other.

"Pathological or not," snapped Horker, "I can resent your remarks! I've considered several times varying my treatment with another solid cut to the jaw!" He rose from his chair, stamping viciously toward the other.

"A moment," said Nicholas Devine. "Do you know what you've done? Have you any idea what you've done?" He turned cool, mocking, red-glinting eyes on the Doctor.

"Huh?" Horker paused as if puzzled. "What I've done? What do you mean?"

"You don't know, then." The other gave a satyric smile. "You're stupid; I gave you the clue, yet you hadn't the intelligence to follow it. Do you know what I am?" He leaned forward, his eyes leering evilly into the Doctor's. "I'll tell you. I'm a question of synapses. That's all—merely a question of synapses!" He tittered again, horribly. "It still means nothing to you, does it, Doctor?"

"I'll show you what it means!" Horker clenched a massive fist

152

and strode toward the figure, whose eyes stared, steadily, unwinkingly into his own.

"Back!" the being snapped as the great form bent over him. The Doctor paused as if struck rigid, his arm and heavy fist drawn back like the conventional fighting pose of a boxer. "Go back!" repeated the other, rising. Pat whimpered in abject terror as she heard Horker's surprised grunt, and saw him recede slowly, and finally sink into his chair. His bewildered eyes were still fixed on those of Nicholas Devine.

"I'll tell you what you've done!" said the strange being. "You've freed me! There was nothing wrong with your scopolamine. It worked!" He chuckled. "You drugged him and freed me!"

Horker managed a questioning grunt.

"I'm free!" exulted the other. "For the first time I haven't him to fight! He's here, but helpless to oppose me—he's feeble—feeble!" He gave again the horrible tittering chuckle. "See how weak the two of you are against my unopposed powers!" he jeered. "Weaklings—food for my pleasures!"

He turned his eyes, luminous and avid, on Pat. "This time," he said, "there'll be no interruptions. A witness to our experiment will add a delicate touch of pleasure—"

He broke off at the Doctor's sudden movement. Horker had snatched a glistening blue revolver from his pocket, held it leveled at the lust-filled eyes.

"Huh!" growled the Doctor triumphantly. "Do you think I come trailing a maniac without some protection? Especially a vicious one like you?"

Nicholas Devine turned his eyes on his opponent. He stared long and intently.

"Drop it!" he commanded at length. Pat felt a surge of chaotic terror as the weapon clattered to the floor. She turned a frightened glance on Horker's face, and her fright redoubled at the sight of his straining jaw, the perspiration-beaded forehead, and his bewildered eyes. The demon kicked the gun carelessly aside.

"Puerile!" he said contemptuously. He backed away from them, re-seating himself on the couch whence he had risen. He surveyed the pair in sardonic mirth.

"Pat!" muttered the Doctor huskily. "Get out of here, Honey!

He's got some hellish trick of fascination that's paralyzed me. Get out and get help!"

The girl moved as if to rise. Nicholas Devine shifted his eyes for the barest instant to her face; she felt the strength drain out of her body, and she sank weakly to her chair.

"It's useless," she murmured hopelessly to the Doctor. "He's— he's just what I told you—a devil!"

"I guess you were right," mumbled Horker dazedly.

There was a burst of demonic mirth from the being on the couch. "Merely a matter of synapses," he rasped, chuckling. His face changed, took on the familiar coldness, the stony expression Pat had observed there before. "This palls!" he snapped. "I've better amusement—after we've rendered your friend merely an interested on-looker." He narrowed his red eyes as if in thought. "Take off a stocking," he ordered. "Tie his hands to the back of the chair."

"I won't!" said the girl. The eyes shifted to her face. "I won't!" she repeated tremulously as she kicked off a diminutive pump. She shuddered at the gleam in the evil eyes as she stripped the long silken sheath from a white, rounded limb. She slipped a bare foot into the pump and moved reluctantly behind the chair that held the groaning Horker. She took one of the clenched, straining hands, and drew it back, fumbling with shaking fingers as she twisted the strip of thin chiffon. The demon moved closer, standing over her.

"Loose knots!" he snarled abruptly. He knocked her violently away with a stinging slap across her cheek, and seized the strip in his own hands. He drew the binding tight, twisting it about the lowest rung of the chair's ladder back. Horker was forced to lean awkwardly to the rear; in this unbalanced position it was quite impossible to rise.

Nicholas Devine turned away from the straining, perspiring Doctor, and advanced toward Pat, who cowered against the shattered cabinet.

"Now!" he muttered. "The experiment!" He chuckled raspingly. "What delicacy of degradation! Your lover and your guardian angel—both helpless watchers! Excellent! Oh, very excellent!"

He grasped her wrist, drawing her after him to the center of the room, into the full view of the horrified, staring eyes of Horker.

The Dark Other

"Always before," continued her tormentor, "these hands have
prepared you for the rites—the ceremony that failed on two other
occasions to transpire. Would it add a poignancy to the torture if
I made you strip this body of yours with your own hands? Or will
they suffer more watching me? Which do you think?"

Pat closed her eyes in helpless resignation to her fate. "Nick!"
she moaned. "Oh, Nick dearest!"

"Not this time!" sneered the other. "Your friend and protector,
the Doctor, has thoughtfully eliminated your sweetheart as a factor.
He struggles too feebly for me to feel."

"Nick!" she murmured again. "Dr. Carl!"

But the Doctor, now pulling painfully at his bonds, could only
groan in distraction, and curse the unsuspected strength of sheer
chiffon. He writhed miserably at the chafing of his wrists; his strange
paralysis had departed, but he was quite helpless to assist Pat.

"I think," said the cold tones of Nicholas Devine, "that the more
delicate torture lies in your willingness. Let us see."

He drew her into his arms. He twisted a hand in her hair, jerked
her head violently backward, and pressed avid lips to hers. She
struggled a little, but hopelessly, automatically. At last she lay quite
passive, quite motionless, supported by his arms, and making not the
slightest response to his kiss.

"Are you mine?" he queried fiercely, releasing her lips. "Are you
mine now?"

She shook her head without opening her eyes. "No," she said
dully. "Not now, or ever."

Again he crushed her, while the Doctor looked on in helpless,
bewildered, voiceless anger. This time his kiss was painful, burning,
searing. Again that unholy fascination and unnatural delight in her
own pain stirred her, and it took what little effort she was able to
make to keep from responding. After a long interval, his lips again
withdrew.

"Are you mine?" he repeated. She made no answer; she was gasping, and tears glistened under her closed eyelids, from the pain of her
crushed lips. Again he kissed her, and again the wild abandonment to
evil suffused her. She was suddenly responding to his agonizing caress;
she was clinging fiercely to his torturing lips, feeling an unholy exaltation in the pain of his tearing fingers in the flesh of her back.

155

"Yours!" she murmured in response to his query. She heard her voice repeat madly, "Yours! Yours! Yours!"

"Do you yield willingly?" came the icy tones of the demon.

"Yes—yes—yes! Willingly!"

"Take off your clothes!" sounded the terrible, overpowering voice. He thrust her from him, so that she staggered dizzily backward. She stood swaying; the voice repeated its command, the girl's eyes widened wildly; she had the appearance of one in an ecstasy, a religious fervor. She raised her hand with a jerky impulsive gesture to the neck of her frock, still pinned together in the makeshift repairs of the evening.

There came a strange interruption. The Doctor, helpless on-looker, had at length evolved an idea out of the bewilderment in his mind. He opened his mouth and emitted a tremendous, deep, ear shattering bellow!

Nicholas Devine sent the girl spinning to the floor with a vicious shove, and turned his blazing eyes on Horker, who was drawing in his breath for a repetition of his roar. "Quiet!" he rasped, his red orbs boring down at the other. "Quiet, or I'll muffle you!" Closing his eyes, the Doctor repeated his mighty shout.

The demon snatched the blanket from the couch, tossing it over the figure of the Doctor, where it became a billowing, writhing heap of brown wool. He turned his gaze on Pat, who was just struggling to her feet, and moved as if to advance toward her.

He paused. She had retrieved the Doctor's revolver from the floor, and now faced him with the madness gone out of her eyes, supporting the weapon with both hands, the muzzle wavering toward his face.

"Drop it!" he commanded. She felt a recurrence of fascination, and an impulse to obey. Out of the corner of her eye, she saw the Doctor's head emerging from the blanket as he shook it off.

"Drop it!" repeated Nicholas Devine.

She closed her eyes, shutting out the vision of his dominant visage. With a surge of terror, she squeezed the trigger, staggering back to the couch at the roar and the recoil.

She opened her eyes. Nicholas Devine lay in the center of the room on his face; a crimson spot was matting the hair on the back of his head. She saw the Doctor raise a free hand; he was working clear of his bonds.

"Pat!" he said softly. He looked at her pale, sickened features. "Honey," he said, "sit down till I get free. Sit down, Pat; you look faint."

"Never faint!" murmured the girl, and pitched backward to the couch, with one clad and one bare leg hanging in curious limpness over the edge.

31. "Not Humanly Possible"

Pat opened weary eyes and gazed at a blank, uninformative ceiling. It was some moments before she realized that she was lying on the couch in the room of Nicholas Devine. Somebody had placed her there, presumably, since she was quite unaware of the circumstances of her awakening. Then recollection began to form—Dr. Carl, the other, the roar of a shot. After that, nothing save a turmoil ending in blankness.

A sound of movement beside her drew her attention. She turned her head and perceived Dr. Horker kneeling over a form on the floor, fingering a white bandage about the head of the figure. Her recollections took instant form; she remembered the catastrophes of the evening—last night, rather, since dawn glowed dully in the window. She had shot Nick! She gave a little moan and pushed herself to a sitting position.

The Doctor glanced at her with a sick, shaky smile. "Hello," he said. "Come to, have you? Sorry I couldn't give you any attention." He gave the bandage a final touch. "Here's a job I had no heart for," he muttered. "Better for everyone to let things happen without interference."

The girl, returning to full awareness, noticed now that the bandage consisted of strips of the Doctor's shirt. She glanced fearfully at the still features of Nicholas Devine; she saw pale cheeks and closed eyes, but indubitably not the grim mien of the demon.

"Dr. Carl!" she whispered. "He isn't—he isn't—"

"Not yet."

"But will he—?"

"I don't know. That's a bad spot, a wound in the base of the brain. You'd best know it now, Pat, but also realize that nothing can happen to you. I'll see to that!"

"To me!" she said dully. "What difference does that make? It's Nick I want saved."

"I'll do my best for you, Honey," said Horker with almost a hint of reluctance. "I've phoned Briggs General for an ambulance. Your faint lasted a full quarter hour," he added.

"What can we tell them?" asked the girl. "What can we say?"

"Don't you say anything, Pat. I'm not on the board for nothing." He rose from his knees, glancing out of the window into the cool dawn. "Queer neighborhood!" he said. "All that yelling and a shot, and still no sign of interest from the neighbors. That's Chicago, though," he mused. "Lucky for us, Pat; we can handle the thing quietly now."

But the girl was staring dully at the still figure on the floor. "Oh God!" she said huskily. "Help him, Dr. Carl!"

"I'll do my best," responded Horker gloomily. "I was a good surgeon before I specialized in psychiatry. Brain surgery, too; it led right into my present field."

Pat said nothing, but dropped her head on her hands and stared vacantly before her.

"Better for you, and for him too, if I fail," muttered the Doctor.

His words brought a reply. "You won't fail," she said tensely. "You won't!"

"Not voluntarily, I'm afraid," he growled morosely. "I've still a little respect for medical ethics, but if ever a case—" His voice trailed into silence as from somewhere in the dawn sounded the wail of a siren. "There's the ambulance," he finished.

Pat sat unmoving as the sounds from outdoors detailed the stopping of the vehicle before the house. She heard the Doctor descending the steps, and the creak of the door. Though it took place before her eyes, she scarcely saw the white-coated youths as they lifted the form of Nicholas Devine and bore it from the room on a stretcher, treading with carefully broken steps to prevent the swaying of the support. Dr. Horker's order to follow made no impression on her; she sat dully on the couch as the chamber emptied.

Why, she wondered, had the thought of Nick's death disturbed her so? Wasn't it but a short time since they had both contemplated it? What had occurred to alter that determination? Nick was dying, she thought mournfully; all that remained was for her to follow. There on the floor lay the revolver, and on the table, glistening in the wan light, reposed the untouched lethal draft. That was the preferable way, she mused, staring fixedly at its glowing contour.

But suppose Nick weren't to die—she'd have abandoned him to his terrible doom, left him to face a situation far more ominous than any unknown terrors beyond death. She shook her head distractedly, and looked up to meet the eyes of Dr. Horker, who was watching her gravely in the doorway.

"Come on, Pat," he said gently.

She rose, followed him down the stairs and out into the morning light. The driver of the ambulance stared curiously at her disheveled, bedraggled figure, but she was so weary and forlorn that even the effort of brushing away the black strands of hair that clouded her smoke-dark eyes was beyond her. She slumped into the seat of the Doctor's car and sighed in utter exhaustion.

"Rush it!" Horker called to the driver ahead. "I'll follow you."

The car swept into motion, and the swift cool morning air beating against her face from the open window restored some clarity to her mind. She fixed her eyes on the rear of the speeding vehicle they followed.

"Is there any hope at all?" she queried despondently.

"I don't know, Pat. I can't tell yet. When you closed your eyes, he half turned, dodged; the bullet entered his skull near the base, near the cerebellum. If it had pierced the cerebellum, his heart and breathing must have stopped instantly. They didn't, however, and that's a mildly hopeful sign. Very mildly hopeful, though."

"Do you know now what that devil—what the attack was?"

"No, Pat," Horker admitted. "I don't. Call it a devil if you like; I can't name it any better." His voice changed to a tone of wonder. "Pat, I can't understand that paralyzing fascination the thing exerted. I—any medical man—would say that mental dominance of that sort doesn't exist."

"Hypnotism," the girl suggested.

"Bah! Every psychiatrist uses hypnotism in his business; it's part of some treatments. There's nothing of fascination about it; no dominance of one will over another, despite the popular view. That's natural and understandable; this was like—well, like the exploded claims of Mesmerism. I tell you, it's not humanly possible—and yet I felt it!"

"Not humanly possible," murmured Pat. "That's the answer, then, Dr. Carl. Maybe now you'll believe in my devil."

"I'm tempted to."

"You'll have to! Can't you see it, Dr. Carl? Even his name, Nick—that's a colloquialism for the devil, isn't it?"

"And Devine, I suppose," said Horker, "refers to his angelic ancestry. Devils are only fallen angels, aren't they?"

"All right," said Pat wearily. "Make fun of it. You'll see!"

"I'm not making fun of your theory, Honey. I can't offer a better one myself. I never saw nor heard of anything similar, and I'm not in position to ridicule any theory."

"But you don't believe me."

"Of course I don't, Pat. You're weaving an intricate fairy tale about a pathological condition and a fortuitous suggestiveness in names. Whatever the condition is—and I confess I don't understand it—it's something rational, and those things can be treated."

"Treated by exorcism," said the girl. "That's the only way anyone ever succeeded in casting out a devil."

The Doctor made no answer. The wailing vehicle ahead of them swung rapidly out of sight into an alley, and Horker halted his car before the gray facade of Briggs General.

"Come in here," he said, helping Pat to alight. "You'll want to wait, won't you?"

"How long," she queried listlessly, "before—before you'll know?"

"Perhaps immediately. The only chance is to get that bullet out at once—if there's still time for it."

She followed him into the building, past a desk where a white-clad girl regarded her curiously, and up an elevator. He led her into a small office.

"Sit here," he said gently, and disappeared.

She sat dully in the chair he had indicated, and minutes passed. She made no attempt to think; the long, cataclysmic night had exhausted her powers. She simply sat and suffered; the deep scratches of fingernails burned in the flesh of her back, her cheek pained from the violent slap, and her head and jaw ached from that first blow, the one that had knocked her unconscious last evening. But these twinges were minor; they were merely physical, and the hurts of the demon had struck far deeper than any physical injury. The damage to her spirit was by all odds the more painful; it numbed her mind and dulled her thoughts, and she simply sat idle and stared at the blank wall.

She had no conception of the interval before Dr. Horker returned. He entered quietly, and began rinsing his hands at a basin in the corner.

"Is it over?" she asked listlessly.

"Not even begun," he responded. "However, it isn't too late. He'll be ready in a moment or so."

"I wish it were over," she murmured. "One way or the other."

"I too!" said the Doctor. "With all my heart, I wish it were over! If there were anyone within call who could handle it, I'd turn it to him gladly. But there isn't!"

He moved again toward the door, leaning out and glancing down the hall.

"You stay here," he admonished her. "Don't try to find us; I want no interruptions, no matter what enters that mind of yours!"

"You needn't worry," she said soberly. "I'm not fool enough for that." She leaned wearily back in the chair, closing her eyes. A long interval passed; she was vaguely surprised to see the Doctor still standing in the doorway when she opened her eyes. She had fancied him already in the midst of his labor.

"What will you do?" she asked.

"About what?"

"I mean what sort of operation will it need? Probing or what?"

"Oh," he said. "I'll have to trephine him. Must get that bullet."

"What's that—trephine?"

He glanced down the hall. "They're ready," he said, and turned to go. At the door he paused. "Trephining is to open a little door in the skull. If your devil is in his head, we'll have it out along with the bullet."

His footsteps receded down the hall.

32. Revelation

"Is it over now?" Queried Pat tremulously as the Doctor finally reappeared. The interminable waiting had left her even more worn, and her pallid features bore the marks of strain.

"Twenty minutes ago," said Horker. His face too bore evidence of tension; moreover, there was a puzzled, dubious expression in his eyes that frightened Pat. She was too apprehensive to risk a question as to the outcome, and simply stared at him with wide, fearful, questioning eyes.

"I called up your home," he said irrelevantly. "I told them you left with me early this morning. Your mother's still in bed, although it's after ten." He paused. "Slip in without anyone seeing you, will you, Honey? And rumple up your bed."

"If I haven't lost my key," she said, still with the question in her eyes.

"It's in the mailbox. Magda found it on the porch this morning. I talked to her."

She could bear the uncertainty no longer. "Tell me!" she demanded.

"It's all right, I think."

"You mean—he'll live?"

The Doctor nodded. "I think so." He turned his puzzled eyes on her.

"Oh!" breathed Pat. "Thank God!"

"You wanted him back, Honey, didn't you?" Horker's tone was gentle.

"Oh, yes!"

"Devil and all?"

"Yes—devil and all!" she echoed. Suddenly she sensed something strange in the other's manner. She perceived the uncertainty in his visage, and felt a rising trepidation. "What's the matter?" she queried anxiously. "You're not telling me everything! Tell me, Dr. Carl!"

163

"There's something else," he said. "I'm not sure, Pat, but I think—I hope—you've got him back without the devil!"

"He's cured?" Her voice was incredulous; she did not dare accept the Doctor's meaning.

"I hope so. At least I located the cause."

"What was it?" she demanded, an unexpected vigor livening her tired body. "What was that devil? Tell me! I want to know, Dr. Carl!"

"I think the best name for it is a tumor," he said slowly. "I told them in there it was a tumor. I wish I knew myself."

"A tumor! I don't understand!"

"I don't either, Pat—not fully. It's something on or beyond the border of medical knowledge. I don't think any living authority could classify it definitely."

"But tell me!" she cried fiercely. "Tell me!"

"Well, Honey—I'll try." He paused thoughtfully. "Cancers and tumors—sarcomas—are curious things, Dear. Doctors aren't at all sure just what they are. And one of their peculiarities is that they sometimes seem to be trying to develop into separate entities, trying to become human by feeding like parasites on their hosts. Do you understand?"

"No," said the girl. "I'm sorry, Dr. Carl, but I don't."

"I mean," he continued, "that sometimes these growths seem to be trying to develop into—into organisms. I've seen them, for instance—every surgeon has—with bones developing. I've seen one with a rather perfect jaw-bone, and little teeth, and hair. As if," he added, "it were making a sort of attempt to become human, in a primitive, disorganized fashion. Now do you see what I mean?"

"Yes," said the girl, with a violent shudder. "Dr. Carl, that's horrible!"

"Life sometimes is," he agreed. "Well," he continued slowly, "I opened up our patient's skull at the point where the fluoroscope indicated the bullet. I trephined it, and there, pierced by the shot, was this—" He hesitated, "—this tumor."

"Did you—remove it?"

"Of course. But it wasn't a natural sort of brain tumor, Honey. It was a little cerebrum, apparently joined to a Y-shaped branch of the

164

spinal cord. A little brain, Pat—no larger than your small fist, but deeply convoluted, and with the pre-Rolandic area highly developed."

"What's pre-Rolandic, Dr. Carl?" asked Pat, shivering.

"The seat of the motor nerves. The home, you might say, of the will. This brain was practically all will—and I wonder," he said musingly, "if that explains the ungodly, evil fascination the creature could command. A brain that was nothing but pure willpower, relieved by its parasitic nature of all the distractions of a directing body! I wonder—" He fell silent.

"Tell me the rest!" she said frantically.

"That's all, Honey. I removed it, and I guess I'm the only surgeon in the world who ever removed a brain from a human skull without killing the patient! Luckily, he had two of them!"

"Oh God!" murmured the girl faintly. She turned to Horker. "But he will live?"

"I think so. Your shot killed the devil, it seems." He frowned. "I said it was a tumor; I told them it was a tumor, but I'm not sure. Perhaps, just as some people are born with six fingers or toes on each member, he was born with two brains. It's possible; one developed normally, humanly, and the other—into that creature we faced last night. I don't know!"

"It's what I said," asserted Pat. "It's a devil, and what you've just told me about tumors proves it. They're devils, that's all, and someday some student is going to cut one loose and raise it to maturity outside a human body, and you'll see what a devil is really like! And go ahead and laugh!"

"I'm not laughing, Pat. I'd be the last one to laugh at your theory, after facing that thing last night. It had satanic powers, all right—that paralyzing fascination! You felt it too; it wasn't just a mental lapse on my part, was it?"

"I felt it, Dr. Carl! I'd felt it before that; I was always helpless in the presence of it."

"Could it," he asked, "have imposed its will actively on yours? I mean, could it have made you actually do what it asked there at the end, just before I recovered enough sense to let out that bellow?"

"To take off—my dress?" She shivered. "I don't know, Dr. Carl.—I'm afraid so." She looked at him appealingly. "Why did I yield to it so?" she cried. "What made me find such a fierce pleasure in its kisses—in its blows and scratches, and the pain it inflicted on me? Why was that, Dr. Carl?"

"Why," he countered, "do gangsters' girls and apache women enjoy the cruelties perpetrated on them by their men? There's a little masochism in most women, and that—creature was sadistic, perverted, abnormal, and somehow dominating. It took an unfair advantage of you, Pat; don't blame yourself."

"It was—utterly evil!" she muttered. "It was the ultimate in everything unholy."

"It was an aberrant brain," said Horker. "You can't judge it by human standards, since it wasn't actually human. It was, I suppose, just what you said—a devil. I didn't even keep it," he added grimly. "I destroyed it."

"Do you know what it meant by saying it was a question of synapses?" she asked.

"That was queer!" The Doctor's voice was puzzled. "That remark implies that the thing itself knew what it was. How? It must have possessed knowledge that the normal brain lacked."

"Was it a question of synapses?"

"In a sense it was. The nerves from the two rival brains must have met in a synaptic juncture. The oftener the aberrant brain gained control, the easier it became for it to repeat the process, as the synapse, so to speak, wore thin. That's why the attacks intensified so horribly toward the end; the habit was being formed."

"Last night was the very worst!"

"Of course. As the thing itself pointed out, I made the mistake of drugging the normal brain and giving the other complete control of the body. At other times, there'd always been the rivalry to weaken whichever was dominant."

"Does that mean," asked Pat anxiously, "that Nick's character will be changed now?"

"I think so. I think you'll find him less meek, less gentle, than heretofore. More spirited, perhaps, since his energies won't be drained so constantly by the struggle."

"I don't care!" she said. "I'd like that, and anyway, it doesn't make a bit of difference to me as long as he's just—*my* Nick."

The Doctor gave her a tender smile. "Let's go home," he said, pinching her cheek in his great hand.

166

"Can you leave him?"

"I'll run back after a while, Honey. I think he'll do." He took her hand, drawing her after him. "Don't forget to slip in unseen, Pat, and rumple up your bed."

"Rumple it!" She gave him a weary smile. "I'll be in it!"

"Good idea. You look a bit worn out, Honey, and we can't have you getting sick now, or even pull a temporary faint like that one last night."

"I didn't faint!"

"Maybe not," grinned Horker. "Perhaps the proceedings grew a little boring, and you just lay down on the couch for a nap. It *was* a dull evening."

Stories

Proteus Island

The brown Maori in the bow of the outrigger stared hard at Austin Island slowly swimming nearer; then he twisted to fix his anxious brown eyes on Carver. "Taboo!" he exclaimed. "Taboo! *Aussitan* taboo!"

Carver regarded him without change of expression. He lifted his gaze to the island. With an air of sullen brooding the Maori returned to his stroke. The second Polynesian threw the zoologist a pleading look.

"Taboo," he said. "*Aussitan* taboo!"

The white man studied him briefly, but said nothing. The soft brown eyes fell and the two bent to their work. But as Carver stared eagerly shoreward there was a mute, significant exchange between the natives.

The proa slid over green combers toward the foam-skirted island, then began to sheer off as if reluctant to approach. Carver's jaw squared. "*Malloa*! Put in, you chocolate pig. Put in, do you hear?"

He looked again at the land. Austin Island was not traditionally sacred, but these natives had a fear of it for some reason. It was not the concern of a zoologist to discover why. The island was uninhabited and had been charted only recently. He noted the fern forests ahead, like those of New Zealand, the Kauri pine and dammar—dark wood hills, a curve of white beach, and between them a moving dot—an *apteryx mantelli*, thought Carver—a kiwi.

The proa worked cautiously shoreward.

"Taboo," Malloa kept whispering. "Him plenty *bunyip*!"

"Hope there is," the white man grunted. "I'd hate to go back to Jameson and the others at Macquarie without at least one little *bunyip*, or anyway a ghost of a fairy." He grinned. "*Bunyip Carveris*. Not bad, eh? Look good in natural-history books with pictures."

On the approaching beach the kiwi scuttled for the forest—if it was a kiwi after all. It looked queer, somehow, and Carver squinted after it. Of course, it had to be an apteryx; these islands of the New

Zealand group were too deficient in fauna for it to be anything else. One variety of dog, one sort of rat, and two species of bat—that covered the mammalian life of New Zealand.

Of course, there were the imported cats, pigs and rabbits that ran wild on the North and Middle Islands, but not here. Not on the Aucklands, not on Macquarie, least of all here on Austin, out in the lonely sea between Macquarie and the desolate Balleny Islands, far down on the edge of Antarctica. No; the scuttling dot must have been a kiwi.

The craft grounded. Kolu, in the bow, leaped like a brown flash to the beach and drew the proa above the gentle inwash of the waves. Carver stood up and stepped out, then paused sharply at a moan from Malloa in the stern.

"See!" he gulped. "The trees, *wahi*! The *bunyip* trees!"

Carver followed his pointing figure. The trees—what about them? There they were beyond the beach as they had fringed the sands of Macquarie and of the Aucklands. Then he frowned. He was no botanist; that was Halburton's field, back with Jameson and the *Fortune* at Macquarie Island. He was a zoologist, aware only generally of the variations of flora. Yet he frowned.

The trees were vaguely queer. In the distance they had resembled the giant ferns and towering kauri pine that one would expect. Yet here, close at hand, they had a different aspect—not a markedly different one, it is true, but none the less, a strangeness. The kauri pines were not exactly kauri, nor were the tree ferns quite the same Cryptogamia that flourished on the Aucklands and Macquarie. Of course, those islands were many miles away to the north, and certain local variations might be expected. All the same—

"Mutants," he muttered, frowning. "Tends to substantiate Darwin's isolation theories. I'll have to take a couple of specimens back to Halburton."

"*Wahi*," said Kolu nervously, "we go back now?"

"Now!" exploded Carver. "We just got here! Do you think we came all the way from Macquarie for one look? We stay here a day or two, so I have a chance to take a look at this place's animal life. What's the matter, anyway?"

"The trees, *wahi*!" wailed Malloa. "*Bunyip*!—the walking trees, the talking trees!"

172

"Bah! Walking and talking, eh?" He seized a stone from the pebbled beach and sent it spinning into the nearest mass of dusky green. "Let's hear 'em say a few cuss words, then."

The stone tore through leaves and creepers, and the gentle crash died into motionless silence. Or not entirely motionless; for a moment something dark and tiny fluttered there, and then soared briefly into black silhouette against the sky. It was small as a sparrow, but bat like, with membranous wings. Yet Carver stared at it amazed, for it trailed a twelve-inch tail, thin as a pencil, but certainly an appendage no normal bat ought to possess.

For a moment or two the creature fluttered awkwardly in the sunlight, its strange tail lashing, and then it swooped again into the dusk of the forest whence his missile had frightened it. There was only an echo of its wild, shrill cry remaining, something that sounded like "*Wheer! Whe-e-e-r!*"

"What the devil!" said Carver. "There are two species of Chiroptera in New Zealand and neighboring islands, and that was neither of them! No bat has a tail like that!"

Kolu and Malloa were wailing in chorus. The creature had been too small to induce outright panic, but it had flashed against the sky with a sinister appearance of abnormality. It was a monstrosity, an aberration, and the minds of Polynesians were not such as to face unknown strangeness without fear. Nor for that matter, reflected Carver, were the minds of whites; he shrugged away a queer feeling of apprehension. It would be sheer stupidity to permit the fears of Kolu and Malloa to influence a perfectly sane zoologist.

"Shut up!" he snapped. "We'll have to trap that fellow, or one of his cousins. I'll want a specimen of his tribe. Rhimolophidæ, I'll bet a trade dollar, but a brand-new species. We'll net one tonight."

The voices of the two brown islanders rose in terror. Carver cut in sharply on the protests and expostulations and fragmentary descriptions of the honors of *bunyips*, walking and talking trees, and the bat-winged spirits of evil.

"Come on," he said gruffly. "Turn out the stuff in the proa. I'll look along the beach for a stream of fresh water. Mawson reported water on the north side of the island."

Malloa and Kolu were muttering as he turned away. Before him the beach stretched white in the late afternoon sun; at his left rolled

173

the blue Pacific and at his right slumbered the strange, dark, dusky quarter; he noted curiously the all but infinite variety of the vegetable forms, marveling that there was scarcely a tree or shrub that he could identify with any variety common on Macquarie or the Aucklands, or far-away New Zealand. But, of course, he mused, he was no botanist.

Anyway, remote islands often produced their own particular varieties of flora and fauna. That was part of Darwin's original evolution theory, this idea of isolation. Look at Mauritius and its dodo, and the Galapagos turtles, or for that matter, the kiwi of New Zealand, or the gigantic, extinct moa. And yet—he frowned over the thought—one never found an island that was entirely covered by its own unique forms of plant life. Windblown seeds or ocean borne debris always caused an interchange of vegetation among islands; birds carried seeds clinging to their feathers, and even the occasional human visitors aided in the exchange.

Besides, a careful observer like Mawson in 1911 would certainly have reported the peculiarities of Austin Island. He hadn't; nor, for that matter, had the whalers, who touched here at intervals as they headed into the Antarctic, brought back any reports. Of course, whalers had become very rare of late years; it might have been a decade or more since one had made anchorage at Austin. Yet what change could have occurred in ten or fifteen years?

Carver came suddenly upon a narrow tidal arm into which dropped a tinkling trickle of water from a granite ledge at the verge of the jungle. He stooped, moistened his finger, and tasted it. It was brackish but drinkable, and therefore quite satisfactory. He could hardly expect to find a larger stream on Austin, since the watershed was too small on an island only seven miles by three. With his eyes he followed the course of the brook upward into the tangle of fern forest, and a flash of movement arrested his eyes. For a moment he gazed in complete incredulity, knowing that he couldn't possibly be seeing—what he was seeing!

The creature had apparently been drinking at the brink of the stream, for Carver glimpsed it first in kneeling position. That was part of the surprise—the fact that it was kneeling—for no animal save man ever assumes that attitude, and this being, whatever it might be, was not human.

Wild, yellow eyes glared back at him, and the thing rose to an erect posture. It was a biped, a small travesty of man, standing no more than twenty inches in height. Little clawed fingers clutched at hanging creepers. Carver had a shocked glimpse of a body covered in patches with ragged gray fur, of an agile tail, of needle-sharp teeth in a little red mouth. But mostly he saw only malevolent yellow eyes and a face that was not human, yet had a hideous suggestion of humanity gone wild, a stunning miniature synthesis of manlike and feline characteristics.

Carver had spent much time in the wastelands of the planet. His reaction was almost in the nature of a reflex, without thought or volition; his blue-barreled gun leaped and flashed as if it moved of itself. This automatism was a valuable quality in the wilder portions of the earth; more than once he had saved his life by shooting first when startled, and reflecting afterward. But the quickness of the reaction did not lend itself to accuracy.

His bullet tore a leaf at the very cheek of the creature. The thing snarled, and then, with a final flash of yellow flame from its wild eyes, leaped headlong into the tangle of foliage and vanished.

Carver whistled. "What in Heaven's name," he muttered aloud, "was that?" But he had small time for reflection; long shadows and an orange tint to the afternoon light warned that darkness—sudden, twilightless darkness—was near. He turned back along the curving beach toward the outrigger.

A low coral spit hid the craft and the two Maoris, and the ridge jutted like a bar squarely across the face of the descending sun. Carver squinted against the light and trudged thoughtfully onward—to freeze into sudden immobility at the sound of a terrified scream from the direction of the proa!

He broke into a run. It was no more than a hundred yards to the coral ridge, but so swiftly did the sun drop in these latitudes that dusk seemed to race him to the crest. Shadows skittered along the beach as he leaped to the top and stared frantically toward the spot where his craft had been beached.

Something was there. A box—part of the provisions from the proa. But the proa itself—was gone!

Then he saw it, already a half dozen cables' lengths out in the bay. Malloa was crouching in the stern, Kolu was partly hidden by the sail, as the craft moved swiftly and steadily out toward the darkness gathering in the north.

His first impulse was to shout, and shout he did. Then he realized that they were beyond earshot, and very deliberately, he fired his revolver three times. Twice he shot into the air, but since Malloa cast not even a glance backward, the third bullet he sent carefully in the direction of the fleeing pair. Whether or not it took effect he could not tell, but the proa only slid more swiftly into the black distance.

He stared in hot rage after the deserters until even the white sail had vanished; then he ceased to swear, sat glumly on the single box they had unloaded, and fell to wondering what had frightened them. But that was something he never discovered.

Full darkness settled. In the sky appeared the strange constellations of the heaven's under hemisphere; southeast glowed the glorious Southern Cross, and south the mystic Clouds of Magellan. But Carver had no eyes for these beauties; he was already long familiar with the aspect of the Southern skies.

He mused over his situation. It was irritating rather than desperate, for he was armed, and even had he not been, there was no dangerous animal life on these tiny islands south of the Aucklands, nor, excepting man, on New Zealand itself. But not even man lived in the Aucklands, or on Macquarie, or here on remote Austin.

Malloa and Kolu had been terrifically frightened, beyond doubt; but it took very little to rouse the superstitious fears of a Polynesian. A strange species of bat was enough, or even a kiwi passing in the shadows of the brush, or merely their own fancies, stimulated by whatever wild tales had ringed lonely Austin Island with taboos.

And as for rescue, that too was certain. Malloa and Kolu might recover their courage and return for him. If they didn't, they still might make for Macquarie Island and the Fortune expedition. Even if they did what he supposed they naturally would do—head for the Aucklands, and then to their home on the Chathams—still Jameson would begin to worry in three or four days, and there'd be a search made.

There was no danger, he told himself—nothing to worry about. Best thing to do was simply to go about his work. Luckily, the box on which he sat was the one that contained his cyanide jar for insect specimens, nets, traps, and snares. He could proceed just as planned, except that he'd have to devote some of his time to hunting and preparing food.

Carver lighted his pipe, set about building a fire of the plentiful driftwood, and prepared for the night. He delivered himself of a few choice epithets descriptive of the two Maoris as he realized that his comfortable sleeping bag was gone with the proa, but the fire would serve against the chill of the high Southern latitude. He puffed his pipe reflectively to its end, lay down near his driftwood blaze, and prepared to sleep.

When, seven hours and fifty minutes later, the edge of the sun dented the eastern horizon, he was ready to admit that the night was something other than a success. He was hardened to the tiny, persistent fleas that skipped out of the sand, and his skin had long been toughened to the bloodthirsty night insects of the islands. Yet he had made a decided failure at the attempt to sleep.

Why? It surely couldn't be nervousness over the fact of strange surroundings and loneliness. Alan Carver had spent too many nights in wild and solitary places for that. Yet the night sounds had kept him in a perpetual state of half-wakeful apprehension, and at least a dozen times he had started to full consciousness in a sweat of nervousness. Why?

He knew why. It was the night sounds themselves. Not their loudness nor their menace, but their—well, their variety. He knew what darkness ought to bring forth in the way of noises; he knew every bird call and bat squeak indigenous to these islands. But the noises of night here on Austin Island had refused to conform to his pattern of knowledge. They were strange, unclassified, and far more varied than they should have been; and yet, even through the wildest cry, he fancied a disturbing note of familiarity.

Carver shrugged. In the clear daylight his memories of the night seemed like foolish and perverse notions, quite inexcusable in the mind of one as accustomed to lonely places as himself. He heaved his powerful form erect, stretched, and gazed toward the matted tangle of plant life under the tree ferns.

He was hungry, and somewhere in there was breakfast, either fruit or bird. Those represented the entire range of choice, since he was not at present hungry enough to consider any of the other possible variations—rat, bat, or dog. That covered the fauna of these islands.

Did it, indeed? He frowned as sudden remembrance struck him. What of the wild, yellow-eyed imp that had snarled at him from the brook side? He had forgotten that in the excitement of the desertion of Kolu and Malloa. That was certainly neither bat, rat, nor dog. What was it?

Still frowning, he felt his gun, glancing to assure himself of its readiness. The two Maoris might have been frightened away by an imaginary menace, but the thing by the brook was something he could not ascribe to superstition. He had seen that. He frowned more deeply as he recalled the tailed bat of earlier in the preceding evening. That was no native fancy either.

He strode toward the fern forest. Suppose Austin Island did harbor a few mutants, freaks, and individual species. What of it? So much the better; it justified the *Fortune* expedition. It might contribute to the fame of one Alan Carver, zoologist, if he were the first to report this strange, insular animal world. And yet—it was queer that Mawson had said nothing of it, nor had the whalers.

At the edge of the forest he stopped short. Suddenly he perceived what was responsible for its aspect of queerness. He saw what Malloa had meant when he gestured toward the trees. He gazed incredulously, peering from tree to tree. It was true. There were no related species. There were no two trees alike. Not two alike. Each was individual in leaf, bark, stem. There were no two the same. No two trees were alike!

But that was impossible. Botanist or not, he knew the impossibility of it. It was all the more impossible on a remote islet where inbreeding must of necessity take place. The living forms might differ from those of other islands, but not from each other—at least, not in such incredible profusion. The number of species must be limited by the very intensity of competition on an island. Must be!

Carver stepped back a half dozen paces, surveying the forest wall. It was true. There were ferns innumerable; there were pines; there were deciduous trees—but there were, in the hundred yard stretch he could scan accurately, no two alike! No two, even, with enough similarity to be assigned to the same species, perhaps not even to the same genus.

He stood frozen in uncomprehending bewilderment. What was the meaning of it? What was the origin of this unnatural plenitude of species and genera? How could any one of the numberless forms reproduce unless there were somewhere others of its kind to fertilize it? It was true, of course, that blossoms on the same tree could cross-fertilize each other, but where, then, were the offspring? It is a fundamental aspect of nature that from acorns spring oaks, and from kauri cones spring kauri pines.

In utter perplexity, he turned along the beach, edging away from the wash of the waves into which he had almost backed. The solid wall of forest was immobile save where the sea breeze ruffled its leaves, but all that Carver saw was the unbelievable variety of those leaves. Nowhere—nowhere—was there a single tree that resembled any he had seen before.

There were compound leaves, and digitate, palmate, cordate, acuminate, bipinnate, and ensiform ones. There were specimens of every variety he could name, and even a zoologist can name a number if he has worked with a botanist like Halburton. But there were no specimens that looked as if they might be related, however distantly, to any one of the others. It was as if, on Austin Island, the walls between the genera had dissolved, and only the grand divisions remained.

Carver had covered nearly a mile along the beach before the pangs of hunger recalled his original mission to his mind. He had to have food of some sort, animal or vegetable. With a feeling of distinct relief, he eyed the beach birds quarreling raucously up and down the sand; at least, they were perfectly normal representatives of the genus Larus. But they made, at best, but tough and oily fare, and his glance returned again to the mysterious woodlands.

He saw now a trail or path, or perhaps just a chance thinning of the vegetation along a subsoil ridge of rock, that led into the green shades, slanting toward the forested hill at the western end of the island. That offered the first convenient means of penetration he had encountered, and in a moment he was slipping through the dusky aisle, watching sharply for either fruit or bird.

He saw fruit in plenty. Many of the trees bore globes and ovoids of various sizes, but the difficulty, so far as Carver was concerned, was that he saw none he could recognize as edible. He dared not chance biting into some poisonous variety, and Heaven alone knew what wild and deadly alkaloids this queer island might produce.

Birds fluttered and called in the branches, but for the moment he saw none large enough to warrant a bullet. And besides, another queer fact had caught his attention; he noticed that the farther he proceeded from the sea, the more bizarre became the infinite forms of the trees of the forest. Along the beach he had been able at least to assign an individual growth to its family, if not its genus, but here even those distinctions began to vanish.

He knew why. "The costal growths are crossed with strays from other islands," he muttered. "But in here they've run wild. The whole island's run wild."

The movement of a dark mass against the leaf-sprinkled sky caught his attention. A bird? If it were, it was a much larger one than the inconsiderable passerine songsters that fluttered about him. He raised his revolver carefully, and fired.

The weird forest echoed to the report. A body large as a duck crashed with a long, strange cry, thrashed briefly among the grasses of the forest floor, and was still. Carver hurried forward to stare in perplexity at his victim.

It was not a bird. It was a climbing creature of some sort, armed with viciously sharp claws and wicked, needle-pointed white teeth in a triangular little red mouth. It resembled quite closely a small dog—if one could imagine a tree-climbing dog—and for a moment Carver froze in surprise at the thought that he had inadvertently shot somebody's mongrel terrier, or at least some specimen of Canis.

But the creature was no dog. Even disregarding its plunge from the treetops, Carver could see that. The retractile claws, five on the forefeet, four on the hind, were evidence enough, but stronger still was the evidence of those needle teeth. This was one of the Felidae. He could see further proof in the yellow, slitted eyes that glared at him in moribund hate, to lose their fire now in death. This was no dog, but a cat!

His mind flashed to that other apparition on the bank of the stream. That had borne a wild aspect of feline nature, too. What was the meaning of it? Cats that looked like monkeys; cats that looked like dogs!

He had lost his hunger. After a moment he picked up the furry body and set off toward the beach. The zoologist had superseded the man; this dangling bit of disintegrating protoplasm was no longer food, but a rare specimen. He had to get to the beach to do what he could to preserve it. It would be named after him—*Felis Carveri*—doubtless.

A sound behind him brought him to an abrupt halt. He peered cautiously back through the branch-roofed tunnel. He was being trailed. Something, bestial or human, lurked back there in the forest shadows. He saw it—or them—dimly, as formless as darker shades in the shifting array that marked the wind-stirred leaves.

For the first time, the successive mysteries began to induce a sense of menace. He increased his pace. The shadows slid and skittered behind him, and, lest he ascribe the thing to fancy, a low cry of some sort, a subdued howl, rose in the dusk of the forest at his left, and was answered at his right.

He dared not run, knowing that the appearance of fear too often brought a charge from both beasts and primitive humans. He moved as quickly as he could without the effect of flight from danger, and at last saw the beach. There in the opening he would at least distinguish his pursuers, if they chose to attack.

But they didn't. He backed away from the wall of vegetation, but no forms followed him. Yet they were there. All the way back to the box and the remains of his fire, he knew that just within the cover of the leaves lurked wild forms.

The situation began to prey on his mind. He couldn't simply remain on the beach indefinitely, waiting for an attack. Sooner or later he'd have to sleep, and then—Better to provoke the attack at once, see what sort of creatures he faced, and try to drive them off or exterminate them. He had, after all, plenty of ammunition.

He raised his gun, aimed at the skittering shadow, and fired. There was a howl that was indubitably bestial; before it had quivered into silence, others answered. Then Carver started violently backward, as the bushes quivered to the passage of bodies, and he saw what sort of beings had lurked there.

A line of perhaps a dozen forms leaped from the fringe of underbrush to the sand. For the space of a breath they were motionless, and Carver knew that he was in the grip of a zoologist's nightmare, for no other explanation was at all adequate.

The pack was vaguely doglike; but by no means did its members resemble the indigenous hunting dogs of New Zealand, nor the dingoes of Australia. Nor, for that matter, did they resemble any other dogs in his experience, nor, if the truth be told, any dogs at all, except perhaps in their lupine method of attack, their subdued yelps, their slavering mouths, and the arrangement of their teeth—what Carver could see of that arrangement.

But the fact that bore home to him now was another stunning repetition of all his observations of Austin Island—they did not resemble each other! Indeed, it occurred to Carver with the devastating force of a blow that, so far on this mad island, he had seen no two living creatures, animal or vegetable, that appeared to belong to related species!

The nondescript pack inched forward. He saw the wildest extremes among the creatures—beings with long hind legs and short forelimbs; a creature with hairless, thorn-scarred skin and a face like the half-human visage of a werewolf; a tiny, rat-sized thing that yelped with a shrill, yapping voice; and a mighty, barrel-chested creature whose body seemed almost designed for erect posture, and who loped on its hinder limbs with its forepaws touching the ground at intervals like the knuckles of an orang utan. That particular being was a horrible, yellow-fanged monstrosity, and Carver chose it for his first bullet.

The thing dropped without a sound; the slug had split its skull. As the report echoed back and forth between the hills on the east and west extremities of Austin, the pack answered with a threatening chorus of bays, howls, growls, and shrieks. They shrank back momentarily from their companion's body, then came menacingly forward.

Again Carver fired. A red-eyed hopping creature yelped and crumpled. The line halted nervously, divided now by two dead forms. Their cries were no more than a muffled growling as they eyed him with red and yellowish orbs.

He started suddenly as a different sound rose, a cry whose nature he could not determine, though it seemed to come from a point where the forested bank rose sharply in a little cliff. It was as if some watcher urged on the nondescript pack, for they gathered courage again to advance. And it was at this moment that a viciously flung stone caught the man painfully on the shoulder.

He staggered, then scanned the line of brush. A missile meant humankind. The mad island harbored something more than aberrant beasts.

A second cry sounded, and another stone hummed past his ear. But this time he had caught the flash of movement at the top of the cliff, and he fired instantly.

There was a scream. A human figure reeled from the cover of foliage, swayed, and pitched headlong into the brush at the base, ten feet below. The pack of creatures broke howling, as if their courage had vanished before this evidence of power. They fled like shadows into the forest.

But something about the figure that had fallen from the cliff struck Carver as strange. He frowned, waiting a moment to assure himself that the nondescript pack had fled, and that no other menace lurked in the brush, then he darted toward the place where his assailant had fallen.

The figure was human, beyond doubt—or was it? Here on this mad island where species seemed to take any form, Carver hesitated to make even that assumption. He bent over his fallen foe, who lay face down, then turned the body over. He stared.

It was a girl. Her face, still as the features of the Buddha of Nikko, was young and lovely as a Venetian bronze figurine, with delicate features that even in unconsciousness had a *wildness* apparent in them. Her eyes, closed though they were, betrayed a slight, dryad like slant.

The girl was white, though her skin was sun-darkened almost to a golden hue. Carver was certain of her color, nevertheless, for at the edges of her single garment—an untanned hide of leopard-like fur, already stiffening and cracking—her skin showed whiter.

Had he killed her? Curiously perturbed, he sought for the wound, and found it, at last, in a scarcely bleeding graze above her right knee. His shot had merely spun her off balance; it was the ten-foot fall from the cliff that had done the damage, of which the visible evidence was a reddening bruise of her left temple. But she was living. He swung her hastily into his arms and bore her across the beach, away from the brush in which her motley pack was doubtless still lurking.

He shook his nearly empty canteen, then tilted her head to pour water between her lips. Instantly her eyes flickered open, and for a moment she stared quite uncomprehendingly into Carver's eyes, not twelve inches from her own. Then her eyes widened, not so much in terror as in startled bewilderment; she twisted violently from his arms, tried twice to rise, and twice fell back as her legs refused to support her. At last she lay quite passive, keeping her fascinated gaze on his face.

But Carver received a shock as well. As her lids lifted, he started at the sight of the eyes behind them. They were unexpected, despite the hint given by their ever-so-faint Oriental cast, for they flamed upon him in a tawny hue. They were amber, almost golden, and wild as the eyes of a votary of Pan. She watched the zoologist with the intentness of a captive bird, but not with a bird's timidity, for he saw her hand fumbling for the pointed stick or wooden knife in the thong about her waist.

He proffered the canteen, and she shrank away from his extended hand. He shook the container, and at the sound of gurgling liquid, she took it gingerly, tilted a trickle into her hand, and then, to Carver's surprise, smelled it, her dainty nostrils flaring as widely as her diminutive, up tilted nose permitted. After a moment she drank from her cupped palm, poured another trickle, and drank that. It did not occur to her, apparently, to drink from the canteen.

Her mind cleared. She saw the two motionless bodies of the slain creatures, and murmured a low sound of sorrow. When she moved as if to rise, her gashed knee pained her, and she turned her strange eyes on Carver with a renewed expression of fear. She indicated the red streak of the injury.

"*C'm on?*" she said with a questioning inflection.

Carver realized that the sound resembled English words through accident only. "Where to?" He grinned.

She shook a puzzled head. "*Bu-r-r-o-o-om!*" she said. "*Zee-e-e-e!*"

He understood that. It was her attempt to imitate the sound of his shot and the hum of the bullet. He tapped the revolver. "Magic!" he said warningly. "Bad medicine. Better be good girl, see?" It was obvious that she didn't understand. "*Thumbi?*" he tried. "You Maori?"

No result save a long look from slanting, golden eyes.

"Well," he grunted, "*Sprechen zie Deutsch*, then? Or Kanaka? Or—what the devil! That's all I know—*Latinum intelligisne?*"

"*Cm on?*" she said faintly, her eyes on the gun. She rubbed the scratch on her leg and the bruise on her temple, apparently ascribing both to the weapon.

"All right," Carver acceded grimly. He reflected that it could do no harm to impress the girl with his powers. "I'll come on. Watch this!"

He leveled his weapon at the first target he saw—a dead branch that jutted from a drifted log at the end of the coral spit. It was thick as his arm, but it must have been thoroughly rotted, for instead of stripping a bit of bark as he expected, the heavy slug shattered the entire branch.

"O-o-oh!" gasped the girl, clapping her hands over her ears. Her eyes flickered sidewise at him; then she scrambled wildly to her feet. She was in sheer panic.

"No, you don't!" he snapped. He caught her arm. "You stay right here!"

For a moment he was amazed at the lithe strength of her. Her free arm flashed upward with the wooden dagger, and he caught that wrist as well. Her muscles were like tempered steel wires. She twisted frantically; then, with sudden yielding, stood quietly in his grasp, as if she thought, "What use to struggle with a god?"

He released her. "Sit down!" he growled.

She obeyed his gesture rather than his voice. She sat on the sand before him, gazing up with a trace of fear but more of wariness in her honey-hued eyes.

"Where are your people?" he asked sharply, pointing at her and then waving in an inclusive gesture at the forest.

She stared without comprehension, and he varied his symbolism. "Your home, then?" he pantomimed the act of sleeping.

The result was the same, simply a troubled look from her glorious eyes.

"Now what the devil!" he muttered. "You have a name, haven't you? A name? Look!" He tapped his chest. "Alan. Get it? Alan. Alan."

That she understood instantly. "Alan," she repeated dutifully, looking up at him.

But when he attempted to make her assign a name to herself, he failed utterly. The only effect of his efforts was a deepening of the perplexity in her features. He reverted, at last, to the effort to make her indicate in some fashion the place of her home and people, varying his gestures in every way he could devise. And at last she seemed to comprehend.

She rose doubtfully to her feet and uttered a strange, low, mournful cry. It was answered instantly from the brush, and Carver stiffened as he saw the emergence of that same motley pack of non-descript beings. They must have been watching, lurking just beyond view. Again they circled the two slain members as they advanced.

Carver whipped out his revolver. His movement was followed by a wail of anguish from the girl, who flung herself before him, arms outspread as if to shield the wild pack from the menace of the weapon. She faced him fearfully, yet defiantly, and there was puzzled questioning in her face as well. It was as if she accused the man of ordering her to summon her companions only to threaten them with death.

He stared. "O.K.," he said at last. "What's a couple of rare specimens on an island that's covered with 'em? Send 'em away."

She obeyed his gesture of command. The weird pack slunk silently from view, and the girl backed hesitantly away as if to follow them, but halted abruptly at Carver's word. Her attitude was a curious one, partly fear, but more largely composed, it seemed, of a sort of fascination, as if she did not quite understand the zoologist's nature.

This was a feeling he shared to a certain extent, for there was certainly something mysterious in encountering a white girl on this mad Austin Island. It was as if there were one specimen, and only one, of every species in the world here on this tiny islet, and she were the representative of humanity. But still he frowned perplexedly into her wild, amber eyes.

It occurred to him again that on the part of Austin he had traversed he had seen no two creatures alike. Was this girl, too, a mutant, a variant of some species other than human, who had through mere chance adopted a perfect human form? As, for instance, the doglike cat whose body still lay on the sand where he had flung it. Was she, perhaps, the sole representative of the human form on the island, Eve before Adam, in the garden? There had been a woman before Adam, he mused.

186

"We'll call you Lilith," he said thoughtfully. The name fitted her wild, perfect features and her flame-hued eyes. Lilith, the mysterious being whom Adam found before him in Paradise, before Eve was created. "Lilith," he repeated. "Alan—Lilith. See?" She echoed the sounds and the gesture. Without question she accepted the name he had given her, and that she understood the sound as a name was evident by her response to it. For when he uttered it a few minutes later, her amber eyes flashed instantly to his face and remained in a silent question.

Carver laughed and resumed his puzzled thoughts. Reflectively, he produced his pipe and packed it, then struck a match and lighted it. He was startled by a low cry from the girl Lilith, and looked up to see her extended hand. For a moment he failed to perceive what it was she sought, and then her fingers closed around the hissing stem of the match! She had tried to seize the flame as one takes a fluttering bit of cloth.

She screamed in pain and fright. At once the pack of nondescripts appeared at the edge of the forest, voicing their howls of anger, and Carver whirled again to meet them. But again Lilith, recovering from the surprise of the burn, halted the pack with her voice, and sent them slinking away into the shadows. She sucked her scorched fingers and turned widened eyes to his face. He realized with a start of disbelief that the girl did not comprehend fire!

There was a bottle of alcohol in the box of equipment; he produced it and, taking Lilith's hand, bound a moistened strip of handkerchief about her two blistered fingers, though he knew well enough that alcohol was a poor remedy for burns. He applied the disinfectant to the bullet graze on her knee; she moaned softly at the sting, then smiled as it lessened, while her strange amber eyes followed fixedly the puffs of smoke from his pipe, and her nostrils quivered to the pungent tobacco odor.

"Now what," queried Carver, smoking reflectively, "am I going to do with you?"

Lilith had apparently no suggestion. She simply continued her wide-eyed regard.

"At least," he resumed, "you ought to know what's good to eat on this crazy island. You do eat, don't you?" He pantomimed the act.

The girl understood instantly. She rose, stepped to the spot where the body of the doglike cat lay, and seemed for an instant to sniff its scent. Then she removed the wooden knife from her girdle, placed one bare foot upon the body, and hacked and tore a strip of flesh from it. She extended the bloody chunk to him, and was obviously surprised at his gesture of refusal.

After a moment she withdrew it, glanced again at his face, and set her own small white teeth in the meat. Carver noted with interest how daintily she managed even that difficult maneuver, so that her soft lips were not stained by the slightest drop of blood.

But his own hunger was unappeased. He frowned over the problem of conveying his meaning, but at last hit upon a means. "Lilith!" he said sharply. Her eyes flashed at once to him. He indicated the meat she held, then waved at the mysterious line of trees. "Fruit," he said. "Tree meat. See?" He went through the motions of eating.

Again the girl understood instantly. It was odd, he mused, how readily she comprehended some things, while others equally simple seemed utterly beyond her. Queer, as everything on Austin Island was queer. Was Lilith, after all, entirely human? He followed her to the tree line, stealing a sidelong look at her wild, flame-colored eyes, and her features, beautiful, but untamed, dryad like, elfin—wild.

She scrambled up the crumbling embankment and seemed to vanish magically into the shadows. For a moment Carver felt a surge of alarm as he clambered desperately after her; she could elude him here as easily as if she were indeed a shadow herself. True, he had no moral right to restrain her, save the hardly tenable one given by her attack; but he did not want to lose her—not yet. Or perhaps not at all.

"Lilith!" he shouted as he topped the cliff.

She appeared almost at his elbow. Above them twined a curious vine like a creeping conifer of some kind, bearing white-greenish fruits the size and shape of a pullet's egg. Lilith seized one, halved it with agile fingers, and raised a portion to her nostrils. She sniffed carefully, daintily, then flung the fruit away.

"*Pah bo!*" she said, wrinkling her nose distastefully.

She found another sort of queerly unprepossessing fruit composed of five finger-like protuberances from a fibrous disk, so that the whole bore the appearance of a large, malformed hand. This she sniffed as carefully as she had the other, then smiled sidewise up at him.

"*Bo!*" she said, extending it.

Carver hesitated. After all, it was not much more than an hour ago that the girl had been trying to kill him. Was it not entirely possible that she was now pursuing the same end, offering him a poisonous fruit?

She shook the unpleasantly bulbous object. "*Bo!*" she repeated, and then, exactly as if she understood his hesitancy, she broke off one of the fingers and thrust it into her own mouth. She smiled at him.

"Good enough, Lilith." He grinned, taking the remainder.

It was much pleasanter to the tongue than to the eye. The pulp had a tart sweetness that was vaguely familiar to him, but he could not quite identify the taste. Nevertheless, encouraged by Lilith's example, he ate until his hunger was appeased.

The encounter with Lilith and her wild pack had wiped out thoughts of his mission. Striding back toward the beach he frowned, remembering that he was here as Alan Carver, zoologist, and in no other role. Yet—where could he begin? He was here to classify and to take specimens, but what was he to do on a mad island where every creature was of an unknown variety? There was no possibility of classification here, because there were no classes. There was only one of everything—or so it appeared.

Rather than set about a task futile on the very face of it, Carver turned his thoughts another way. Somewhere on Austin was the secret of this riotous disorder, and it seemed better to seek the ultimate key than to fritter away his time at the endless task of classifying. He would explore the island. Some strange volcanic gas, he mused vaguely, or some queer radioactive deposit—analogous to Morgan's experiments with X-rays on germ plasm. Or—or something else. There must be some answer.

"Come on, Lilith," he ordered, and set off toward the west, where the hill seemed to be higher than the opposing eminence at the island's eastern extremity.

The girl followed with her accustomed obedience, with her honey-hued eyes fastened on Carver in that curious mixture of fear, wonder, and—perhaps—a dawning light of worship.

The zoologist was not too preoccupied with the accumulation of mysteries to glance occasionally at the wild beauty of her face, and once he caught himself trying to picture her in civilized attire—her mahogany hair confined under one of the current tiny hats, her lithe body sheathed in finer textile than the dried and cracking skin she wore, her feet in dainty leather, and her ankles in chiffon. He scowled and thrust the visualization away, but whether because it seemed too anomalous or too attractive he did not trouble to analyze.

He turned up the slope. Austin was heavily wooded, like the Aucklands, but progress was easy, for it was through a forest, not a jungle. A mad forest, true enough, but still comparatively clear of underbrush.

A shadow nickered, then another. But the first was only a queen's pigeon, erecting its glorious feather crest, and the second only an owl parrot. The birds on Austin were normal; they were simply the ordinary feathered life of the southern seas. Why? Because they were mobile; they traveled, or were blown by storms, from island to island.

It was mid-afternoon before Carver reached the peak, where a solemn outcropping of black basalt rose treeless, like a forester's watchtower. He clambered up its eroded sides and stood with Lilith beside him, gazing out across the central valley of Austin Island to the hill at the eastern point, rising until its peak nearly matched their own. Between sprawled the wild forest, in whose depths blue-green shadows shifted in the breeze like squalls visible here and there on the surface of a calm lake. Some sort of soaring bird circled below, and far away, in the very center of the valley, was the sparkle of water. That, he knew must be the rivulet he had already visited. But nowhere—nowhere at all—was there any sign of human occupation to account for the presence of Lilith—no smoke, no clearing, nothing.

The girl touched his arm timidly, and gestured toward the opposite hill.

"*Pah bo!*" she said tremulously. It must have been quite obvious to her that he failed to understand, for she amplified the phrase. "*R-r-r-r!*" she growled, drawing her perfect lips into an imitation of a snarl. "*Pah bo, lay shot.*" She pointed again toward the east.

Was she trying to tell him that some fierce beasts dwelt in that region? Carver could not interpret her symbolism in any other way, and the phrase she had used was the same she had applied to the poisonous fruit.

He narrowed his eyes as he gazed intently toward the eastern eminence, then started. There was something, not on the opposing hill, but down near the flash of water midway between.

At his side hung the prism binoculars he used for identifying birds. He swung the instrument to his eyes. What he saw, still not clearly enough for certainty, was a mound or structure, vine-grown and irregular. But it might be the roofless walls of a ruined cottage.

The sun was sliding westward. Too late in the day now for exploration, but tomorrow would do. He marked the place of the mound in his memory, then scrambled down.

As darkness approached, Lilith began to evince a curious reluctance to move eastward, hanging back, sometimes dragging timidly at his arm. Twice she said "No, no!" and Carver wondered whether the word was part of her vocabulary or whether she had acquired it from him. Heaven knew, he reflected amusedly, that he had used the word often enough, as one might use it to a child.

He was hungry again, despite the occasional fruits Lilith had plucked for him. On the beach he shot a magnificent Cygnus Atratus, a black Australian swan, and carried it with its head dragging, while Lilith, awed by the shot, followed him now without objection.

He strode along the beach to his box; not that that stretch was any more desirable than the next, but if Kolu and Malloa were to return, or were to guide a rescue expedition from the *Fortune*, that was the spot they'd seek first.

He gathered driftwood, and, just as darkness fell, lighted a fire.

He grinned at Lilith's start of panic and her low "O-o-oh!" of sheer terror as the blaze of the match caught and spread. She remembered her scorched fingers, doubtless, and she circled warily around the flames, to crouch behind him where he sat plucking and cleaning the great bird.

She was obviously quite uncomprehending as he pierced the fowl with a spit and set about roasting it, but he smiled at the manner in which her sensitive nostrils twitched at the combined odor of burning wood and cooking meat.

When it was done, he cut her a portion of the flesh, rich and fat like roast goose, and he smiled again at her bewilderment. She ate it, but very gingerly, puzzled alike by the heat and the altered taste; beyond question she would have preferred it raw and bleeding. When she had finished, she scrubbed the grease very daintily from her fingers with wet sand at a tidal pool.

Carver was puzzling again over what to do with her. He didn't want to lose her, yet he could hardly stay awake all night to guard her. There were the ropes that had lashed his case of supplies; he could, he supposed, tie her wrists and ankles; but somehow the idea appealed to him not at all. She was too naive, too trusting, too awe-struck and worshipful. And besides, savage or not, she was a white girl over whom he had no conceivable rightful authority.

At last he shrugged and grinned across the dying fire at Lilith, who had lost some of her fear of the leaping flames. "It's up to you," he remarked amiably. "I'd like you to stick around, but I won't insist on it."

She answered his smile with her own quick, flashing one, and the gleam of eyes exactly the color of the flames they mirrored, but she said nothing. Carver sprawled in the sand; it was cool enough to dull the activities of the troublesome sand fleas, and after a while he slept.

His rest was decidedly intermittent. The wild chorus of night sounds disturbed him again with its strangeness, and he woke to see Lilith staring fixedly into the fire's dying embers. Some time later he awakened again; now the fire was quite extinct, but Lilith was standing. While he watched her silently, she turned toward the for-est. His heart sank; she was leaving.

But she paused. She bent over something dark—the body of one of the creatures he had shot. The big one, it was; he saw her struggle to lift it, and, finding the weight too great, drag it laboriously to the coral spit and roll it into the sea.

Slowly she returned; she gathered the smaller body into her arms and repeated the act, standing motionless for long minutes over the black water. When she returned once more she faced the rising moon for a moment, and he saw her eyes glistening with tears. He knew he had witnessed a burial.

He watched her in silence. She dropped to the sand near the black smear of ashes; but she seemed in no need of sleep. She stared so fixedly and so apprehensively toward the east that Carver felt a sense of foreboding. He was about to raise himself to sitting position when Lilith, as if arriving at a decision after long pondering, sud-denly sprang to her feet and darted across the sand to the trees.

Startled, he stared into the shadows, and out of them drifted that same odd call he had heard before. He strained his ears, and was certain he heard a faint yelping among the trees. She had summoned her pack. Carver drew his revolver quietly from its holster and half rose on his arm.

Lilith reappeared. Behind her, darker shadows against the shadowy growths, lurked wild forms, and Carver's hand tightened on the grip of his revolver.

But there was no attack. The girl uttered a low command of some sort, the slinking shadows vanished, and she returned alone to her place on the sand.

The zoologist could see her face, silver-pale in the moonlight, as she glanced at him, but he lay still in apparent slumber, and Lilith, after a moment, seemed ready to imitate him. The apprehension had vanished from her features; she was calmer, more confident. Carver realized why, suddenly; she had set her pack to guard against whatever danger threatened from the east.

Dawn roused him. Lilith was still sleeping, curled like a child on the sand, and for some time he stood gazing down at her. She was very beautiful, and now, with her tawny eyes closed, she seemed much less mysterious; she seemed no island nymph or dryad, but simply a lovely, savage, primitive girl. Yet he knew—or he was beginning to suspect—the mad truth about Austin Island. If the truth were what he feared, then he might as well fall in love with a sphinx, or a mermaid, or a female centaur, as with Lilith.

He steeled himself. "Lilith!" he called gruffly.

She awoke with a start of terror. For a moment she faced him with sheer panic in her eyes; then she remembered, gasped, and smiled tremulously. Her smile made it very hard for him to remember what it was that he feared in her, for she looked beautifully and appealingly human save for her wild, flame-colored eyes, and even what he fancied he saw in those might be but his own imagining.

She followed him toward the trees. There was no sign of her bestial body-guards, though Carver suspected their nearness. He breakfasted again on fruits chosen by Lilith, selected unerringly, from the almost infinite variety, by her delicate nostrils. Carver mused interestedly that smell seemed to be the one means of identifying genera on this insane island.

Smell is chemical in nature. Chemical differences meant glandular ones, and glandular differences, in the last analysis, probably accounted for racial ones. Very likely the differences between a cat, say, and a dog was, in the ultimate sense, a glandular difference. He scowled at the thought and stared narrowly at Lilith; but, peer as he might, she seemed neither more nor less than an unusually lovely little savage—except for her eyes.

He was moving toward the eastern part of the island, intending to follow the brook to the site of the ruined cabin, if it was a ruined cabin. Again he noted the girl's nervousness as they approached the stream that nearly bisected this part of the valley. Certainly, unless her fears were sheer superstition, there was something dangerous there. He examined his gun again, then strode on.

At the bank of the brook Lilith began to present difficulties. She snatched his arm and tugged him back, wailing, "No, no, no!" in frightened repetition.

When he glanced at her in impatient questioning, she could only repeat her phrase of yesterday. "*Lay shot,*" she said, anxiously and fearfully. "*Lay shot!*"

"Humph!" he growled. "A cannon's the only bird I ever heard of that could—" He turned to follow the watercourse into the forest.

Lilith hung back. She could not bring herself to follow him there. For an instant he paused, looking back at her slim loveliness, then turned and strode on. Better that she remained where she was. Better if he never saw her again, for she was too beautiful for close proximity. Yet Heaven knew, he mused, that she looked human enough.

But Lilith rebelled. Once she was certain that he was determined to go on, she gave a frightened cry. "Alan!" she called. "Alan!"

He turned, astonished that she remembered his name, and found her darting to his side. She was pallid, horribly frightened, but she would not let him go alone.

Yet there was nothing to indicate that this region of the island was more dangerous than the rest. There was the same mad profusion of varieties of vegetation, the same unclassifiable leaves, fruits, and flowers. Only—or he imagined this—there were fewer birds.

One thing slowed their progress. At times the eastern bank of the rivulet seemed more open than their side, but Lilith steadfastly refused to permit him to cross. When he tried it, she clung so desperately and so violently to his arms that he at last yielded, and plowed his way through the underbrush on his own bank. It was as if the watercourse were a dividing line, a frontier, or—he frowned—a border.

By noon they had reached a point which Carver knew must be close indeed to the spot he sought. He peered through the tunnel that arched over the course of the brook, and there ahead, so overgrown that it blended perfectly with the forest wall, he saw it.

It was a cabin, or the remains of one. The log walls still stood, but the roof, doubtless of thatch, had long ago disintegrated. But what struck Carver first was the certainty, evident in design, in window openings, in doorway, that this was no native hut. It had been a white man's cabin of perhaps three rooms.

It stood on the eastern bank; but by now the brook had narrowed to a mere rill, gurgling from pool to tiny rapids. He sprang across, disregarding Lilith's anguished cry. But at a glimpse of her face he did pause. Her magnificent honey-hued eyes were wide with fear, while her lips were set in a tense little line of grimmest determination. She looked as an ancient martyr must have looked marching out to face the lions, as she stepped deliberately across to his side. It was almost as if she said, "If you are bound to die, then I will die beside you."

Yet within the crumbling walls there was nothing to inspire fear. There was no animal life at all, except a tiny, rat-like being that skittered out between the logs at their approach. Carver stared around him at the grassy and fern grown interior, at the remnants of decaying furniture and the fallen debris. It had been years since this place had known human occupants, a decade at the very least.

His foot struck something. He glanced down to see a human skull and a human femur in the grass. And then other bones, though none of them were in a natural position. Their former owner must have died there where the ruined cot sagged, and been dragged here by—well, by whatever it was that had feasted on human carrion.

He glanced sidewise at Lilith, but she was simply staring affrightedly toward the east. She had not noticed the bones, or if she had, they had meant nothing to her. Carver poked gingerly among them for some clue to the identity of the remains, but there was nothing save a corroded belt buckle. That, of course, was a little; it had been a man, and most probably a white man.

Most of the debris was inches deep in the accumulation of loam. He kicked among the fragments of what must once have been a cupboard, and again his foot struck something hard and round—no skull this time, but an ordinary jar.

He picked it up. It was sealed, and there was something in it. The cap was hopelessly stuck by the corrosion of years; Carver smashed the glass against a log. What he picked from the fragments was a notebook, yellow-edged and brittle with time. He swore softly as a dozen leaves disintegrated in his hands, but what remained seemed stronger. He hunched down on the log and scanned the all-but-obliterated ink.

There was a date and a name. The name was Ambrose Callan, and the date was October 25th, 1921. He frowned. In 1921 he had been—let's see, he mused; fifteen years ago—he had been in grade school. Yet the name Ambrose Callan had a familiar ring to it.

He read more of the faded, written lines, then stared thoughtfully into space. That was the man, then. He remembered the Callan expedition because as a youngster he had been interested in far places, exploration, and adventure, as what youngster isn't? Professor Ambrose Callan of Northern; he began to remember that Morgan had based some of his work with artificial species—synthetic evolution—on Callan's observations.

But Morgan had only succeeded in creating a few new species of fruit fly, of Drosophila, by exposing germ plasm to hard X-rays. Nothing like this—this madhouse of Austin Island. He stole a look at the tense and fearful Lilith, and shuddered, for she seemed so lovely—and so human. He turned his eyes to the crumbling pages and read on, for here at last he was close to the secret.

He was startled by Lilith's sudden wail of terror. "*Lay shot!*" she cried. "Alan, *lay shot.*"

He followed her gesture, but saw nothing. Her eyes were doubtless sharper than his, yet—There! In the deep afternoon shadows of the forest something moved. For an instant he saw it clearly—a malevolent pygmy like the cat-eyed horror he had glimpsed drinking from the stream. Like it? No, the same; it must be the same, for here on Austin no creature resembled another, nor ever could, save by the wildest of chances.

196

The creature vanished before he could draw his weapon, but in the shadows lurked other figures, other eyes that seemed alight with nonhuman intelligence. He fired, and a curious squawling cry came back, and it seemed to him that the forms receded for a time. But they came again, and he saw without surprise the nightmare horde of creatures.

He stuffed the notebook in his pocket and seized Lilith's wrist, for she stood as if paralyzed by horror. He backed away out of the doorless entrance, over the narrow brook. The girl seemed dazed, half hypnotized by the glimpses of the things that followed them. Her eyes were wide with fear, and she stumbled after him unseeing. He sent another shot into the shadows.

That seemed to rouse Lilith. "*Lay shot!*" she whimpered, then gathered her self-control. She uttered her curious call, and somewhere it was answered, and yet further off, answered again.

Her pack was gathering for her defense, and Carver felt a surge of apprehension for his own position. Might he not be caught between two enemies?

He never forgot that retreat down the course of the little stream. Only delirium itself could duplicate the wild battles he witnessed, the unearthly screaming, the death grips of creatures not quite natural, things that fought with the mad frenzy of freaks and outcasts. He and Lilith must have been slain immediately save for the intervention of her pack; they slunk out of the shadows with low, bestial noises, circling Carver cautiously, but betraying no scrap of caution against—the other things.

He saw or sensed something that had almost escaped him before. Despite their forms, whatever their appearance happened to be, Lilith's pack was doglike. Not in looks, certainly; it was far deeper than that. In nature, in character; that was it.

And their enemies, wild creatures of nightmare though they were, had something feline about them. Not in appearance, no more than the others, but in character and actions. Their method of fighting, for instance—all but silent, with deadly claw and needle teeth, none of the fencing of canine nature, but with the leap and talons of feline. But their aspect, their—their *catness* was more submerged by their outward appearance, for they ranged from the semi-human form of the little demon of the brook to ophidianheaded things as heavy and lithe as a panther. And they fought with a ferocity and intelligence that was itself abnormal.

Carver's gun helped. He fired when he had any visible target, which was none too often; but his occasional hits seemed to instill respect into his adversaries.

Lilith, weaponless save for stones and her wooden knife, simply huddled at his side as they backed slowly toward the beach. Their progress was maddeningly slow, and Carver began to note apprehensively that the shadows were stretching toward the east, as if to welcome the night that was sliding around from that half of the world. Night meant—destruction.

If they could attain the beach, and if Lilith's pack could hold the others at bay until Carver could build a fire, they might survive. But the creatures that were allied with Lilith were being overcome. They were hopelessly outnumbered. They were being slain more rapidly with each one that fell, as ice melts more swiftly as its size decreases.

Carver stumbled backward into orange-tinted sunlight. The beach! The sun was already touching the coral spit, and darkness was a matter of minutes—brief minutes.

Out of the brush came the remnants of Lilith's pack, a half dozen nondescripts, snarling, bloody, panting, and exhausted. For the moment they were free of their attackers, since the catlike fiends chose to lurk among the shadows. Carver backed farther away, feeling a sense of doom as his own shadow lengthened in the brief instant of twilight that divided day from night in these latitudes. And then swift darkness came just as he dragged Lilith to the ridge of the coral spit.

He saw the charge impending. Weird shadows detached themselves from the deeper shadows of the trees. Below, one of the nondescripts whined softly. Across the sand, clear for an instant against the white ground coral of the beach, the figure of the small devil with the half-human posture showed, and a malevolent sputtering snarl sounded. It was exactly as if the creature had leaped forward like a leader to exhort his troops to charge.

Carver chose that figure as his target. His gun flashed; the snarl became a squawl of agony, and the charge came.

Lilith's pack crouched; but Carver knew that this was the end.

He fired. The flickering shadows came on. The magazine emptied; there was no time now to reload, so he reversed the weapon, clubbed it. He felt Lilith grow tense beside him.

And then the charge halted. In unison, as if at command, the shadows were motionless, silent save for the low snarling of the dying creature on the sand. When they moved again, it was away—toward the trees!

Carver gulped. A faint shimmering light on the wall of the forest caught his eye, and he spun. It was true! Down the beach, down there where he had left his box of supplies, a fire burned, and rigid against the light, facing toward them in the darkness, were human figures. The unknown peril of fire had frightened off the attack.

He stared. There in the sea, dark against the faint glow of the west, was a familiar outline. The *Fortune*. The men there were his associates; they had heard his shots and lighted the fire as a guide.

"Lilith!" he choked. "Look there. Come on!"

But the girl held back. The remnant of her pack slunk behind the shelter of the ridge of coral, away from the dread fire. It was no longer the fire that frightened Lilith, but the black figures around it, and Alan Carver found himself suddenly face to face with the hardest decision of his life.

He could leave her here. He knew she would not follow, knew it from the tragic light in her honey-hued eyes. And beyond all doubt that was the best thing to do; for he could not marry her. Nobody could ever marry her, and she was too lovely to take among men who might love her—as Carver did. But he shuddered a little as a picture flashed in his mind. Children! What sort of children would Lilith bear? No man could dare chance the possibility that Lilith, too, was touched by the curse of Austin Island.

He turned sadly away—a step, two steps, toward the fire. Then he turned.

"Come, Lilith," he said gently, and added mournfully, "other people have married, lived, and died without children. I suppose we can, too."

The *Fortune* slid over the green swells, northward toward New Zealand. Carver grinned as he sprawled in a deck chair. Halburton was still gazing reluctantly at the line of blue that was Austin Island.

"Buck up, Vance," Carver chuckled. "You couldn't classify that flora in a hundred years, and if you could, what'd be the good of it? There's just one of each, anyway."

"I'd give two toes and a finger to try," said Halburton. "You had the better part of three days there, and might have had more if you hadn't winged Malloa. They'd have gone home to the Chathams sure, if your shot hadn't got his arm. That's the only reason they made for Macquarie."

"And lucky for me they did. Your fire scared off the cats."

"The cats, eh? Would you mind going over the thing again, Alan? It's so crazy that I haven't got it all yet."

"Sure. Just pay attention to teacher and you'll catch on." He grinned. "Frankly, at first I hadn't a glimmering of an idea myself. The whole island seemed insane. No two living things alike! Just one of each genus, and all unknown genera at that. I didn't get a single clue until after I met Lilith. Then I noticed that she differentiated by smell. She told good fruits from poisonous ones by the smell, and she even identified that first cat-thing I shot by smell. She'd eat that because it was an enemy, but she wouldn't touch the dog-things I shot from her pack."

"So what?" asked Halburton, frowning.

"Well, smell is a chemical sense. It's much more fundamental than outward form, because the chemical functioning of an organism depends on its glands. I began to suspect right then that the fundamental nature of all the living things on Austin Island was just the same as anywhere else. It wasn't the nature that was changed, but just the form. See?"

"Not a bit."

"You will. You know what chromosomes are, of course. They're the carriers of heredity, or rather, according to Weissman, they carry the genes that carry the determinants that carry heredity. A human being has forty-eight chromosomes, of which he gets twenty-four from each parent."

"So," said Halburton, "has a tomato."

"Yes, but a tomato's forty-eight chromosomes carry a different heredity, else one could cross a human being with a tomato. But to return to the subject, all variations in individuals come about from the manner in which chance shuffles these forty-eight chromosomes with their load of determinants. That puts a pretty definite limit on the possible variations.

"For instance, eye color has been located on one of the genes on the third pair of chromosomes. Assuming that this gene contains twice as many brown-eye determinants as blue-eye ones, the chances are two to one that the child of whatever man or woman owns that particular chromosome will be brown-eyed—if his mate has no marked bias either way. See?"

"I know all that. Get along to Ambrose Callan and his notebook."

"Coming to it. Now remember that these determinants carry all heredity, and that includes shape, size, intelligence, character, coloring—everything. People—or plants and animals—can vary in the vast number of ways in which it is possible to combine forty-eight chromosomes with their cargo of genes and determinants. But that number is not infinite. There are limits, limits to size, to coloring, to intelligence. Nobody ever saw a human race with sky-blue hair, for instance."

"Nobody'd ever want to!" grunted Halburton.

"And," proceeded Carver, "that is because there are no blue-hair determinants in human chromosomes. But—and here comes Callan's idea—suppose we could increase the number of chromosomes in a given ovum. What then? In humans or tomatoes, if, instead of forty-eight, there were four hundred eighty, the possible range of variation would be ten times as great as it is now.

"In size, for instance, instead of the present possible variation of about two and a half feet, they might vary twenty-five feet! And in shape—a man might resemble almost anything! That is, almost anything within the range of the mammalian orders. And in intelligence—" He paused thoughtfully.

"But how," cut in Halburton, "did Callan propose to accomplish the feat of inserting extra chromosomes? Chromosomes themselves are microscopic; genes are barely visible under the highest magnification, and nobody ever saw a determinant."

"I don't know how," said Carver gravely. "Part of his notes crumbled to dust, and the description of his method must have gone with those pages. Morgan uses hard radiations, but his object and his results are both different. He doesn't change the number of chromosomes."

He hesitated. "I think Callan used a combination of radiation and injection," he resumed. "I don't know. All I know is that he stayed on Austin four or five years, and that he came with only his wife. That part of his notes is clear enough. He began treating the vegetation near his shack, and some cats and dogs he had brought. Then he discovered that the thing was spreading like a disease."

"Spreading?" echoed Halburton.

"Of course. Every tree he treated strewed multi-chromosomed pollen to the wind, and as for the cats—Anyway, the aberrant pollen fertilized normal seeds, and the result was another freak, a seed with the normal number of chromosomes from one parent and ten times as many from the other. The variations were endless. You know how swiftly kauri and tree ferns grow, and these had a possible speed of growth ten times as great.

"The freaks overran the island, smothering out the normal growths. And Callan's radiations, and perhaps his injections, too, affected Austin Island's indigenous life—the rats, the bats. They began to produce mutants. He came in 1918, and by the time he realized his own tragedy, Austin was an island of freaks where no child resembled its parents save by the merest chance."

"His own tragedy? What do you mean?"

"Well, Callan was a biologist, not an expert in radiation. I don't know exactly what happened. Exposure to X-rays for long periods produces burns, ulcers, malignancies. Maybe Callan didn't take proper precautions to shield his device, or maybe he was using a radiation of peculiarly irritating quality. Anyway, his wife sickened first—an ulcer that turned cancerous.

"He had a radio—a wireless, rather, in 1921—and he summoned his sloop from the Chathams. It sank off that coral spit, and Callan, growing desperate, succeeded somehow in breaking his wireless. He was no electrician, you see.

"Those were troubled days, after the close of the War. With Callan's sloop sunk, no one knew exactly what had become of him, and after a while he was forgotten. When his wife died, he buried her; but when he died there was no one to bury him. The descendants of what had been his cats took care of him, and that was that."

"Yeah? What about Lilith?"

"Yes," said Carver soberly. "What about her? When I began to

suspect the secret of Austin Island, that worried me. Was Lilith really quite human? Was she, too, infected by the taint of variation, so
that her children might vary as widely as the offspring of the—cats?
She spoke not a word of any language I knew—or I thought so,
anyway—and I simply couldn't fit her in. But Callan's diary and
notes did it for me."

"How?"

"She's the daughter of the captain of Callan's sloop, whom he
rescued when it was wrecked on the coral point. She was five years
old then, which makes her almost twenty now. As for language—
well, perhaps I should have recognized the few halting words she
recalled. *C'm on*, for instance, was *comment*—that is, 'how?' And
pah bo was simply *pas bon*, not good. That's what she said about the
poisonous fruit. And *lay shot* was *les chats*, for somehow she remembered, or sensed, that the creatures from the eastern end were cats.

"About her, for fifteen years, centered the dog creatures, who
despite their form were, after all, dogs by nature, and loyal to their
mistress. And between the two groups was eternal warfare."

"But are you sure Lilith escaped the taint?"

"Her name's Lucienne," mused Carver, "but I think I prefer Lilith." He smiled at the slim figure clad in a pair of Jameson's trousers
and his own shirt, standing there in the stern looking back at Austin.
"Yes, I'm sure. When she was cast on the island, Callan had already
destroyed the device that had slain his wife and was about to kill
him. He wrecked his equipment completely, knowing that in the
course of time the freaks he had created were doomed."

"Doomed?"

"Yes. The normal strains, hardened by evolution, are stronger.
They're already appearing around the edges of the island, and some
day Austin will betray no more peculiarities than any other remote
islet. Nature always reclaims her own."

The Adaptive Ultimate

Dr. Daniel Scott, his dark and brilliant eyes alight with the fire of enthusiasm, paused at last and stared out over the city, or that portion of it visible from the office windows of Herman Bach—the Dr. Herman Bach of Grand Mercy Hospital. There was a moment of silence; the old man smiled a little indulgently, a little wistfully, at the face of the youthful biochemist.

"Go on, Dan," he said. "So it occurred to you that getting well of a disease or injury is merely a form of adaptation—then what?"

"Then," flashed the other, "I began to look for the most adaptive of living organisms. And what are they? Insects! Insects, of course. Cut off a wing, and it grows back. Cut off a head, stick it to the headless body of another of the same species, and that grows back on. And what's the secret of their great adaptability?"

Dr. Bach shrugged. "What is?"

Scott was suddenly gloomy. "I'm not sure," he muttered. "It's glandular, of course—a matter of hormones." He brightened again. "But I'm off the track. So then I looked around for the most adaptive insect. And which is that?"

"Ants?" suggested Dr. Bach. "Bees? Termites?"

"Bah! They're the most highly evolved, not the most adaptable. No; there's one insect that is known to produce a higher percentage of mutants than any other, more freaks, more biological sports. The one Morgan used in his experiments on the effect of hard X-rays on heredity—the fruit fly, the ordinary fruit fly. Remember? They have reddish eyes, but under X-rays they produced white-eyed offspring—and that was a true mutation, because the white eyes bred true! Acquired characteristics can't be inherited, but these were. Therefore—"

"I know," interrupted Dr. Bach.

Scott caught his breath. "So I used fruit flies," he resumed. "I putrefied their bodies, injected a cow, and got a serum at last, after weeks of clarifying with albumen, evaporating *in vacuo*, rectifying with—But

204

you're not interested in the technique. I got a serum. I tried it on tubercular guinea pigs, and"—he paused dramatically—"it cured! They adapted themselves to the tubercle bacillus. I tried it on a rabid dog. He adapted. I tried it on a cat with a broken spine. That knit. And now, I'm asking you for the chance to try it on a human being!"

Dr. Bach frowned. "You're not ready," he grunted. "You're not ready by two years. Try it on an anthropoid. Then try it on yourself. I can't risk a human life in an experiment that's as raw as this."

"Yes, but I haven't got anything that needs curing, and as for an anthropoid, you get the board to allow funds to buy an ape—if you can. I've tried."

"Take it up with the Stoneman Foundation, then."

"And have Grand Mercy lose the credit? Listen, Dr. Bach, I'm asking for just one chance—a charity case—anything."

"Charity cases are human beings." The old man scowled down at his hands. "See here, Dan. I shouldn't even offer this much, because it's against all medical ethics, but if I find a hopeless case—utterly hopeless, you understand—where the patient himself consents, I'll do it. And that's the final word."

Scott groaned. "And try to find a case like that. If the patient's conscious, you think there's hope, and if he isn't how can he consent? That settles it!"

But it didn't. Less than a week later Scott looked suddenly up at the annunciator in the corner of his tiny laboratory. "Dr. Scott," it rasped. "Dr. Scott. Dr. Scott. To Dr. Bach's office."

He finished his titration, noted the figures, and hurried out. The old man was pacing the floor nervously as Scott entered.

"I've got your case, Dan," he muttered. "It's against all ethics—yet I'll be damned if I can see how you can do this one any harm. But you'd better hurry. Come on—isolation ward."

They hurried. In the tiny cubical room Scott stared appalled. "A girl!" he muttered.

She could never have been other than drab and plain, but lying there with the pallor of death already on her cheeks, she had an appearance of somber sweetness. Yet that was all the charm she could ever have possessed; her dark, cropped, oily hair was unkempt and stringy, her features flat and unattractive. She breathed with an almost inaudible rasp, and her eyes were closed.

"Do you," asked Scott, "consider this a test? She's all but dead now."

Dr. Bach nodded. "Tuberculosis," he said, "final stage. Her lungs are hemorrhaging—a matter of hours."

The girl coughed; flecks of blood appeared on her pallid lips. She opened dull, watery blue eyes.

"So!" said Bach, "conscious, eh? This is Dr. Scott. Dan, this is—uh"—he peered at the card at the foot of the bed—"Miss—uh—Kyra Zelas. Dr. Scott has an injection, Miss Zelas. As I warned you, it probably won't help, but I can't see how it can hurt. Are you willing?"

She spoke in faint, gurgling tones. "Sure, I'm through anyway. What's the odds?"

"All right. Got the hypo, Dan?" Bach took the tube of water-clear serum. "Any particular point of injection? No? Give me the cubital, then."

He thrust the needle into the girl's arm. Dan noted that she did not even wince at the bite of the steel point, but lay stoical and passive as thirty c. c. of liquid flowed into her veins. She coughed again, then closed her eyes.

"Come out of here," ordered Bach gruffly, as they moved into the hall, "I'm damned if I like this. I feel like a dirty dog."

He seemed to feel less canine, however, the following day. "That Zelas case is still alive," he reported to Scott. "If I dared trust my eyes, I'd say she's improved a little. A very little. I'd still call it hopeless."

But the following day Scott found himself seated in his office with a puzzled expression in his old gray eyes. "Zelas is better," he muttered. "No question of it. But you keep your head, Dan. Such miracles have happened before, and without serums. You wait until we've had her under long observation."

By the end of the week it became evident that the observation was not to be long. Kyra Zelas flourished under their gaze like some swift-blooming tropical weed. Queerly, she lost none of her pallor, but flesh softened the angular features, and a trace of light grew in her eyes.

"The spots on her lungs are going," muttered Bach. "She's stopped coughing, and there's no sign of bugs in her culture. But the queerest thing, Dan—and I can't figure it out, either—is the way she reacts to abrasions and skin punctures. Yesterday I took a blood specimen for a Wasserman, and—this sounds utterly mad—the puncture closed almost before I had a c. c! Closed and healed!"

And in another week, "Dan, I can't see any reason for keeping Kyra here. She's well. Yet I want her where we can keep her under observation. There's a queer mystery about this serum of yours. And besides, I hate to turn her out to the sort of life that brought her here."

"What did she do?"

"Sewed. Piece work in some sweatshop, when she could work at all. Drab, ugly, uneducated girl, but there's something appealing about her. She adapts quickly."

Scott gave him a strange look. "Yes," he said, "she adapts quickly."

"So," resumed Bach, "it occurred to me that she could stay at my place. We could keep her under observation, you see, and she could help the housekeeper. I'm interested—damn' interested. I think I'll offer her the chance."

Scott was present when Dr. Bach made his suggestion. The girl Kyra smiled. "Sure," she said. Her pallid, plain face lighted up. "Thanks."

Bach gave her the address. "Mrs. Getz will let you in. Don't do anything this afternoon. In fact, it might not hurt you to simply walk in the park for a few hours."

Scott watched the girl as she walked down the hall toward the elevator. She had filled out, but she was still spare to the point of emaciation, and her worn black suit hung on her as if it were on a frame of sticks. As she disappeared, he moved thoughtfully about his duties, and a quarter hour later descended to his laboratory.

On the first floor, turmoil met him. Two officers were carrying in the body of a nondescript old man, whose head was a bloody ruin. There was a babble of excited voices, and he saw a crowd on the steps outside.

"What's up?" he called. "Accident?"

"Accident!" snapped an officer. "Murder, you mean. Woman steps up to this old guy, picks a hefty stone from the park border, slugs him, and takes his wallet. Just like that!"

Scott peered out of the window. The Black Maria was backing

toward a crowd on the park side of the street. A pair of hulking po-
licemen flanked a thin figure in black, thrusting it toward the doors
of the vehicle.

Scott gasped. It was Kyra Zelas!

A week later Dr. Bach stared into the dark fireplace of his living
room. "It's not our business," he repeated.

"My God!" blazed Scott. "Not our business! How do we know
we're not responsible? How do we know that our injection didn't
unsettle her mind? Glands can do that; look at Mongoloid idiots and
cretins. Our stuff was glandular. Maybe we drove her crazy!"

"All right," said Bach. "Listen. We'll attend the trial tomorrow,
and if it looks bad for her, we'll get hold of her lawyer and let him
put us on the stand. We'll testify that she's just been released after a
long and dangerous illness, and may not be fully responsible. That's
entirely true."

Mid-morning of the next day found them hunched tensely on
benches in the crowded courtroom. The prosecution was opening;
three witnesses testified to the event.

"This old guy buys peanuts for the pigeons. Yeah, I sell 'em to
him every day—or did. So this time he hasn't any change, and he
pulls out his wallet, and I see it's stuffed with bills. And one minute
later I see the dame pick up the rock and conk him. Then she grabs
the dough—"

"Describe her, please."

"She's skinny, and dressed in black. She ain't no beauty, neither. Brownish hair, dark eyes, I don't know whether dark-blue
or brown."

"Your witness!" snapped the prosecutor.

A young and nervous individual—appointed by the court, the
paper said—rose. "You say," he squeaked, "that the assailant had
brown hair and dark eyes?"

"Yeah."

"Will the defendant please rise?"

Her back was toward Scott and Bach as Kyra Zelas arose, but
Scott stiffened. Something strangely different about her appearance;
surely her worn black suit no longer hung so loosely about her.
What he could see of her figure seemed—well, magnificent.

"Take off your hat, Miss Zelas," squeaked the attorney.

Scott gasped. Radiant as aluminum glowed the mass of hair she revealed!

"I submit, your honor, that this defendant does not possess dark hair, nor, if you will observe, dark eyes. It is, I suppose, conceivable that she could somehow have bleached her hair while in custody, and I therefore"—he brandished a pair of scissors—"submit a lock to be tested by any chemist the court appoints. The pigmentation is entirely natural. And as for her eyes—does my esteemed opponent suggest that they, too are bleached?"

He swung on the gaping witness. "Is this lady the one you claim to have seen committing the crime?"

The man goggled. "Uh—I can't—say."

"Is she?"

"N-no!"

The speaker smiled. "That's all. Will you take the stand, Miss Zelas?"

The girl moved lithe as a panther. Slowly she turned, facing the court. Scott's brain whirled, and his fingers dug into Bach's arm. Silver-eyed, aluminum-haired, alabaster pale, the girl on the stand was beyond doubt the most beautiful woman he had ever seen!

The attorney was speaking again. "Tell the court in your own words what happened, Miss Zelas."

Quite casually the girl crossed her trim ankles and began to speak. Her voice was low, resonant, and thrilling; Scott had to fight to keep his attention on the sense of her words rather than the sound.

"I had just left Grand Mercy Hospital," she said, "where I had been ill for some months. I had crossed the park when suddenly a woman in black rushed at me, thrust an empty wallet into my hands, and vanished. A moment later I was surrounded by a screaming crowd, and—well, that's all."

"An empty wallet, you say?" asked the defense lawyer. "What of the money found in your own bag, which my eminent colleague believes stolen?"

"It was mine," said the girl, "about seven hundred dollars."

Bach hissed, "That's a lie! She had two dollars and thirty-three cents on her when we took her in."

"Do you mean you think she's the same Kyra Zelas we had at the hospital?" gasped Scott.

"I don't know. I don't know anything, but if I ever touch that damned serum of yours—Look! Look, Dan!" This last was a tense whisper.

"What?"

"Her hair! When the sun strikes it!"

Scott peered more closely. A vagrant ray of noon sunlight filtered through a high window, and now and again the swaying of a shade permitted it to touch the metallic radiance of the girl's hair. Scott stared and saw; slightly but unmistakable, whenever the light touched that glowing aureole, her hair darkened from bright aluminum to golden blond!

Something clicked in his brain. There was a clue somewhere—if he could but find it. The pieces of the puzzle were there, but they were woefully hard to fit together. The girl in the hospital and her reaction to incisions; this girl and her reaction to light.

"I've got to see her," he whispered. "There's something I have to find—Listen!"

The speaker was orating. "And we ask the dismissal of the whole case, your honor, on the grounds that the prosecution has utterly failed even to identify the defendant."

The judge's gavel crashed. For a moment his aging eyes rested on the girl with the silver eyes and incredible hair, then: "Case dismissed!" he snapped. "Jury discharged!"

There was a tumult of voices. Flashlights shot instantaneous sheets of lightning. The girl on the witness stand rose with perfect poise, smiled with lovely, innocent lips, and moved away. Scott waited until she passed close at hand then:

"Miss Zelas!" he called.

She paused. Her strange silver eyes lighted with unmistakable recognition. "Dr. Scott!" said the voice of tinkling metal. "And Dr. Bach!"

She was, then. She was the same girl. This was the drab sloven of the isolation ward, this weirdly beautiful creature of exotic coloring. Staring, Scott could trace now the very identity of her features, but changed as by a miracle.

He pushed through the mob of photographers, press men, and curiosity seekers. "Have you a place to stay?" he asked. "Dr. Bach's offer still stands."

She smiled. "I am very grateful," she murmured, and then, to the crowd of reporters. "The doctor is an old friend of mine." She was completely at ease, unruffled, poised.

Something caught Scott's eye, and he purchased a paper, glancing quickly at the photograph, the one taken at the moment the girl had removed her hat. He started; her hair showed raven black! There was a comment below the picture, too, to the effect that "her striking hair photographs much darker than it appears to the eye."

He frowned. "This way," he said to the girl, then goggled in surprise again. For in the broad light of noon her complexion was no longer the white of alabaster; it was creamy tan, the skin of one exposed to long hours of sunlight; her eyes were deep violet, and her hair—that tiny wisp unconcealed by her hat—was as black as the basalt columns of hell!

Kyra had insisted on stopping to purchase a substitute for the worn black suit, and had ended by acquiring an entire outfit. She sat now curled in the deep davenport before the fireplace in Dr. Bach's library, sheathed in silken black from her white throat to the tiny black pumps on her feet. She was almost unearthly in her weird beauty, with her aluminum hair, silver eyes, and marble-pale skin against the jet silk covering.

She gazed innocently at Scott. "But why shouldn't I?" she asked. "The court returned my money; I can buy what I please with it."

"Your money?" he muttered. "You had less than three dollars when you left the hospital."

"But this is mine now."

"Kyra," he said abruptly, "where did you get that money?"

Her face was saint like in its purity. "From the old man."

"You—you did murder him!"

"Why, of course I did."

He choked. "My Lord!" he gasped. "Don't you realize we'll have to tell?"

She shook her head, smiling, gently from one to the other of them. "No, Dan. You won't tell, for it wouldn't do any good. I can't be tried twice for the same crime. Not in America."

"But why, Kyra? Why did you—"

"Would you have me resume the life that sent me into your hands? I needed money; money was there; I took it."

"But murder!"

"It was the most direct way."

"Not if you happened to be punished for it," he returned grimly.

"But I wasn't," she reminded him gently.

He groaned. "Kyra," he said, shifting the subject suddenly, "why do your eyes and skin and hair darken in sunlight or when exposed to flashlight?"

She smiled. "Do they?" she asked. "I hadn't noticed." She yawned, stretched her arms above her head and her slim legs before her. "I think I shall sleep now," she announced. She swept her magnificent eyes over them, rose, and disappeared into the room Dr. Bach had given her—his own.

Scott faced the older man, his features working in emotion. "Do you see?" he hissed. "Good Lord, do you see?"

"Do you, Dan?"

"Part of it. Part of it, anyway."

"And I see part as well."

"Well," said Scott, "here it is as I see it. That serum—that accursed serum of mine—has somehow accentuated this girl's adaptability to an impossible degree. What is it that differentiates life from non-living matter? Two things, irritation and adaptation. Life adapts itself to its environment, and the greater the adaptability, the more successful the organism.

"Now," he proceeded, "all human beings show a very considerable adaptivity. When we expose ourselves to sunlight, our skin shows pigmentation—we tan. That's adaptation to an environment containing sunlight. When a man loses his right hand, he learns to use his left. That's another adaptation. When a person's skin is punctured, it heals and rebuilds, and that's another angle of the same thing. Sunny regions produce dark-skinned, dark-haired people; northern lands produce blonds—and that's adaptation again.

"So what's happened to Kyra Zelas, by some mad twist I don't understand, is that her adaptive powers have been increased to an extreme. She adapts instantly to her environment; when sun strikes her, she tans at once, and in shade she fades immediately. In sunlight her hair and eyes are those of a tropical race; in shadow, those of a Northerner. And—good Lord, I see it now—when she was faced with danger there in the courtroom, faced by a jury and judge who were men, she adapted to that! She met that danger, not only by changed appearance, but by a beauty so great, that she couldn't have been convicted!" He paused. "But how? How?"

"Perhaps medicine can tell how," said Bach. "Undoubtedly man is the creature of his glands. The differences between races—white, red, black, yellow—is doubtless glandular. And perhaps the most effective agent of adaptation is the human brain and neural system, which in itself is controlled partly by a little greasy mass on the floor of the brain's third ventricle, before the cerebellum, and supposed by the ancients to be the seat of the soul.

"I mean, of course, the pineal gland. I suspect that what your serum contains is the long-sought hormone *pinealin*, and that it has caused hypertrophy of Kyra's pineal gland. And Dan, do you realize that if her adaptability is perfect, she's not only invincible, but invulnerable?"

"That's true!" gulped Scott. "Why, she couldn't be electrocuted, because she'd adapt instantly to an environment containing an electric current, and she couldn't be killed by a shot, because she'd adapt to that as quickly as to your needle pricks. And poison—but there must be a limit somewhere!"

"There doubtless is," observed Bach. "I hardly believe she could adapt herself to an environment containing a fifty-ton locomotive passing over her body. And yet there's an important point we haven't considered. Adaptation itself is of two kinds."

"Two kinds?"

"Yes. One kind is biological; the other, human. Naturally a biochemist like you would deal only with the first, and equally naturally a brain surgeon like me has to consider the second as well. Biological adaptation is what all life—plant, animal, and human—possesses, and it is merely conforming to one's environment. A chameleon, for instance, shows much the same ability as Kyra herself, and so, in lesser degree, does the arctic fox, white in winter, brown in summer; or the snowshoe rabbit, for that matter, or the weasel. All life conforms to its environment to a great extent, because if it doesn't, it dies. But human life does more."

"More?"

"Much more. Human adaptation is not only conformity to environment, but also the actual changing of environment to fit human needs! The first cave man who left his cave to build a grass hut changed his environment, and so, in exactly the same sense, did Steinmetz, Edison, and as far as that goes, Julius Caesar and Napoleon. In fact, Dan, all human invention, genius, and military leadership boils down to that one fact—changing the environment instead of conforming to it."

He paused, then continued, "Now we know that Kyra possesses the biological adaptivity. Her hair and eyes prove that. But what if she possesses the other to the same degree? If she does, God knows what the result will be. We can only watch to see what direction she takes—watch and hope."

"But I don't see," muttered Scott, "how that could be glandular."

"Anything can be glandular. In a mutant—and Kyra's as much a mutant as your white-eyed fruit flies—anything is possible." He frowned reflectively. "If I dared phrase a philosophical interpretation, I'd say that Kyra—perhaps—represents a stage in human evolution. A mutation. If one ventured to believe that, then de Vries and Weissman are justified."

"The mutation theory of evolution, you mean?"

"Exactly. You see, Dan, while it is very obvious from fossil remains that evolution occurred, yet it is very easy to prove it couldn't possibly have occurred!"

"How?"

"Well, it couldn't have occurred slowly, as Darwin believed, for many reasons. Take the eye, for instance. He thought that very gradually, over thousands of generations, some sea creature developed a spot on its skin that was sensitive to light, and that this gave it an advantage over its blind fellows. Therefore its kind survived and others perished. But see here. If this eye developed slowly, why did the very first ones, the ones that couldn't yet see, have any better chance than the others? And take a wing. What good is a wing until you can fly with it? Just because a jumping lizard had a tiny fold of skin between foreleg and breast wouldn't mean that that lizard could survive where others died. What kept the wing developing to a point where it could actually have value?"

"What did?"

"De Vries and Weissman say nothing did. They answer that evolution must have progressed in jumps, so that when the eye appeared, it was already efficient enough to have survival value, and likewise the wing. Those jumps they named mutations. And in that sense, Dan, Kyra's a mutation, a jump from the human to—something else. Perhaps the superhuman."

Scott shook his head in perplexity. He was thoroughly puzzled, completely baffled, and more than a little unnerved. In a few moments more he bade Bach good night, wandered home, and lay for hours in sleepless thought.

The next day Bach managed a leave of absence for both of them from Grand Mercy, and Scott moved in. This was in part simply out of his fascinated interest in the case of Kyra Zelas, but in part it was altruistic. She had confessedly murdered one man; it occurred to Scott that she might with no more compunction murder Dr. Bach, and he meant to be at hand to prevent it.

He had been in her company no more than a few hours before Bach's words on evolution and mutations took on new meaning. It was not only Kyra's chameleon like coloring, nor her strangely pure and saint like features, nor even her incredible beauty. There was something more; he could not at once identify it, but decidedly the girl Kyra was not quite human.

The event that impressed this on him occurred in the late afternoon. Bach was away on personal business, and Scott had been questioning the girl about her own impressions of her experience.

"But don't you know you've changed?" he asked. "Can't you see the difference in yourself?"

"Not I. It is the world that has changed."

"But your hair was black. Now it's light as ashes."

"Was it?" she asked. "Is it?"

He groaned in exasperation. "Kyra," he said, "you must know something about yourself."

Her exquisite eyes turned their silver on him. "I do," she said. "I know that what I want is mine, and"—her pure lips smiled—"I think I want you, Dan."

It seemed to him, that she changed at that moment. Her beauty was not quite as it had been, but somehow more wildly intoxicating than before. He realized what it meant; her environment now contained a man she loved, or thought she loved, and she was adapting to that, too. She was becoming—he shivered slightly—irresistible!

Bach must have realized the situation, but he said nothing. As for Scott, it was sheer torture, for he realized only too well that the girl he loved was a freak, a biological sport, and worse than that, a cold murderess and a creature not exactly human. Yet for the next several days things went smoothly. Kyra slipped easily into the routine; she was ever a willing subject for their inquiries and investigations.

Then Scott had an idea. He produced one of the guinea pigs that he had injected, and they found that the creature evinced the same reaction as Kyra to cuts. They killed the thing by literally cutting it in half with an ax, and Bach examined its brain.

"Right!" he said at last. "It's hypertrophy of the pineal." He stared intently at Scott. "Suppose," he said, "that we could reach Kyra's pineal and correct the hypertrophy. Do you suppose that might return her to normal?"

Scott suppressed a pang of fear. "But why? She can't do any harm as long as we guard her here. Why do we have to gamble with her life like that?"

Bach laughed shortly. "For the first time in my life I'm glad I'm an old man," he said. "Don't you see we have to do something? She's a menace. She's dangerous. Heaven only knows how dangerous. We'll have to try."

Scott groaned and assented. An hour later, under the pretext of experiment, he watched the old man inject five grains of morphia into the girl's arm, watched her frown and blink—and adjust. The drug was powerless.

It was at night that Bach got his next idea. "Ethyl chloride!" he whispered. "The instantaneous anesthetic. Perhaps she can't adjust to lack of oxygen. We'll try."

Kyra was asleep. Silently, carefully, the two crept in, and Scott stared down in utter fascination at the weird beauty of her features, paler than ever in the faint light of midnight. Carefully, so carefully, Bach held the cone above her sleeping face, drop by drop he poured the volatile, sweet-scented liquid into it. Minutes passed.

"That should anaesthetize an elephant," he whispered at last, and jammed the cone full upon her face.

She awoke. Fingers like slim steel rods closed on his wrist, forcing his hand away. Scott seized the cone, and her hand clutched his wrist as well, and he felt the strength of her grasp.

"Stupid," she said quietly, sitting erect. "This is quite useless—look!"

She snatched a paper knife from the table beside the bed. She bared her pale throat to the moonlight, and then, suddenly, drove the knife to its hilt into her bosom!

Scott gulped in horror as she withdrew it. A single spot of blood showed on her flesh, she wiped it away, and displayed her skin, pale, unscarred, beautiful.

"Go away," she said softly, and they departed. The next day she made no reference to the incident. Scott and Bach spent a worried morning in the laboratory, doing no work, but simply talking. It was a mistake, for when they returned to the library, she was gone, having, according to Mrs. Getz, simply strolled out of the door and away. A hectic and hasty search of the adjacent blocks brought no sign of her.

At dusk she was back, pausing hatless in the doorway to permit Scott, who was there alone, to watch the miraculous change as she passed from sunset to chamber, and her hair faded from mahogany to aluminum.

"Hello," she said smiling. "I killed a child."

"What? My Lord, Kyra!"

"It was an accident. Surely you don't feel that I should be punished for an accident, Dan, do you?"

He was staring in utter horror. "How—"

"Oh, I decided to walk a bit. After a block or two, it occurred to me that I should like to ride. There was a car parked there with the keys in it, and the driver was talking on the sidewalk, so I slipped in, started it, and drove away. Naturally I drove rather fast, since he was shouting, and at the second corner I hit a little boy."

"And—you didn't stop?"

"Of course not. I drove around the corner, turned another corner or two, and then parked the car and walked back. The boy was gone, but the crowd was still there. Not one of them noticed me." She smiled her saint like smile. "We're quite safe. They can't possibly trace me."

Scott dropped his head on his hands and groaned. "I don't know what to do!" he muttered. "Kyra, you're going to have to report this to the police."

"But it was an accident," she said gently, her luminous silver eyes pityingly on Scott.

"No matter. You'll have to."

She placed her white hand on his head. "Perhaps to-morrow," she said. "Dan, I have learned something. What one needs in this world is power. As long as there are people in the world with more power than I, I run afoul of them. They keep trying to punish me with their laws—and why? Their laws are not for me. They cannot punish me."

He did not answer.

"Therefore," she said softly, "tomorrow I go out of here to seek power. I will be more powerful than any laws."

That shocked him to action. "Kyra!" he cried. "You're not to try to leave here again." He gripped her shoulders. "Promise me! Swear that you'll not step beyond that door without me!"

"Why, if you wish," she said quietly.

"But swear it! Swear it by everything sacred!"

Her silver eyes looked steadily into his from a face like that of a marble angel. "I swear it," she murmured. "By anything you name, I swear it, Dan."

And in the morning she was gone, taking what cash and bills had been in Scott's wallet, and in Bach's as well. And, they discovered later, in Mrs. Getz's also.

"But if you could have seen her!" muttered Scott. "She looked straight into my eyes and promised, and her face was pure as a Madonna's. I can't believe she was lying."

"The lie as an adaptive mechanism," said Bach, "deserves more attention than it has received. Probably the original liars are those plants and animals that use protective mimicry—harmless snakes imitating poisonous ones, stingless flies that look like bees. Those are living lies."

"But she couldn't—"

"She has, however. What you've told me about her desire for power is proof enough. She's entered the second adaptive phase—that of adapting her environment to herself instead of herself to her environment. How far will her madness—or her genius—carry her? There is very little difference between the two, Dan. And what is left now for us to do but watch?"

"Watch? How? Where is she?"

"Unless I'm badly mistaken, watching her will be easy once she begins to achieve. Wherever she is, I think we—and the rest of the world—will know of it soon enough."

But weeks dropped away without sign of Kyra Zelas. Scott and Bach returned to their duties at Grand Mercy, and down in his laboratory the biochemist disposed grimly of the remains of three guinea pigs, a cat, and a dog, whose killing had been an exhausting and sickening task. In the crematory as well went a tube of water-clear serum.

Then one day the annunciator summoned him to Bach's office, where he found the old man hunched over a copy of the *Post Record*.

"Look here!" he said, indicating a political gossip column called "Whirls of Washington."

Scott read:

"And the surprise of the evening was the soi-disant confirmed bachelor of the cabinet, upright John Callan, who fluttered none other than the gorgeous Kyra Zelas, the lady who affects a dark wig by day and a white by night. Some of us remember her as the acquittee of a murder trial."

Scott looked up. "Callan, eh? Secretary of the treasury, no less! When she said power she meant power, apparently."

"But will she stop there?" mused Bach gloomily. "I have a premonition that she's just beginning."

"Well, actually, how far can a woman go?"

The old man looked at him. "A woman? This is Kyra Zelas, Dan. Don't set your limits yet. There will be more of her."

Bach was right. Her name began to appear with increasing frequency, first in social connections, then with veiled references to secret intrigues and influences.

Thus: "Whom do the press boys mean by the tenth cabineteer?" Or later: "Why not a secretary of personal relations? She has the powers; give her the name." And still later: "One has to go back to Egypt for another instance of a country whose exchequer was run by a woman. And Cleopatra busted that one."

Scott grinned a little ruefully to himself as he realized that the thrusts were becoming more indirect, as if the press itself were be-

ginning to grow cautions. It was a sign of increasing power, for
nowhere are people as sensitive to such trends as among the Washington correspondents. Kyra's appearance in the public prints began
to be more largely restrained to purely social affairs, and usually in
connection with John Callan, the forty-five-year-old bachelor secretary of the treasury.

Waking or sleeping, Scott never for a moment quite forgot her,
for there was something mystical about her, whether she were mad
or a woman of genius, whether freak or superwoman. The only
thing he did forget was a thin girl with drab features and greasy black
hair who had lain on a pallet in the isolation ward and coughed up
flecks of blood.

It was no surprise to either Scott or Dr. Bach to return one
evening to Bach's residence for a few hours' conversation, and find
there, seated as comfortably as if she had never left it, Kyra Zelas.
Outwardly she had changed but little; Scott gazed once more in
fascination on her incredible hair and wide, innocent silver eyes.
She was smoking a cigarette, and she exhaled a long, blue plume of
smoke and smiled up at him.

He hardened himself. "Nice of you to honor us," he said coldly.
"What's the reason for this visit? Did you run out of money?"

"Money? Of course not. How could I run out of money?"

"You couldn't, not as long as you replenished your funds the
way you did when you left."

"Oh, that!" she said contemptuously. She opened her handbag,
indicating a green mass of bills. "I'll give that back, Dan. How much
was it?"

"To hell with the money!" he blazed. "What hurts me is the
way you lied. Staring into my eyes as innocent as a baby, and lying
all the time!"

"Was I?" she asked. "I won't lie to you again, Dan. I promise."

"I don't believe you," he said bitterly. "Tell us what you're doing here, then."

"I wanted to see you. I haven't forgotten what I said to you,
Dan." With the words she seemed to grow more beautiful than
ever, and this time poignantly wistful as well.

"And have you," asked Bach suddenly, "abandoned your idea
of power?"

"Why should I want power?" she rejoined innocently, flashing her magnificent eyes to him.

"But you said," began Scott impatiently, "that you—"

"Did I?" There was a ghost of a smile on her perfect lips. "I won't lie to you, Dan," she went on, laughing a little. "If I want power, it is mine for the taking—more power than you dream."

"Through John Callan?" he rasped.

"He offers a simple way," she said impassively. "Suppose, for instance, that in a day or so he were to issue a statement—a supremely insulting statement—about the war debts. The administration couldn't afford to reprimand him openly, because most of the voters feel that a supremely insulting statement is called for. And if it were insulting enough—and I assure you it would be—you would see the animosity of Europe directed westward.

"Now, if the statement were one that no national government could ignore and yet keep its dignity in the eyes of its people, it would provoke counter-insults. And there are three nations—you know their names as well as I—who await only such a diversion of interest. Don't you see?" She frowned.

"How stupid you both are!" she murmured, and then, stretching her glorious figure and yawning, "I wonder what sort of empress I would make. A good one, doubtless."

But Scott was aghast. "Kyra, do you mean you'd urge Callan into such a colossal blunder as that?"

"Urge him!" she echoed contemptuously. "I'd force him."

"Do you mean you'd do it?"

"I haven't said so," she smiled. She yawned again, and snapped her cigarette into the dark fireplace. "I'll stay here a day or two," she added pleasantly, rising. "Goodnight."

Scott faced Dr. Bach as she vanished into the old man's chamber. "Damn her!" he grated, his lips white. "If I believed she meant all of that—"

"You'd better believe it," said Bach.

"Empress, eh! Empress of what?"

"Of the world, perhaps. You can't set limits to madness or genius."

"We've got to stop her!"

"How? We can't keep her locked up here. In the first place, she'd doubtless develop strength enough in her wrists to break the locks on the doors, and if she didn't, all she'd need to do is shout for help from a window."

"We can have her adjudged insane!" flared Scott. "We can have her locked up where she can't break out or call for help."

"Yes, we could. We could if we could get her committed by the Sanity Commission. And if we got her before them, what chance do you think we'd have?"

"All right, then," said Scott grimly, "we're going to have to find her weakness. Her adaptability can't be infinite. She's immune to drugs and immune to wounds, but she can't be above the fundamental laws of biology. What we have to do is to find the law we need."

"You find it then," said Bach gloomily.

"But we've got to do something. At least we can warn people—" He broke off, realizing the utter absurdity of the idea.

"Warn people!" scoffed Bach. "Against what? We'd be the ones to go before the Sanity Commission then. Callan would ignore us with dignity, and Kyra would laugh her pretty little laugh of contempt, and that would be that."

Scott shrugged helplessly. "I'm staying here to-night," he said. "At least we can talk to her again tomorrow."

"If she's still here," remarked Bach ironically.

But she was. She came out as Scott was reading the morning papers alone in the library, and sat silently opposite him, garbed in black silk lounging pajamas against which her alabaster skin and incredible hair glowed in startling contrast. He watched skin and hair turn faintly golden as the morning sun lightened the chamber. Somehow it angered him that she should be so beautiful and at the same time deadly with an inhuman deadliness.

He spoke first. "You haven't committed any murders since our last meeting, I hope." He said it spitefully, viciously.

She was quite indifferent. "Why should I? It has not been necessary."

"You know, Kyra," he said evenly, "that you ought to be killed."

"But not by you, Dan. You love me."

He said nothing. The fact was too obvious to deny.

"Dan," she said softly, "if you only had my courage, there is no height we might not reach together. No height—if you had the courage to try. That is why I came back here, but—" She shrugged. "I go back to Washington tomorrow."

Later in the day Scott got Bach alone. "She's going tomorrow!" he said tensely. "Whatever we can do has to be done tonight."

The old man gestured helplessly. "What can we do? Can you think of any law that limits adaptability?"

"No, but—" He paused suddenly. "By Heaven!" he cried. "I can! I've got it!"

"What?"

"The law! A fundamental biological law that must be Kyra's weakness!"

"But what?"

"This! No organism can live in its own waste products! Its own waste is poison to any living thing!"

"But—"

"Listen. Carbon dioxide is a human waste product. Kyra can't adapt to an atmosphere of carbon dioxide!"

Bach stared. "By Heaven!" he cried. "But even if you're right, how—"

"Wait a minute. You can get a couple of cylinders of carbonic acid gas from Grand Mercy. Can you think of any way of getting the gas into her room?"

"Why—this is an old house. There's a hole from her room to the one I'm using, where the radiator connection goes through. It's not tight; we could get a rubber tube past the pipe."

"Good!"

"But the windows! She'll have the windows open."

"Never mind that," said Scott. "See that they're soaped so they'll close easily, that's all."

"But even if it works, what good—Dan! You don't mean to kill her?"

He shook his head. "I—couldn't," he whispered. "But once she's helpless, once she's overcome—if she is—you'll operate. That operation on the pineal you suggested before. And may Heaven forgive me!"

Scott suffered the tortures of the damned that evening. Kyra was, if possible, lovelier than ever, and for the first time she seemed to exert herself to be charming. Her conversation was literally brilliant;

she sparkled, and over and over Scott found himself so fascinated that the thought of the treachery he planned was an excruciating pain. It seemed almost a blasphemy to attempt violence against one whose outward appearance was so pure, so innocent, so saint like.

"But she isn't quite—human!" he told himself. "She's not an angel but a female demon, a—what were they called?—an incubus!"

Despite himself, when at last Kyra yawned luxuriously and dropped her dainty feet to the floor to depart, he pleaded for a few moments more.

"But it's early," he said, "and tomorrow you leave."

"I will return, Dan. This is not the end for us."

"I hope not," he muttered miserably, watching the door of her room as it clicked shut.

He gazed at Bach. The older man, after a moment's silence, whispered, "It is likely that she sleeps almost at once. That's also a matter of adaptability."

In tense silence they watched the thin line of light below the closed door. Scott started violently when, after a brief interval, her shadow crossed it and it disappeared with a faint click.

"Now, then," he said grimly. "Let's get it over."

He followed Bach into the adjacent room. There, cold and metallic, stood the gray cylinders of compressed gas. He watched as the old man attached a length of tubing, ran it to the opening around the steam pipe, and began to pack the remaining space with wet cotton.

Scott turned to his own task. He moved quietly into the library. With utmost stealth he tried the door of Kyra's room; it was unlocked as he had known it would be, for the girl was supremely confident of her own invulnerability.

For a long moment he gazed across at the mass of radiant silver hair on her pillow, then, very cautiously, he placed a tiny candle on the chair by the window, so that it should be at about the level of the bed, lighted it with a snap of his cigarette lighter, withdrew the door key, and departed.

He locked the door on the outside, and set about stuffing the crack below it with cotton. It was far from air-tight, but that mattered little, he mused, since one had to allow for the escape of the replaced atmosphere.

He returned to Bach's room. "Give me a minute," he whispered. "Then turn it on."

He stepped to a window. Outside was a two-foot ledge of stone, and he crept to this precarious perch. He was visible from the street below, but not markedly noticeable, for he was directly above an areaway between Bach's house and its neighbor. He prayed fervently that he might escape attention.

He crept along the ledge. The two windows of Kyra's chamber were wide, but Bach had done his work. They slid downward without a creak, and he pressed close against the glass to peer in.

Across the room glowed the faint and steady flame of his little taper. Close beside him, within a short arm's length had no pane intervened, lay Kyra, quite visible in the dusk. She lay on her back, with one arm thrown above her unbelievable hair, and she had drawn only a single sheet over her. He could watch her breathing, quiet, calm, peaceful.

It seemed as if a long time passed. He fancied at last that he could hear the gentle hiss of gas from Bach's window, but he knew that that must be fancy. In the chamber he watched there was no sign of anything unusual; the glorious Kyra slept as she did everything else—easily, quietly, and confidently.

Then there was a sign. The little candle flame, burning steadily in the draughtless air, flickered suddenly. He watched it, certain now that its color was changing. Again it flickered, flared for a moment, then died. A red spark glowed on the wick for a bare instant, then that was gone.

The candle flame was smothered. That meant a concentration of eight or ten per cent of carbon dioxide in the room's temperature—far too high to support ordinary life. Yet Kyra was living. Except that her quiet breathing seemed to have deepened, she gave not even a sign of inconvenience. She had adapted to the decreased oxygen supply.

But there must be limits to her powers. He blinked into the darkness. Surely—surely her breathing was quickening. He was positive now; her breast rose and fell in convulsive gasps, and somewhere in his turbulent mind the scientist in him recorded the fact.

"Cheyne-Stokes breathing," he muttered. In a moment the violence of it would waken her.

It did. Suddenly the silver eyes started open. She brushed her hand across her mouth, then clutched at her throat. Aware instantly of danger, she thrust herself erect, and her bare legs flashed as she pushed herself from the bed. But she must have been dazed, for she turned first to the door.

He saw the unsteadiness in her movements. She twisted the doorknob, tugged frantically, then whirled toward the window. He could see her swaying as she staggered through the vitiated air, but she reached it. Her face was close to his, but he doubted if she saw him, for her eyes were wide and frightened, and her mouth and throat were straining violently for breath. She raised her hand to smash the pane; the blow landed, but weakly, and the window shook but did not shatter,

Again her arm rose, but that blow was never delivered. For a moment she stood poised, swaying slowly, then her magnificent eyes misted and closed, she dropped to her knees, and at last collapsed limply on the floor.

Scott waited a long, torturing moment, then thrust up the window. The rush of lifeless air sent him whirling dizzily on his dangerous perch, and he clutched the casement. Then a slow breeze moved between the buildings, and his head cleared.

He stepped gingerly into the chamber. It was stifling, but near the open window he could breathe. He kicked thrice against Bach's wall.

The hiss of gas ceased. He gathered Kyra's form in his arms, waited until he heard the key turn, then dashed across the room and into the library.

Bach stared as if fascinated at the pure features of the girl. "A goddess overcome," he said. "There is something sinful about our part in this."

"Be quick!" snapped Scott. "She's unconscious, not anaesthetized. God knows how quickly she'll readjust."

But she had not yet recovered when Scott laid her on the operating table in Bach's office, and drew the straps about her arms and body and slim bare legs. He looked down on her still, white face and bright hair, and he felt his heart contract with pain to see them darken ever so faintly and beautifully under the brilliant operating light, rich in actinic rays.

"You were right," he whispered to the unhearing girl. "Had I your courage there is nothing we might not have attained together."

Bach spoke brusquely. "Nasal?" he asked. "Or shall I trephine her?"

"Nasal."

"But I should like a chance to observe the pineal gland. This case is unique, and—"

"Nasal!" blazed Scott. "I won't have her scarred!"

Bach sighed and began. Scott, despite his long hospital experience, found himself quite unable to watch this operation; he passed the old man his instruments as needed, but kept his eyes averted from the girl's passive and lovely face.

"So!" said Bach at last. "It is done." For the first time he himself had a moment's leisure to survey Kyra's features.

Bach started violently. Gone was the exquisite aluminum hair, replaced by the stringy, dark, and oily locks of the girl in the hospital! He pried open her eye, silver no longer, but pallid blue. Of all her loveliness, there remained—what? A trace, perhaps; a trace in the saint like purity of her pale face, and in the molding of her features. But a flame had died; she was a goddess no longer, but a mortal—a human being. The superwoman had become no more than a suffering girl.

An ejaculation had almost burst from his lips when Scott's voice stopped him.

"How beautiful she is!" he whispered.

Bach stared. He realized suddenly that Scott was not seeing her as she was, but as she once had been. To his eyes, colored by love, she was still Kyra the magnificent.

Pygmalion's Spectacles

'But what is reality?' asked the gnome-like man. He gestured at the tall banks of buildings that loomed around Central Park, with their countless windows glowing like the cave fires of a city of Cro-Magnon people. 'All is dream, all is illusion; I am your vision as you are mine.'

Dan Burke, struggling for clarity of thought through the fumes of liquor, stared without comprehension at the tiny figure of his companion. He began to regret the impulse that had driven him to leave the party to seek fresh air in the park, and to fall by chance into the company of this diminutive old madman. But he had needed escape; this was one party too many, and not even the presence of Claire with her trim ankles could hold him there. He felt an angry desire to go home—not to his hotel, but home to Chicago and to the comparative peace of the Board of Trade. But he was leaving tomorrow anyway.

'You drink,' said the elfin, bearded face, 'to make real a dream. Is it not so? Either to dream that what you seek is yours, or else to dream that what you hate is conquered. You drink to escape reality, and the irony is that even reality is a dream.'

'Cracked!' thought Dan again.

'Or so,' concluded the other, 'says the philosopher Berkeley.'

'Berkeley?' echoed Dan. His head was clearing; memories of a sophomore course in Elementary Philosophy drifted back. 'Bishop Berkeley, eh?'

'You know him, then? The philosopher of Idealism—no?—the one who argues that we do not see, feel, hear, taste the object, but that we have only the sensation of seeing, feeling, hearing, tasting.'

'I—sort of recall it.'

'Hah! But sensations are mental phenomena. They exist in our minds. How, then, do we know that the objects themselves do not exist only in our minds?' He waved again at the light-flecked buildings. 'You do not see that wall of masonry; you perceive only a sensation, a feeling of sight. The rest you interpret.'

'You see the same thing,' retorted Dan.

'How do you know I do? Even if you knew that what I call red would not be green could you see through my eyes—even if you knew that, how do you know that I too am not a dream of yours?'

Dan laughed. 'Of course nobody knows anything. You just get what information you can through the windows of your five senses, and then make your guesses. When they're wrong, you pay the penalty.' His mind was clear now save for a mild headache. 'Listen,' he said suddenly. 'You can argue a reality away to an illusion; that's easy. But if your friend Berkeley is right, why can't you take a dream and make it real? If it works one way, it must work the other.'

The beard waggled; elf-bright eyes glittered queerly at him. 'All artists do that,' said the old man softly. Dan felt that something more quivered on the verge of utterance.

'That's an evasion,' he grunted. 'Anybody can tell the difference between a picture and the real thing, or between a movie and life.'

'But,' whispered the other, 'the realer the better, no? And if one could make a—a movie very real indeed, what would you say then?'

'Nobody can, though.'

The eyes glittered strangely again. 'I can!' he whispered. 'I did!'

'Did what?'

'Made real a dream.' The voice turned angry. 'Fools! I bring it here to sell to Westman, the camera people, and what do they say? 'It isn't clear. Only one person can use it at a time. It's too expensive.' Fools! Fools!'

'Huh?'

'Listen! I'm Albert Ludwig—Professor Ludwig.' As Dan was silent, he continued, 'It means nothing to you, eh? But listen—a movie that gives one sight and sound. Suppose now I add taste, smell, even touch, if your interest is taken by the story. Suppose I make it so that you are in the story, you speak to the shadows, and the shadows reply, and instead of being on a screen, the story is all about you, and you are in it. Would that be to make real a dream?'

'How the devil could you do that?'

'How? How? But simply! First my liquid positive, then my magic spectacles. I photograph the story in a liquid with light-sensitive chromates. I build up a complex solution—do you see? I add taste chemically and sound electrically. And when the story is recorded, then I put the solution in my spectacles—my movie projector. I electrolyze the solution, the story, sight, sound, smell, taste all!'

'Touch?'

'If your interest is taken, your mind supplies that.' Eagerness crept into his voice. 'You will look at it, Mr.—'

'Burke,' said Dan. 'A swindle!' he thought. Then a spark of recklessness glowed out of the vanishing fumes of alcohol. 'Why not?' he grunted.

He rose; Ludwig, standing, came scarcely to his shoulder. A queer gnome-like old man, Dan thought as he followed him across the park and into one of the scores of apartment hotels in the vicinity.

In his room Ludwig fumbled in a bag, producing a device vaguely reminiscent of a gas mask. There were goggles and a rubber mouth-piece; Dan examined it curiously, while the little bearded professor brandished a bottle of watery liquid.

'Here it is!' he gloated. 'My liquid positive, the story. Hard photography—infernally hard, therefore the simplest story. A Utopia— just two characters and you, the audience. Now, put the spectacles on. Put them on and tell me what fools the Westman people are!' He decanted some of the liquid into the mask, and trailed a twisted wire to a device on the table. 'A rectifier,' he explained. 'For the electrolysis.'

'Must you use all the liquid?' asked Dan. 'If you use part, do you see only part of the story? And which part?'

'Every drop has all of it, but you must fill the eye-pieces.' Then as Dan slipped the device gingerly on, 'So! Now what do you see?'

'Not a damn thing. Just the windows and the lights across the street.'

'Of course. But now I start the electrolysis. Now!'

There was a moment of chaos. The liquid before Dan's eyes clouded suddenly white, and formless sounds buzzed. He moved to tear the device from his head, but emerging forms in the mistiness caught his interest. Giant things were writhing there.

The scene steadied; the whiteness was dissipating like mist in summer. Unbelieving, still gripping the arms of that unseen chair, he was staring at a forest. But what a forest! Incredible, unearthly, beautiful! Smooth holes ascended inconceivably toward a brightening sky, trees bizarre as the forests of the Carboniferous age. Infinite-

ly overhead swayed misty fronds, and the verdure showed brown
and green in the heights. And there were birds—at least, curiously
loving pipings and twitterings were all about him though he saw no
creatures—thin elfin whistlings like fairy bugles sounded softly.

He sat frozen, entranced. A louder fragment of melody drifted
down to him, mounting in exquisite, ecstatic bursts, now clear as
sounding metal, now soft as remembered music. For a moment he
forgot the chair whose arms he gripped, the miserable hotel room
invisibly about him, old Ludwig, his aching head. He imagined
himself alone in the midst of that lovely glade. 'Eden!' he muttered,
and the swelling music of unseen voices answered.

Some measure of reason returned. 'Illusion!' he told himself.
Clever optical devices, not reality. He groped for the chair's arm,
found it, and clung to it; he scraped his feet and found again an in-
consistency. To his eyes the ground was mossy verdure; to his touch
it was merely a thin hotel carpet.

The elfin buglings sounded gently. A faint, deliciously sweet per-
fume breathed against him; he glanced up to watch the opening
of a great crimson blossom on the nearest tree, and a tiny reddish
sun edged into the circle of sky above him. The fairy orchestra
swelled louder in its light, and the notes sent a thrill of wistfulness
through him. Illusion? If it were, it made reality almost unbearable; he wanted to believe that somewhere—somewhere this side of
dreams, there actually existed this region of loveliness. An outpost
of Paradise? Perhaps.

And then—far through the softening mists, he caught a movement that was not the swaying of verdure, a shimmer of silver more
solid than mist. Something approached. He watched the figure as it
moved, now visible, now hidden by trees; very soon he perceived
that it was human, but it was almost upon him before he realized
that it was a girl.

She wore a robe of silvery, half-translucent stuff, luminous as
starbeams; a thin band of silver bound glowing black hair about her
forehead, and other garment or ornament she had none. Her tiny
white feet were bare to the mossy forest floor as she stood no more
than a pace from him, staring dark-eyed. The thin music sounded
again; she smiled.

Dan summoned stumbling thoughts. Was this being also—illusion? Had she no more reality than the loveliness of the forest? He opened his lips to speak, but a strained excited voice sounded in his ears. 'Who are you?' Had he spoken? The voice had come as if from another, like the sound of one's words in fever.

The girl smiled again. 'English!' she said in queer soft tones. 'I can speak a little English.' She spoke slowly, carefully. 'I learned it from!'—she hesitated—'my mother's father, whom they call the Gray Weaver.'

Again came the voice in Dan's ears. 'Who are you?'

'I am called Galatea,' she said. 'I came to find you.'

'To find me?' echoed the voice that was Dan's.

'Leucon, who is called the Gray Weaver, told me,' she explained smiling. 'He said you will stay with us until the second noon from this.' She cast a quick slanting glance at the pale sun now full above the clearing, then stepped closer. 'What are you called?'

'Dan,' he muttered. His voice sounded oddly different.

'What a strange name!' said the girl. She stretched out her bare arm. 'Come,' she smiled.

Dan touched her extended hand, feeling without any surprise the living warmth of her fingers. He had forgotten the paradoxes of illusion; this was no longer illusion to him, but reality itself. It seemed to him that he followed her, walking over the shadowed turf that gave with springy crunch beneath his tread, though Galatea left hardly an imprint. He glanced down, noting that he himself wore a silver garment, and that his feet were bare; with the glance he felt a feathery breeze on his body and a sense of mossy earth on his feet.

'Galatea,' said his voice. 'Galatea, what place is this? What language do you speak?'

She glanced back laughing. 'Why, this is Paracosma, of course, and this is our language.'

'Paracosma,' muttered Dan. 'Paracosma!' A fragment of Greek that had survived somehow from a sophomore course a decade in the past came strangely back to him. Paracosma! Land-beyond-the-world!

Galatea cast a smiling glance at him. 'Does the real world seem strange,' she queried, 'after that shadow land of yours?'

'Shadow land?' echoed Dan, bewildered. 'This is shadow, not my world.'

The girl's smile turned quizzical. 'Poof!' she retorted with an impudently lovely pout. 'And I suppose, then, that I am the phantom instead of you!' She laughed. 'Do I seem ghostlike?'

Dan made no reply; he was puzzling over unanswerable questions as he trod behind the lithe figure of his guide. The aisle between the unearthly trees widened, and the giants were fewer. It seemed a mile, perhaps, before a sound of tinkling water obscured that other strange music; they emerged on the bank of a little river, swift and crystalline, that rippled and gurgled its way from glowing pool to flashing rapids, sparkling under the pale sun. Galatea bent over the brink and cupped her hands, raising a few mouthfuls of water to her lips; Dan followed her example, finding the liquid stinging cold.

'How do we cross?' he asked.

'You can wade up there'—the dryad who led him gestured to a sun-lit shallows above a tiny falls—'but I always cross here.' She poised herself for a moment on the green bank, then dove like a silver arrow into the pool. Dan followed; the water stung his body like champagne, but a stroke or two carried him across to where Galatea had already emerged with a glistening of creamy bare limbs. Her garment clung tight as a metal sheath to her wet body; he felt a breathtaking thrill at the sight of her. And then, miraculously, the silver cloth was dry, the droplets rolled off as if from oiled silk, and they moved briskly on.

The incredible forest had ended with the river; they walked over a meadow studded with little, many-hued, starshaped flowers, whose fronds underfoot were soft as a lawn. Yet still the sweet pipings followed them, now loud, now whisper-soft, in a tenuous web of melody.

'Galatea!' said Dan suddenly. 'Where is the music coming from?'

She looked back amazed. 'You silly one!' she laughed. 'From the flowers, of course. See!' she plucked a purple star and held it to his ear; true enough, a faint and plaintive melody hummed out of the blossom. She tossed it in his startled face and skipped on.

A little copse appeared ahead, not of the gigantic forest trees, but of lesser growths, bearing flowers and fruits of iridescent colors, and a tiny brook bubbled through. And there stood the objective of their journey—a building of white, marble-like stone, single-storied and vine-covered, with broad glassless windows. They trod upon a path of bright pebbles to the arched entrance, and here, on an intricate stone bench, sat a gray-bearded patriarchal individual. Galatea addressed him in a liquid language that reminded Dan of the flower pipings; then she turned. 'This is Leucon,' she said, as the ancient rose from his seat and spoke in English.

'We are happy, Galatea and I, to welcome you, since visitors are a rare pleasure here, and those from your shadowy country most rare.'

Dan uttered puzzled words of thanks, and the old man nodded, reseating himself on the carven bench; Galatea skipped through the arched entrance, and Dan, after an irresolute moment, dropped to the remaining bench. Once more his thoughts were whirling in perplexed turbulence. Was all this indeed but illusion? Was he sitting, in actuality, in a prosaic hotel room, peering through magic spectacles that pictured this world about him, or was he, transported by some miracle, really sitting here in this land of loveliness? He touched the bench; stone, hard and unyielding, met his fingers.

'Leucon,' said his voice, 'how did you know I was coming?'

'I was told,' said the other.

'By whom?'

'By no one.'

'Why—someone must have told you!'

The Gray Weaver shook his solemn head. 'I was just told.'

Dan ceased his questioning, content for the moment to drink in the beauty about him, and then Galatea returned bearing a crystal bowl of the strange fruits. They were piled in colorful disorder, red, purple, orange and yellow, pear-shaped, egg-shaped, and clustered spheroids—fantastic, unearthly. He selected a pale, transparent ovoid, bit into it, and was deluged by a flood of sweet liquid, to the amusement of the girl. She laughed and chose a similar morsel; biting a tiny puncture in the end, she squeezed the contents into her mouth. Dan took a different sort, purple and tart as Rhenish wine, and then another, filled with edible, almond-like seeds. Galatea laughed delightedly at his surprises, and even Leucon smiled a gray smile. Finally Dan tossed the last husk into the brook beside them, where it danced briskly toward the river.

'Galatea,' he said, 'do you ever go to a city? What cities are in Paracosma?'

'Cities? What are cities?'

'Places where many people live close together.'

'Oh,' said the girl frowning. 'No. There are no cities here.'

'Then where are the people of Paracosma? You must have neighbors.'

The girl looked puzzled. 'A man and a woman live off there,' she said, gesturing toward a distant blue range of hills dim on the horizon. 'Far away over there. I went there once, but Leucon and I prefer the valley.'

'But Galatea!' protested Dan. 'Are you and Leucon alone in this valley? Where—what happened to your parents—your father and mother?'

'They went away. That way—toward the sunrise. They'll return some day.'

'And if they don't?'

'Why, foolish one! What could hinder them?'

'Wild beasts,' said Dan. 'Poisonous insects, disease, flood, storm, lawless people, death!'

'I never heard those words,' said Galatea. 'There are no such things here.' She sniffed contemptuously. 'Lawless people!'

'Not—death?'

'What is death?'

'It's—' Dan paused helplessly. 'It's like falling asleep and never waking. It's what happens to everyone at the end of life.'

'I never heard of such a thing as the end of life!' said the girl decidedly. 'There isn't such a thing.'

'What happens, then,' queried Dan desperately, 'when one grows old?'

'Nothing, silly! No one grows old unless he wants to, like Leucon. A person grows to the age he likes best and then stops. It's a law!'

Dan gathered his chaotic thoughts. He stared into Galatea's dark, lovely eyes. 'Have you stopped yet?'

The dark eyes dropped; he was amazed to see a deep, embarrassed flush spread over her cheeks. She looked at Leucon nodding reflectively on his bench, then back to Dan, meeting his gaze.

'Not yet,' she said.

'And when will you, Galatea?'

'When I have had the one child permitted me. You see—' she stared down at her dainty toes—'one cannot—bear children—afterwards.'

'Permitted? Permitted by whom?'

'By a law.'

'Laws! Is everything here governed by laws? What of chance and accidents?'

'What are those—chance and accidents?'

'Things unexpected—things unforeseen.'

'Nothing is unforeseen,' said Galatea, still soberly. She repeated slowly, 'Nothing is unforeseen.' He fancied her voice was wistful.

Leucon looked up. 'Enough of this,' he said abruptly. He turned to Dan, 'I know these words of yours—chance, disease, death. They are not for Paracosma. Keep them in your unreal country.'

'Where did you hear them, then?'

'From Galatea's mother,' said the Gray Weaver, 'who had them from your predecessor—a phantom who visited here before Galatea was born.'

Dan had a vision of Ludwig's face. 'What was he like?'

'Much like you.'

'But his name?'

The old man's mouth was suddenly grim. 'We do not speak of him,' he said and rose, entering the dwelling in cold silence.

'He goes to weave,' said Galatea after a moment. Her lovely piquant face was still troubled.

'What does he weave?'

'This.' She fingered the silver cloth of her gown. 'He weaves it out of metal bars on a very clever machine. I do not know the method.'

'Who made the machine?'

'It was here.'

'But—Galatea! Who built the house? Who planted these fruit trees?'

'They were here. The house and trees were always here,' She lifted her eyes. 'I told you everything had been foreseen, from the beginning until eternity—everything. The house and trees and machine were ready for Leucon and my parents and me. There is a place for my child, who will be a girl, and a place for her child—and so on forever.'

Dan thought a moment. 'Were you born here?'

'I don't know.' He noted in sudden concern that her eyes were glistening with tears.

'Galatea, dear! Why are you unhappy? What's wrong?'

'Why, nothing!' She shook her black curls, sniffed suddenly at him. 'What could be wrong? How can one be unhappy in Paracosma?' She sprang erect and seized his hand. 'Come! Let's gather fruit for tomorrow.'

She darted off in a whirl of flashing silver, and Dan followed her around the wing of the edifice. Graceful as a dancer she leaped for a branch above her head, caught it laughingly, and tossed a great golden globe to him. She loaded his arms with the bright prizes and sent him back to the bench, and when he returned, she piled it so full of fruit that a deluge of colorful spheres dropped around him. She laughed again, and sent them spinning into the brook with thrusts of her rosy toes, while Dan watched her with an aching wistfulness. Then suddenly she was facing him; for a long, tense instant they stood motionless, eyes upon eyes, and then she turned away and walked slowly around to the arched portal. He followed her with his burden of fruit; his mind was once more in a turmoil of doubt and perplexity.

The little sun was losing itself behind the trees of that colossal forest to the west, and a coolness stirred among long shadows. The brook was purple-hued in the dusk, but its cheery notes mingled still with the flower music. Then the sun was hidden; the shadow fingers darkened the meadow; of a sudden the flowers were still, and the brook gurgled alone in a world of silence. In silence too, Dan entered the doorway.

The chamber within was a spacious one, flooded with large black and white squares; exquisite benches of carved marble were here and there. Old Leucon, in a far corner, bent over an intricate, glistening mechanism, and as Dan entered he drew a shining length of silver cloth from it, folded it, and placed it carefully aside. There was a curious, unearthly fact that Dan noted; despite windows open to the evening, no night insects circled the globes that glowed at intervals from niches in the walls.

Galatea stood in a doorway to his left, leaning half-wearily against the frame; he placed the bowl of fruit on a bench at the entrance and moved to her side.

'This is yours,' she said, indicating the room beyond. He looked in upon a pleasant, smaller chamber; a window framed a starry square, and a thin, swift, nearly silent stream of water gushed from the mouth of a carved human head on the left wall, curving into a six-foot basin sunk in the floor. Another of the graceful benches covered with the silver cloth completed the furnishings; a single glowing sphere, pendant by a chain from the ceiling, illuminated the room. Dan turned to the girl, whose eyes were still unwontedly serious.

'This is ideal,' he said, 'but, Galatea, how am I to turn out the light?'

'Turn it out?' she said. 'You must cap it—so!' A faint smile showed again on her lips as she dropped a metal covering over the shining sphere. They stood tense in the darkness; Dan sensed her nearness achingly, and then the light was on once more. She moved toward the door, and there paused, taking his hand.

'Dear shadow,' she said softly, 'I hope your dreams are music.' She was gone.

Dan stood irresolute in his chamber; he glanced into the large room where Leucon still bent over his work, and the Gray Weaver raised a hand in a solemn salutation, but said nothing. He felt no urge for the old man's silent company and turned back into his room to prepare for slumber.

Almost instantly, it seemed, the dawn was upon him and bright elfin pipings were all about him, while the odd ruddy sun sent a broad slanting plane of light across the room. He rose as fully aware of his surroundings as if he had not slept at all; the pool tempted him and he bathed in stinging water. Thereafter he emerged into the central chamber, noting curiously that the globes still glowed in dim rivalry to the daylight. He touched one casually; it was cool as metal to his fingers, and lifted freely from its standard. For a moment he held the cold flaming thing in his hands, then replaced it and wandered into the dawn

Galatea was dancing up the path, eating a strange fruit as rosy as her lips. She was merry again, once more the happy nymph who had greeted him, and she gave him a bright smile as he chose a sweet green ovoid for his breakfast.

'Come on!' she called. 'To the river!'

She skipped away toward the unbelievable forest; Dan followed, marveling that her lithe speed was so easy a match for his stronger muscles. Then they were laughing in the pool, splashing about until Galatea drew herself to the bank, glowing and panting. He followed her as she lay relaxed; strangely, he was neither tired nor breathless, with no sense of exertion. A question recurred to him, as yet unasked.

'Galatea,' said his voice, 'whom will you take as mate?'

Her eyes went serious. 'I don't know,' she said. 'At the proper time he will come. That is a law.'

'And will you be happy?'

'Of course.' She seemed troubled. 'Isn't everyone happy?'

'Not where I live, Galatea.'

'Then that must be a strange place—that ghostly world of yours. A rather terrible place.'

'It is, often enough,' Dan agreed. 'I wish—' He paused. What did he wish? Was he not talking to an illusion, a dream, an apparition? He looked at the girl, at her glistening black hair, her eyes, her soft white skin, and then, for a tragic moment, he tried to feel the arms of that drab hotel chair beneath his hands—and failed. He smiled; he reached out his fingers to touch her bare arm, and for an instant she looked back at him with startled, sober eyes, and sprang to her feet.

'Come on! I want to show you my country.' She set off down the stream, and Dan rose reluctantly to follow.

What a day that was! They traced the little river from still pool to singing rapids, and ever about them were the strange twitterings and pipings that were the voices of the flowers. Every turn brought a new vista of beauty; every moment brought a new sense of delight. They talked or were silent; when they were thirsty, the cool river was at hand; when they were hungry, fruit offered itself. When they were tired, there was always a deep pool and a mossy bank; and when they were rested, a new beauty beckoned. The incredible trees towered in numberless forms of fantasy, but on their own side of the river was still the flower-starred meadow. Galatea twisted him a bright-blossomed garland for his head, and thereafter he moved always with a sweet singing about him. But little by little the red sun slanted toward the forest, and the hours dripped away. It was Dan who pointed it out, and reluctantly they turned homeward.

As they returned, Galatea sang a strange song, plaintive and sweet as the medley of river and flower music. And again her eyes were sad.

'What song is that?' he asked.

'It is a song sung by another Galatea,' she answered, 'who is my mother.' She laid her hand on his arm. 'I will make it into English for you.' She sang:

'The River lies in flower and fern,
In flower and fern it breathes a song.
It breathes a song of your return,
Of your return in years too long.
In years too long its murmurs bring
Its murmurs bring their vain replies,
Their vain replies the flowers sing,
The flowers sing, The River lies!'

Her voice quavered on the final notes; there was silence save for the tinkle of water and the flower bugles. Dan said, 'Galatea-' and paused. The girl was again somber-eyed, tearful. He said huskily, 'That's a sad song, Galatea. Why was your mother sad? You said everyone was happy in Paracosma.'

'She broke a law,' replied the girl tonelessly. 'It is the inevitable way to sorrow.' She faced him. 'She fell in love with a phantom!' Galatea said. 'One of your shadowy race, who came and stayed and then had to go back. So when her appointed lover came, it was too late; do you understand? But she yielded finally to the law, and is forever unhappy, and goes wandering from place to place about the world.' She paused. 'I shall never break a law,' she said defiantly.

Dan took her hand. 'I would not have you unhappy, Galatea. I want you always happy.'

She shook her head. 'I am happy,' she said, and smiled a tender, wistful smile.

They were silent a long time as they trudged the way homeward. The shadows of the forest giants reached out across the river as the sun slipped behind them. For a distance they walked hand in hand, but as they reached the path of pebbly brightness near the house, Galatea drew away and sped swiftly before him. Dan followed as quickly as he might; when he arrived, Leucon sat on his bench by the portal, and Galatea had paused on the threshold. She watched his approach with eyes in which he again fancied the glint of tears.

'I am very tired,' she said, and slipped within.

Dan moved to follow, but the old man raised a staying hand.

'Friend from the shadows,' he said, 'will you hear me a moment?'

Dan paused, acquiesced, and dropped to the opposite bench. He felt a sense of foreboding; nothing pleasant awaited him.

'There is something to be said,' Leucon continued, 'and I say it without desire to pain you, if phantoms feel pain. It is this: Galatea loves you, though I think she has not yet realized it.'

'I love her too,' said Dan.

The Gray Weaver stared at him. 'I do not understand. Substance, indeed, may love shadow, but how can shadow love substance?'

'I love her,' insisted Dan.

'Then woe to both of you! For this is impossible in Paracosma; it is a confliction with the laws. Galatea's mate is appointed, perhaps even now approaching.'

'Laws! Laws!' muttered Dan. 'Whose laws are they? Not Galatea's nor mine!'

'But they are,' said the Gray Weaver. 'It is not for you nor for me to criticize them—though I yet wonder what power could annul them to permit your presence here!'

'I had no voice in your laws.'

The old man peered at him in the dusk. 'Has anyone, anywhere, a voice in the laws?' he queried.

'In my country we have,' retorted Dan.

'Madness!' growled Leucon. 'Man-made laws! Of what use are man-made laws with only man-made penalties, or none at all? If you shadows make a law that the wind shall blow only from the east, does the west wind obey it?'

'We do pass such laws,' acknowledged Dan bitterly. 'They may be stupid, but they're no more unjust than yours.'

'Ours,' said the Gray Weaver, 'are the unalterable laws of the world, the laws of Nature. Violation is always unhappiness. I have seen it; I have known it in another, in Galatea's mother, though Galatea is stronger than she.' He paused. 'Now,' he continued, 'I ask only for mercy; your stay is short, and I ask that you do no more harm than is already done. Be merciful; give her no more to regret.'

He rose and moved through the archway; when Dan followed

a moment later, he was already removing a square of silver from his device in the corner. Dan turned silent and unhappy to his own chamber, where the jet of water tinkled faintly as a distant bell.

Again he rose at the glow of dawn, and again Galatea was before him, meeting him at the door with her bowl of fruit. She deposited her burden, giving him a wan little smile of greeting, and stood facing him as if waiting.

'Come with me, Galatea,' he said.

'Where?'

'To the river bank. To talk.'

They trudged in silence to the brink of Galatea's pool. Dan noted a subtle difference in the world about him; outlines were vague, the thin flower pipings less audible and the very landscape was queerly unstable, shifting like smoke when he wasn't looking at it directly. And strangely, though he had brought the girl here to talk to her, he had now nothing to say, but sat in aching silence with his eyes on the loveliness of her face.

Galatea pointed at the red ascending sun. 'So short a time,' she said, 'before you go back to your phantom world. I shall be sorry, very sorry.' She touched his cheek with her fingers. 'Dear shadow!'

'Suppose,' said Dan huskily, 'that I won't go. What if I won't leave here?' His voice grew fiercer. 'I'll not go! I'm going to stay!'

The calm mournfulness of the girl's face checked him; he felt the irony of struggling against the inevitable progress of a dream. She spoke. 'Had I the making of the laws, you should stay. But you can't, dear one. You can't!'

Forgotten now were the words of the Gray Weaver. 'I love you, Galatea,' he said.

'And I you,' she whispered. 'See, dearest shadow, how I break the same law my mother broke, and am glad to face the sorrow it will bring.' She placed her hand tenderly over his. 'Leucon is very wise and I am bound to obey him, but this is beyond his wisdom because he let himself grow old.' She paused. 'He let himself grow old,' she repeated slowly. A strange light gleamed in her dark eyes as she turned suddenly to Dan.

'Dear one!' she said tensely. 'That thing that happens to the old—that death of yours! What follows it?'

'What follows death?' he echoed. 'Who knows?'

'But—' Her voice was quivering. 'But one can't simply vanish! There must be an awakening.'

'Who knows?' said Dan again. 'There are those who believe we wake to a happier world, but—' He shook his head hopelessly.

'It must be true! Oh, it must be!' Galatea cried. 'There must be more for you than the mad world you speak of!' She leaned very close. 'Suppose, dear,' she said, 'that when my appointed lover arrives, I send him away. Suppose I bear no child, but let myself grow old, older than Leucon, old until death. Would I join you in your happier world?'

'Galatea!' he cried distractedly. 'Oh, my dearest—what a terrible thought!'

'More terrible than you know,' she whispered, still very close to him. 'It is more than violation of a law; it is rebellion. Everything is planned, everything was foreseen, except this; and if I bear no child, her place will be left unfilled, and the places of her children, and of their children, and so on until some day the whole great plan of Paracosma fails of whatever its destiny was to be.' Her whisper grew very faint and fearful. 'It is destruction, but I love you more than I fear death!'

Dan's arms were about her. 'No, Galatea! No! Promise me!'

She murmured, 'I can promise and then break my promise.' She drew his head down; their lips touched, and he felt a fragrance and a taste like honey in her kiss. 'At least,' she breathed. 'I can give you a name by which to love you. Philometros! Measure of my love!'

'A name?' muttered Dan. A fantastic idea shot through his mind—a way of proving to himself that all this was reality, and not just a page that any one could read who wore old Ludwig's magic spectacles. If Galatea would speak his name! Perhaps, he thought daringly, perhaps then he could stay! He thrust her away.

'Galatea!' he cried. 'Do you remember my name?'

She nodded silently, her unhappy eyes on his.

'Then say it! Say it, dear!'

She stared at him dumbly, miserably, but made no sound.

'Say it, Galatea!' he pleaded desperately. 'My name, dear—just my name!' Her mouth moved; she grew pale with effort and Dan could have sworn that his name trembled on her quivering lips, though no sound came.

At last she spoke. 'I can't, dearest one! Oh, I can't. A law forbids it!' She stood suddenly erect, pallid as an ivory carving. 'Leucon calls!' she said, and darted away. Dan followed along the pebbled path, but her speed was beyond his powers; at the portal he found only the Gray Weaver standing cold and stern. He raised his hand as Dan appeared.

'Your time is short,' he said. 'Go, thinking of the havoc you have done.'

'Where's Galatea?' gasped Dan.

'I have sent her away.' The old man blocked the entrance; for a moment Dan would have struck him aside, but something withheld him. He stared wildly about the meadow—there! A flash of silver beyond the river, at the edge of the forest. He turned and raced toward it, while motionless and cold the Gray Weaver watched him go.

'Galatea!' he called. 'Galatea!'

He was over the river now, on the forest bank, running through columned vistas that whirled about him like mist. The world had gone cloudy; fine flakes danced like snow before his eyes; Paracosma was dissolving around him. Through the chaos he fancied a glimpse of the girl, but closer approach left him still voicing his hopeless cry of 'Galatea!'

After an endless time, he paused; something familiar about the spot struck him, and just as the red sun edged above him, he recognized the place—the very point at which he had entered Paracosma! A sense of futility overwhelmed him as for a moment he gazed at an unbelievable apparition—a dark window hung in mid-air before him through which glowed rows of electric lights. Ludwig's window!

It vanished. But the trees writhed and the sky darkened, and he swayed dizzily in turmoil. He realized suddenly that he was no longer standing, but sitting in the midst of the crazy glade, and his hands clutched something smooth and hard—the arms of that miserable hotel chair. Then at last he saw her, close before him—Galatea, with sorrow-stricken features, her tear-filled eyes on his. He made a terrific effort to rise, stood erect, and fell sprawling in a blaze of coruscating lights.

He struggled to his knees; walls—Ludwig's room—encompassed

him; he must have slipped from the chair. The magic spectacles lay before him, one lens splintered and spilling a fluid no longer water-clear, but white as milk.

'God!' he muttered. He felt shaken, sick, exhausted, with a bitter sense of bereavement, and his head ached fiercely. The room was drab, disgusting; he wanted to get out of it. He glanced automatically at his watch: four o'clock—he must have sat here nearly five hours. For the first time he noticed Ludwig's absence; he was glad of it and walked dully out of the door to an automatic elevator. There was no response to his ring; someone was using the thing. He walked three flights to the street and back to his own room.

In love with a vision! Worse—in love with a girl who had never lived, in a fantastic Utopia that was literally nowhere! He threw himself on his bed with a groan that was half a sob.

He saw finally the implication of the name Galatea. Galatea—Pygmalion's statue, given life by Venus in the ancient Grecian myth. But his Galatea, warm and lovely and vital, must remain forever without the gift of life, since he was neither Pygmalion nor God.

He woke late in the morning, staring uncomprehendingly about for the fountain and pool of Paracosma. Slow comprehension dawned; how much—how much of last night's experience had been real? How much was the product of alcohol? Or had old Ludwig been right, and was there no difference between reality and dream?

He changed his rumpled attire and wandered despondently to the street. He found Ludwig's hotel at last; inquiry revealed that the diminutive professor had checked out, leaving no forwarding address.

What of it? Even Ludwig couldn't give what he sought, a living Galatea. Dan was glad that he had disappeared; he hated the little professor. Professor? Hypnotists called themselves 'professors.' He dragged through a weary day and then a sleepless night back to Chicago.

It was mid-winter when he saw a suggestively tiny figure ahead of him in the Loop. Ludwig! Yet what use to hail him? His cry was automatic. 'Professor Ludwig!'

The elfin figure turned, recognized him, smiled. They stepped into the shelter of a building.

'I'm sorry about your machine, Professor. I'd be glad to pay for the damage.'

'Ach, that was nothing—a cracked glass. But you—have you been ill? You look much the worse.'

'It's nothing,' said Dan. 'Your show was marvelous, Professor—marvelous! I'd have told you so, but you were gone when it ended.'

Ludwig shrugged. 'I went to the lobby for a cigar. Five hours with a wax dummy, you know!'

'It was marvelous,' repeated Dan.

'So real?' smiled the other. 'Only because you co-operated, then. It takes self-hypnosis.'

'It was real, all right,' agreed Dan glumly. 'I don't understand it—that strange beautiful country.'

'The trees were club-mosses enlarged by a lens,' said Ludwig. 'All was trick photography, but stereoscopic, as I told you—three dimensional. The fruits were rubber; the house is a summer building on our campus—Northern University. And the voice was mine; you didn't speak at all, except your name at the first, and I left a blank for that. I played your part, you see; I went around with the photographic apparatus strapped on my head, to keep the viewpoint always that of the observer. See?' He grinned wryly. 'Luckily I'm rather short, or you'd have seemed a giant.'

'Wait a minute!' said Dan, his mind whirling. 'You say you played my part. Then Galatea—is she real too?'

'She's real enough,' said the Professor. 'My niece, a senior at Northern, and likes dramatics. She helped me out with the thing. Why? Want to meet her?'

Dan answered vaguely, happily. An ache had vanished; a pain was eased. Paracosma was attainable at last!

Printed in the United Kingdom
by Lightning Source UK Ltd.
124680UK00001BA/10/A